Aislinn O'Loughlin

BIG BAD ME

Little
Island
Books create waves

BIG BAD ME
First published in 2022 by
Little Island Books
7 Kenilworth Park
Dublin 6W
Ireland

First published in the USA in 2023

Print ISBN: 978-1-91-507104-0

Cover illustration by Jai McFerran
Designed and typeset by Rosa Devine
Proofread by Emma Dunne
Printed in the UK by CPI

Little Island has received funding to support this book
from the Arts Council of Ireland.

10 9 8 7 6 5 4 3 2 1

For Dave
OK, yes, you were right (this time)

15 ½ years ago…

There was a *smash*!

Dr Sinéad Wilder had half-convinced herself she'd dreamt it, until Katie sat up beside her.

'Mommy? 'a' go bang?'

'Sssh. Nothing, Katie-pie. Go back to sleep.'

Sinéad slid her hand under the pillow, reaching for the … *crap!* Where was it? The stairs creaked. Sinéad tried not to panic.

''a' doin', Mommy?'

'Nothing, I'm not … Everything's fine. Back to sleep, sweetheart. NOW!'

All right, maybe she was panicking a little. Sinéad's fingers curled around metal, but she didn't have time to feel relieved before the door burst open.

Something stumbled in.

Sinéad didn't wait to find out what. She yanked the gun out, fired – and missed. Which is good, because it was Robert. *Just* Robert.

He wasn't OK. 'Madison's gone. The front door's smashed open. But she's been in the lab. There's bits of mice and blood –'

'Blood?' said Katie. (She was two, not deaf.)

Sinéad was already up, snatching more darts off the nightstand. So when Katie reached out, she just scooped her up too. 'It's all right, Katie-pie. It's – it's an adventure. Hey, you want a sleepover with Debbie Next Door?'

Katie nodded. Just as well, because she was not coming with them.

Sinéad wrapped Katie in one of Brendan's old sweaters and snuggled her close, inhaling her husband's scent mingled with their daughter's.

'Sinéad?' said Robert. 'You OK?'

'Me?' Sinéad jogged Katie onto her hip, forcing a smile. 'Always. Let's go.'

* * *

After Brendan's funeral, Debbie had said Sinéad could call in 'any time, for anything' – and if spur-of-the-moment 3AM babysitting wasn't quite what she'd meant, you'd never have guessed from her smile as she took Katie, while Sinéad sped off with Robert in whatever-she-drove-back-then. Whatever it was, it suddenly felt way too small because Robert was getting very upset.

Sinéad glanced at the dart gun in her lap. It was loaded, obviously, but could she drive, aim and fire all at once? Did it even matter? If things went that far, crashing would be the least of her worries.

2

'It'll be grand.' Sinéad had to sound certain, because she wasn't. 'Just take a breath and use that – that thing. The buzzy connection you two have, yeah?'

'The thing,' said Robert. 'Right. Just – just relax. Think of Maddie, and – oh God – Bump!'

'Ah, Bump's fine,' Sinéad said. 'He's a scrapper.'

'She.'

'She?'

'You know, Maddie's convinced,' said Robert. 'She's been eyeing Katie's princess costumes for – oh! LEFT, NOW.'

Well, that worked. Sinéad felt a split-second of relief, before fear kicked in. Because if Robert could feel Madison, that meant –

'She's close,' he said. 'Down there.'

Down that dark creepy cul-de-sac? Of course she was.

Sinéad tried not to shudder as she turned the wheel again.

The headlights caught Madison immediately. Robert didn't even wait for the car to stop before jumping out.

'MADDIE!'

Sinéad yanked the hand-brake and flung her own door open, tripping over the seatbelt as she scrambled out. She hit the ground awkwardly and tried not to think about the crunch of her ankle. It could hurt later.

Madison looked up from the body.

Except, that's not quite right, because *it* wasn't Madison – and *that* was barely a body any more. But Not-Madison – the huge leathery beast with yellow eyes and glinty claws – looked up, licked blood off its snout, then turned to growl at Robert.

'Maddie,' he said, 'it's OK, babe. Just –'

Not-Maddie pounced. Sinéad grabbed the gun.

3

The monster slashed out, catching Robert in the chest and sending him flying. The crack of his skull against the brick wall turned Sinéad's stomach.

But that wasn't the worst bit.

Robert looked up. Or didn't. Because it wasn't Robert any more. His eyes flashed yellow. His muscles ripped through his shirt. His jaw stretched, his fangs lengthened – but that still wasn't the worst.

The worst came when Not-Robert and Not-Maddie leapt, claws flailing as they ripped at each other. Not-Maddie's stomach was as swollen as actual Madison's these days.

Little Bump was right there, in the middle of the fight, and if Not-Robert knew, it didn't care. It slashed down, right across that pregnant belly.

'NO!' Sinéad jumped up, ignoring the pain in her ankle. Her hands were shaking, her palms were slippy with sweat and she was a useless shot at the best of times.

But this wasn't the best of times. So Sinéad fired.

1. Evie

Reader, I was born.

That mightn't surprise you, but I'm sure it surprised me. It certainly surprised me, fifteen and a half years later, when I learned *how* I was born: less 'peaceful-home-birth' than I'd imagined; more 'giant-cage-in-the-basement-birth' – my terrified mom wielding a scalpel while my bio-parents ... well, we'll get to that.

The important thing here is that I was born. And that, growing up, all I knew about the other stuff was this: I was adopted (true); and I'd inherited my bio-mom's red hair (true) and super-dangerous, ultra-rare diabetes (less true).

Sure, maybe it should've seemed odd that my diabetes was so uncommon I couldn't Google it. Or that it caused a burning-allergy to silver, and I had to take special insulin custom-mixed by my mom in her secret, unregulated lab in the basement. (Yep, seeing it all written down, it definitely should've seemed odd.) But it didn't. That was just my life. My slightly unusual, very happy life. Which – and this is the bit you're here for, Reader – was about to fall apart completely.

So let's cut to that, eh?

* * *

The buzzing started in Jolt.

You know Jolt, right? Those generic-cute coffee-shops, with generic-cute artwork and terrible coffee-puns everywhere? (It was December, so we were currently 'Dreaming of a Flat White Christmas'.)

I was in the corner, sipping a sugar-free caramel steamed milk and totally failing to wrap my head around biology homework. Probably not what you'd expect, with my immunology-genius mom and big sister one win off being crowned SciFair Queen for life. But there I was, defying expectations and not understanding the difference between mitosis and ... um ... osmosis? ... when a weird buzz hit right between my eyes.

I dropped my pen, rubbed the buzzing spot, then focused back on my textbook. No, I didn't. I slammed the book shut, then kneaded between my eyes as the buzzing got louder. It felt like a pissed-off bee caught in my brain.

I hoped it wouldn't wind up killing me.

Does that sound melodramatic? It's not. At the time, I really wasn't sure.

Part of my 'normal' over the last few months had involved getting crazy stress-headaches. Not like this buzzing – that was new. Usually it was more ... stabby

6

forehead death-prickles. *Totally typical* given my 'ultra-rare diabetes', apparently. Something to do with hormones and – adrenal spikes (I think?) messing with my blood sugar. So, typical, but potentially life-threatening.

Very reassuring. I could avoid them by staying calm – but you try 'staying calm' while your body's trying to kill you. Or while you've got what was starting to feel like an entire beehive vibrating in your skull.

'Ow!' Maybe I should text Kate. She'd know what to do.

Only, Kate was at the community centre, teaching her adorable class of under-8s judo 'mini-heroes'. If I sent a headache text, she'd ditch them to race to my rescue.

I didn't want that. But I couldn't text Mom. She was on a 'research trip to the Burnaby lab'. She'd probably forgotten she even had a phone.

OK, Evie. Deep breaths, like Kate always says. In, one two – whoa!

The back of my neck bristled, like someone was staring at me.

I looked around, trying not to be the weirdo glaring suspiciously at a room of strangers, even though I totally was. Worse, I was wrong. No-one was looking.

The only guy who caught my eye would've caught anyone's eye – all rugged and handsome with a mess of dark curls and just enough stubble. Very all-Canadian lumberjacky and – *crap!* – he'd just looked at me. Literally, straight into my eyes.

My cheeks burned, and he definitely noticed 'cos his head tilted in either concern or curiosity. I was not maintaining eye contact long enough to figure out which.

I snapped my attention away, squeezing my eyes shut, willing myself to focus on slow, calm breathing instead of the hot woodcutter who'd just caught me gawping.

My forehead stress-prickled, which was definitely bad, so I gripped the arm of the sofa and focused on not freaking out.

'You OK?'

Oh no! I opened my eyes.

Lumberhunk was right there, all handsomely concerned. My heart sped up. The angry bees were gone, but mortified death-prickles spiked in their place.

Stoppit, body! I thought. *Please, I'll drink more water, or eat a carrot or something, just don't awkward me to death in front of the hot guy!*

Lumberhunk smiled. Was he trying to kill me? I had to get out of there.

'Can I sit down?' he asked.

'No!' I jumped up, spilling my drink everywhere as I tried to grab my coat, bag and biology book all at once. Everyone was watching now. Great. 'I – I've gotta go.'

New life goal: Make it out of Jolt without spontaneously combusting from shame.

'Maybe take a sec?' said Lumberhunk. 'Before someone gets hurt?'

I tugged my coat on, ignoring the scarf that flopped out one sleeve as I shoved my arm through. 'No. Dude, you're very handsome, I mean, nice. And handsome. And I know you're trynna help but … you're not. Thanks.'

I said that last word as he passed me my phone (helpfully). My palms were so sweaty it took three goes to jam it into my pocket. I needed my insulin.

'You're welcome,' said Lumberhunk. 'Ouch!'

'SORRY!' I'd swung my backpack into his face as I turned to rush away, hitting every table between mine and the exit. 'Sorry, everyone. Bye!'

I fell out the door, into a puddle of sludgy ex-snow, then picked myself up and hurried off into the freezing Toronto winter.

It was official.

Even if what happened next hadn't happened, I was never going back to Jolt again.

2. Still Evie

'Mom?'

Silence, obviously. I hadn't really expected anything else, but my heart sank anyway.

This was why I'd been waiting for Kate. I hated coming home to an empty house. Maybe I should've been revelling in the freedom but I'm a pack animal, and my den hadn't felt right for the last two weeks, since Mom left.

I dumped my bag and coat on the floor, then took out my phone to text Kate. She'd still be in class, but a quick text like

```
Jolt packed! Homework-ing at home. Gotta be
done for Buffy-fest 😊
```

wasn't too alarming, right? I added a vampire GIF – in case I didn't seem excited enough for tonight's boxset binge-party – then retrieved my insulin from its drawer by the fridge. I wasn't supposed to do this alone, but my head was still spiking after Lumberhunk, and Mom and Kate always said better safe than sorry.

So I jabbed.

The brain-fuzzing was almost instant, and the urge to curl up and cry was strong as ever. If Kate or Mom were here, they would've made a huge batch of steaks to get me back to myself. But they weren't. So I forced back the tears, pulled open the fridge, found a plastic-wrapped slab of steaks and ripped it open.

The surge of sweet, slightly metallic blood-scent was so good I almost grabbed a raw handful and started chomping. I might have – except that angry buzz hit again.

Ow, seriously? I dropped the meat and jabbed my forehead with both hands.

Whatever this buzzing was, it was apparently insulin-resistant.

THUMP-THUMP-THUMP!

And really obnoxious, just like whoever was pounding at my front door right now.

'Leave me ALONE!' I didn't want to talk to anyone. I wanted to eat meat and cry. But the pounding continued, like someone had a personal grudge against my door.

'Fine!' I stumbled down the hall and opened the door. 'What?'

The buzzing stopped.

Lumberhunk smiled. 'Hello, Evie.'

There was more thumping, this time from inside my chest. He was *here*? On my doorstep? How? And why? And –

'You know my name?' That too.

This was too much for my meds-fuzzed brain.

'I do.' His eyes crinkled at the corners. 'And I'm Rom, so now we're even.'

He said it like this was all fine. But it wasn't. 'Dude, did you follow me home?'

'It's called tracking.' Rom laughed. 'And, kinda. Can I come in?'

What? 'No!'

I grabbed for the safety chain, but Rom caught my hand. Hard.

'Ow, let go!'

Rom did, and stepped back. 'Sorry. I just ...' He ran his hand nervously through his snow-coated curls. 'Look, just let me in. We need to talk.'

Seriously? 'Dude, you're a handsome stranger, on my doorstep, at dusk. I am *not* inviting you in. That's, like, Vampires 101!'

I'd only meant it as a joke, but Rom's face darkened so freaking fast I jumped back just as he snarled: 'I AM *NOT* A–'

I slammed the door. Or I tried, but he caught it, flung it wide open and forced his way in. The door bounced off the wall then banged shut behind him.

Oh, crap!

'Evie,' he said, stepping forward, 'don't be scared.'

'I'm not.' I wasn't, I realised.

Something was growling inside me, but it wasn't fear. The urge to rip Rom's head off was sudden and powerful. But he was bigger than me, and clearly unhinged. And Kate's first rule of fighting was, you know, don't. So: 'MOM. Call the cops!'

Rom smirked. 'Sinéad Wilder's not home. And she's *not* your mom.'

12

'Shut up!' The growl inside me became a snarl.

Rom kept talking. 'Just listen, before that girl gets home.'

That girl? 'You mean my sister?'

'SHE'S NOT YOUR SISTER!'

Oh, that's IT! I lunged, shoving Rom hard against the door. The impact snapped his head forward. When he looked up, his eyes were dark and burning. I don't just mean angry – I mean, his eyes were fully black-rimmed, rippling yellow and glowing. OK, *now* I was scared.

He followed me as I backed away.

'Oh, Evie,' he said sadly, 'stop. I'm here to help.'

'I don't want your help,' I said. 'I want you to leave.'

'You want me to save you,' he said. 'You just don't realise it yet.'

Eek, this guy was properly crazy. My head pounded as my fingers tingled, groping behind me for something to whack him with. I kept moving back.

'Do you know how loud you've been calling to me?' he said. 'Sending out your signal, like a rescue flare. So I track you down, I watch you and you're – what? Going to school? Sitting in coffee-shops? Wearing *coats*? You DON'T NEED a coat! You're spectacular, and these *people* –' He spat the word out like a bad taste. 'The ones you think love you? They've turned you into a – a watered-down lab rat!'

My fist clenched around a vase. 'Shut up!'

I smashed it across his head, showering him in stagnant water and dead flowers. He barely flinched.

'All right,' he said. 'Less talk.'

Before I'd even realised Rom had moved, he'd slammed me full-force against the living-room doorway. My muscles felt red-hot, twitching by themselves. I struggled to get free, but this guy was super-strong.

He grabbed my right arm, yanking the sleeve back before holding his left hand up.

Only, slowly, it stopped being a hand. The fingers stretched and curled, the nails clawed – even the skin changed to something leathery and greyish.

'This isn't real,' I cried. 'People can't do this!'

'No,' agreed Rom. 'People can't.'

He slashed down. I didn't mean to shriek, but I did. I'd never felt so much pain.

'Shush.' He forced my arm upwards, showing me the blood against my freckles. 'You're all right. Look.'

He wiped at it with his sleeve. The friction against the cuts made me scream again.

The blood kept coming.

'No!' Rom frowned, wiping more frantically as confused horror spread across his face. 'Oh, Evie. What have they done to you?'

'They?' I stammered, through the pain. '*You* – you stabbed me, freak!'

Rom actually had the nerve to look hurt. 'I'm trying to help. Hang on.' He yanked something from his pocket, flipped the lid off and slammed it into my chest. The full-body jolt was insane.

The pounding in my head became white-hot, searing against my skull like something trying to beat its way out. Without thinking, I shoved Rom into the other side of the doorframe, then doubled over in pain – gripping my head, trying to push the whatever-this-was back. I wanted to curl my fingers into my scalp, rip my skull open, anything to ease the pressure. Everything was on fire; even my vision was blurring.

This was it, the ultimate death-ache. It had to be.

Something howled, but that was far away – through the blinding white light and the rage and the agony. Sounded like an animal. It couldn't have been me.

Then, over all that pain, I became aware of something else.

Or some*one* else. 'Evie? EVIE!'

Katie was right outside the door. *NO!*

A full-body spasm hit, flinging me to the ground on all fours. If the impact hurt, I barely noticed over the feeling of every bone in my body cracking at once.

There was that howling again – then the frantic click of keys in the lock.

No, Kate! Stay out.

The door swung open. I could just make out Kate's blurry form in the doorway. I tried to yell for her to run, but it came out all wrong.

'Oh, look. It's the *sister*.' Rom lunged.

And a second later, he hit the wall head-first. The collision, and possibly the shock of being flipped across the hall by a seventeen-year-old girl, was enough to stun him.

I felt a wave of relief, and my vision cleared up just enough for me to see the ... gun? ... in Kate's hand. She took aim and fired at Rom, like it was something she did every day. The dart hit as he was trying to get to his feet.

He collapsed back against the wall and stayed down.

Then Kate turned to me. She looked scared, but she wasn't hurt. That was something. And she was here.

My heart was still jack-hammering, my skull felt like it was about to splinter, every muscle in my body was burning and there was an unconscious psycho in our hallway – but Kate was here. So it was going to be OK.

'Katie ...' My voice caught in my throat and came out growly.

Kate hadn't budged. She wasn't hurt, right?

I started to stand up, but the moment I moved, Kate raised the dart gun again.

And shot me.

3. Kate

Not-Evie hit the ground.

By the time I'd taken the spare darts from the hidden compartment in the bookcase, my Evie was back. Out cold, but back. I reloaded the gun, tucked it into my waistband and raced over. Her scream was seared into my brain.

What if I hadn't been here? What if I'd left my phone in my backpack, or believed her over-cheery text or – *no!* This was no time to freak out.

Just stop. Breathe. Think. What would Mom do?

Well, for one thing, she wouldn't leave Evie naked in the hallway. So I wrapped my little sister up in her favourite movie-night blanket, carried her to the sofa and laid her down. My inner Mom nodded approvingly. OK, what next?

The monster. I remembered. *Right.*

The big, handsome, unconscious monster. I'd just ... deal with him. Somehow. Hopefully Mom's tranquilliser-and-silver-nitrate formula would keep him out a bit longer. It usually did Evie for around four hours, although her tolerance had sky-rocketed recently. Still, this guy probably hadn't also been taking three preventative shots a day his whole life –

although he was bigger and older, and generally *not* a fifteen-year-old girl, so who knew how he'd metabolise this?

I'd just have to move quickly.

I unlocked the door to Mom's basement, propping it open with my backpack, and had just started dragging the not-person towards it when: 'Kate?'

I spun around. 'Zoe!'

Gorgeous, sweet Zoe King – right there, at the front door I clearly hadn't shut properly. I forced a grin. 'Hey, girlfriend! I ... I mean, girl. Friend. Friend who's ... um, hi. I meant, hi.'

Shut up, Kate.

Zoe giggled. Her cheeks were already winter-rosy, but I'd seen enough blushing to recognise it, even at sub-zero. Then she spotted the not-person.

'Is ... that a body?'

I'd dropped him face down; head towards the basement, feet towards us.

'Nope, art project. Look!' I kicked him, hard. 'Basically a scarecrow.'

Zoe's giggle was half-relief, half-embarrassment. 'It looks so real! Can I –' She pulled her glove off, to touch his leg.

'Don't!' I grabbed her hand. 'It's fragile.'

'You just kicked it.'

'I'm an idiot.'

Zoe laughed. 'No, you're not.'

Wasn't I? Because I was still holding her hand and smiling, with a monster right there. I let go and stepped back.

'Um, I should get back to this. Not going to move itself.' I hoped.

'OK.' Zoe took a deep breath. 'Hey, um, you wanna catch a movie?'

'I can't!'

'Oh.' Zoe's cheeks burned. She looked confused, and a bit hurt. But not as hurt as she'd be if the not-person woke up and ate her.

'Sorry,' I said. 'I've just got a ...'

Monster here. Maybe more on the way, who knows? Mom's been worrying for months about Not-Evie's buzzy monster-radar kicking in, sending out blips between doses. And clearly it's happened, and it could happen again. So now I've gotta uproot my life, shove as much of it as possible into the car and just start driving while Evie's meds hold up enough to silence it. And I don't know if I can ever come back, which sucks. 'Cos I really would love to catch a movie.

'It's fine,' said Zoe. 'I'll just see you at school.'

'Nope.'

'What?'

'Bye, Zoe!' I shut the door. There was a few seconds' beat as she stood there, confused probably, before I heard the snow crunch underfoot as she walked away. *Poor Zoe.*

I dragged the not-person down the hall, struggling under the weight of all that muscle. I made it as far as the first step before the limp monster slipped out of my grip and slid the rest of the way down the stairs.

I cringed as he hit the concrete floor skull-first, but, aside from the sound of breaking cranium, he didn't make a peep. Mom's sedatives really were holding up.

Still, we weren't out of the woods yet.

I took the mouse cages off the shelves by Mom's fake side wall, then dragged the shelves aside. The mice squeaked, and the metal screeched on the concrete. Still the monster didn't budge.

I grabbed a scalpel from Mom's bench, ran my fingers along the wallpaper until I felt the tell-tale crack, then sliced through and pressed down. The 'wall' popped open, revealing the silver-plated bars of Evie's old 'playroom'.

The padlock was open, thank goodness. If Mom still had the key it was on her keyring, wherever she was. Definitely not Burnaby, like we'd told Evie.

The hinges on the cage door creaked as they opened for the first time in – twelve? thirteen? years. Long enough that Evie didn't remember anyway.

The playmat was still in the middle of the room, along with some slightly chewed books and toys. (Evie had stopped *really* savaging things long before we felt safe retiring the playroom.) The place was dusty but you could still see how hard Mom had worked to keep everything fun and happy. Just a nice, colourful room with cute murals, cuddly toys, floor-to-ceiling bars and a massive padlock. I dragged the not-person in, shot another tranq into his leg, then reloaded and shot him again. All that silver would have him feeling like death when he woke up.

Good.

It didn't take long to click the lock shut, pull the shelves back in place and restack them with the cages. I felt awful, leaving the mice. Not-person would definitely eat them once he'd smashed through the cage. Obviously, it was better than eating the neighbours. I just wasn't sure the mice would see it that way.

So, after raiding my mom's supplies for tranqs, dart guns and Evie-meds, I refilled their bowls, adding tranq mix to their water. Maybe they'd still be unconscious when not-person ... you know. They squeaked happily and tucked in.

I felt ill.

* * *

Upstairs, I grabbed whatever was clean from our rooms and shoved it into the biggest bags I could find, adding a couple of the duplicate PJs from the back of Mom's wardrobe for Evie. I filled a couple more bags with toiletries, chargers and our laptops, loaded a cooler bag with meat and stuffed it all into the car.

Then I changed Evie into some non-shredded clothes and sponge-cleaned her arm, which was already starting to heal, despite the silver in the tranq and empty syringe I'd found in the kitchen. She really was getting stronger.

I tried not to think about how she was going to freak out when she woke up.

That was Future Kate's problem. Present Kate had enough to deal with, thanks.

4. Evie

I felt like death.

My entire body ached, everything was somehow burning and freezing all at once, and when I sat up my head threatened to split, as the world blurred into fuzzy spots.

For one happy second, I thought I was just ill. Then everything came flooding back: the crazy-eyed stalker, the claw-hand, the pain, the blood – and Kate. Kate had *shot* me.

No, that couldn't be true. None of this was true! People didn't grow claws; their eyes didn't glow. And Kate wouldn't shoot me: she loved me. No matter what Stalker Rom had said.

The spots in my vision cleared enough for me to realise where I was: the back of Kate's car, in a gas station I didn't recognise, surrounded by barely zipped, overflowing bags of clothes. And no Kate.

Then the door opened beside me. 'Evie! You're awake?'

'Katie!' I launched myself across the seat, yanking her into the car for a hug. 'What's happening? Where are we? Are – are we *running away*?'

'Whoa, slow down!' said Kate. 'Stay calm. Blood sugar, remember?'

'Katie, that guy –'

Kate nodded. 'I know. But you need to rest. You had a seizure.'

'I did?' I didn't remember that, but Kate's nod seemed very certain.

'That guy pumped you full of epinephrine,' she said.

Epi– what? I must have looked as confused as I felt, because Kate said: 'Adrenaline. Sent your blood sugar through the roof. Your synapses went into overdrive, and your poor brain just kept firing out messages until your body freaked out.'

'So you *shot me*?'

'I *sedated* you!' said Kate, with a silent 'silly'. 'You should have seen how you were flailing! Last time that happened, you were three and you concussed yourself for a month. How *is* your head, by the way?'

'My head?' Pounding. Splitting. Threatening to rip open and destroy everything in its path. 'Fine,' I lied. We had bigger problems. 'What happened that monster? Rom? After you shot him?'

Kate shook her head. 'I didn't shoot him. I thought I had, but – he got away. The police are after him, obviously. I just didn't feel safe sticking around.'

Of course she didn't. It wasn't safe. What did the police know about monsters?

'We don't need the police. We need slayers. Or Winchesters. Or – or the kids from *Stranger Things*.'

'*Stranger Things*?' Kate's eyebrows shot up. 'Evie, he's a man, not a demogorgon.'

23

'He's not a man!' I didn't mean to snap that, but I did. 'His eyes turned yellow. And he was crazy strong, and – and his hand turned into a claw and he *stabbed me with it, Katie*!'

'He stabbed you?' said Katie. 'With his claw-hand?'

She didn't believe me. Fair enough, I barely believed me.

'It's true, look!' I shoved my arm out, rolling up my sleeve to reveal ... 'Oh!'

There wasn't even a scratch. 'Wait, maybe it's my other arm.'

'You don't remember where he stabbed you?'

'No, I do. I just ...' I rolled up my other sleeve anyway.

Nothing. What the hell?

Kate must've seen my panic. She pulled me in for another squeeze.

'He did jab you, Evie,' she said, 'with the epi-pen, remember? And I'll bet all those synaptic misfires made for some pretty vivid hallucinations and messed with your memory. That sort of crap can feel very real.'

Hallucinations? Was that all this was?

'So it's just a combination of scary human and out-of-control blood sugar?' I winced, as the fake-memory of his flashing eyes replayed through my head. 'That's messed up.'

Kate nodded sympathetically. 'I'm sorry. I wish I could fix this but – oh!'

She pulled a cooler bag from under the passenger seat and pushed it into my lap.

'Here! I can't erase imaginary monsters, but this should defeat that lukewarm death feeling. Open it.'

The sweet-metallic scent of bloody steak hit like a delicious sledge-hammer. My stomach growled. I still felt cold

and achy and slightly insane, but suddenly, more than anything, I felt hungry. I ripped straight into a raw steak with my
teeth. If Kate was grossed out, she didn't show it.

'The iron will balance your blood sugar,' she said. 'Plus,
they won't keep outside the fridge, so eat up!' She slid into
the driver's seat. 'And buckle up. We're going on a Wilder
sisters road trip!'

5. Kate

It was just before midnight when our headlights gleamed against the happy-looking billboard with *Welcome to Brightside* splashed across a floral background.

If Evie had been awake, she would've said it was just the sort of sign that winds up battered and bloody by the end of the horror movie. It was only missing the word 'Hell' graffiti-ed over 'Brightside' in dripping red paint – and a population counter whizzing down to zero. But Evie had dozed off hours ago, no tranqs required.

The poor thing was wiped. She'd been through hell herself today and her body knew the truth even if she didn't yet. I would tell her. Just not right now. Right now, I needed to focus on finding Mom.

It had been two weeks since she'd headed off in search of Evie's parents, desperately hoping that Robert had made more progress on a cure than we had. Because Not-Evie was getting stronger, and that was dangerous for everyone.

She hadn't told me where she was going, but the last contact I'd had was a text ten days ago, telling me she might be out of coverage for a bit so not to panic. I had been panicking, as time went on. But pretending to Evie that everything was OK had helped me convince myself too. Until now.

This wasn't OK. This was horrible – and we needed our mom.

According to her online banking, Mom had used her debit card in Brightside a bunch of times since she'd left. The last time was nine days ago – twenty-four dollars in a place called Ray's, and a load of cash at an ATM straight after.

No account activity since.

Mom wouldn't be delighted I hacked her account from my phone but, in my defence, using some version of Dad's name and birthday for every password was basically an invitation for cyber-crime. Plus, we had to go *somewhere*.

And sure, maybe the extent of my Brightside research had involved typing it into my GPS and following directions. But that did tell me it was a little town in the middle of nowhere. Probably the safest place in the world to lie low for a few days.

Of course, if I'd been a bit less panicked, I might have wondered why Mom would go looking for two dangerous not-people in 'the safest place in the world'. If it had been daylight, I definitely would have noticed all the 'missing person' posters plastered across lamp-posts as I drove towards town. But I hadn't, and it wasn't. So I didn't.

I just kept driving, looking for somewhere to pull over and car-camp for the night.

Then I saw 'Goodman's Guesthouse': three storeys tall with white walls, blue woodwork and a colourful Christmas tree in the window.

It looked nice. More importantly, it looked open, even at midnight. And, according to the neon sign outside, it had **Vacancies**.

Well, that beats sleeping in the car, I thought.

I had no idea what I was getting us into.

6. Evie

The bell on the guesthouse door clattered.

The boy behind the desk jumped to his feet. He was around my age, and cute in a lanky way; his broad shoulders and square jaw looked out of place with his carefully parted brown hair and giant nerd-glasses. It gave him this dorky superhero-waiting-to-fill-out kind of vibe. But I liked dorky superheroes.

He started to smile, then froze and – I swear – *sniffed the air* before slamming his book down and storming across the lobby.

'Out!' he snapped.

'What?' I said.

'GET. OUT!' He was right in my face this time.

Kate pushed between us, shoving him back. 'Pardon me ...' She glanced down at his name-badge. 'Kev.'

'Kevin.'

'Whatever. Talk to my sister like that again, and I'll ram that badge down your throat so hard your duodenum's gonna think it's been promoted to bellhop. Got that?'

Kevin glowered. All right, maybe he wasn't as cute as I'd thought. But he wasn't as scary as he thought either. Especially compared to Kate.

'Kevin? Is someone there?' called a woman from upstairs.

Kevin's face flushed with panic.

Katie grinned. 'Ooh, is that the manager?'

'*I'm* the manager,' hissed Kevin. 'Now get out!'

Kate snorted a very 'no' laugh.

Kevin's jaw set furiously, until the stairs creaked. Then he whipped around and yelled: 'It's no-one, Chris. Go back to – CHRIS, GO BACK TO BED!'

Chris didn't go back to bed. She bounded down the stairs, tying her dressing gown as she came. She was about forty, with a platinum-blond bob and a friendly smile.

'Hey, no-one!' she said. 'Welcome to Goodman's. Can I take your bags?'

OK, I loved her.

As did Kate, judging by how fast her badass scowl morphed into an adorable grin.

'Aw thanks!' She held her gym-bag out.

Kevin snatched it out of her hand, then flung it to the ground.

'Kevin!' gasped Chris.

'Kev!' said Kate.

'It's *Kevin*,' snapped Kevin. 'And, Chris, we need to talk. NOW!'

He jerked his head towards the office behind the desk with wide-eyed urgency. Chris frowned, then sighed.

'Sorry girls,' she said. 'Give us two minutes?'

Kevin threw me a fully murderous glare as they headed into the office. OK, new life goal: Find a guy attractive without him turning out to be a freak.

'You OK?' asked Kate.

'Pfft, yeah!' I said. 'No over-stretched power-tripping dork's getting between us and a bed tonight!'

Besides, Kate looked exhausted. She'd been driving all evening. I wasn't going to make her sleep in the car too.

'All right,' said Kate. 'Let's get cosy, then, since we're not leaving.'

She sat down by the Christmas tree to unzip her boots.

'You get cosy,' I said. 'I'm getting nosy! I wanna know what his problem is.'

I slipped behind the desk, and pressed my ear to the door. Kevin's voice was low and angry, but Chris's was rising – she sounded upset.

'And her sister? You'll send her back out too?'

'That's not her sister. And not my problem.'

'KEVIN!'

'What? It's not!' said Kevin. 'If she wants to ally up and road trip with that abomination, that's her stupid choice. But they're not staying here.'

Abomination? My fists curled as I glanced back at Katie, her Pride badge happily pinned to her dad's leather jacket. Even in Toronto, she'd heard words like 'abomination' a few times. My skin pin-prickled.

'Well, we're not sending them back out to face that psychopath,' said Chris.

Wait, what?

'It's not like we have any other guests,' she continued. 'We can stick 'em in room 2, right next to you. Just in case.'

Great, but did she say ... 'psychopath'? She'd said 'psychopath', right?

'It's not guests I'm worried about, Chrissy,' said Kevin. 'It's you.'

'I'm forty-three!' said Chris. 'I've faced far worse than that teenager. Unless there's another reason you're scared to have her around?' She paused for a beat, and I wished I could have seen Kevin's face as she added, 'She is very pretty.'

Kate was beautiful – all art-student cool, with giant brown eyes and a choppy blond bob framing her heart-shaped face. And Kevin protested a bit too much to pretend he hadn't noticed. 'Ew! Gross, Chrissy.'

'Oh, that's gross?' said Chris. 'But letting Ashton's guys murder them is fine?'

Wait, 'guys'? Like, multiple psychos? Was I hallucinating again?

'You're really not going to let this go, are you?' sighed Kevin. 'OK, one night. For you. But that's it.'

'Sure,' said Chris. 'Wouldn't want you making a friend, would we?'

I'd just raced back around the desk when the door swung open. Chris came out all smiles. Kevin still looked like he wanted to maim someone.

'All right!' said Chris. 'Let's get you girls checked in, Kevin'll take your bags up. Room 2. It's right by his room, in case you need anything.'

She said it so perkily, like Kevin wasn't currently glaring over, trying to eye-murder us. It was only one night, I

32

reminded myself. And we *did* have a violent stalker after us. Plus, apparently someone called Ashton would massacre us if we left?

Unless I'd imagined that, of course.

There was one person who could tell me for sure. So, as Chris and Katie headed to the check-in desk, I joined Kevin by our luggage and swiped Katie's bag from him. 'I'll take that!'

Kevin straightened up, looking half-homicidal, half-confused. 'Why?'

'Because there's a lot of bags,' I said, 'and only one you.'

Kevin glanced over at Chris and Katie, both busy chatting as the computer booted up. Then he turned back to me, with a twisted smirk.

'There's only one of you too, Red,' he hissed. 'You sure you wanna do this?'

OK, he was properly creepy. Whatever. I just needed to hear more about Ashton. After that, Kevin the bigot could shove his head in a blender.

'Let's go.'

7. Evie again

Kevin didn't say a word going up the stairs, although his back managed to look absolutely fuming. It wasn't until we reached the room and I asked 'Who's Ashton?' that he flipped.

'How *dare* you!' He stomped forward, so furious I couldn't help jumping back. His eyes were almost rage-glowing behind his glasses. 'Waltzing into my town – my house – asking about Ashton, as though things like you don't have nightmares about things like him. And like me.'

'You? Dude, don't flatter yourself.'

He wasn't scary, just obnoxious. But he was making my head prickle and my hand twitch with the urge to punch. If he said one more thing about Kate …

'What did you think would happen?' he snarled. 'You and your fake-sister would show up, play dumb and do whatever you want under the radar – 'cos who'd notice another monster when –'

Monster? I'd grabbed that jerk by the throat before I even realised it.

'Shut up,' I snarled. 'Or I'll rip out that over-used voice-box and –'

'OW!' Kevin's yelp snapped me back to myself.

What the hell was I doing?

I let go and stepped back. My fingers were wet. I thought. Until I looked down and realised – those weren't fingers. It was a claw – huge and twisted – like Kate said I'd imagined on Stalker Rom. Except mine was covered in Kevin's blood.

No! I glanced up at him, standing there, bloody and confused – then stared back at my claw. Hand. I was just hallucinating again. This was adrenaline. A blood-sugar spike. That's all.

'This isn't real,' I muttered. 'You're OK. That wasn't real.'

'What? You trying to kill me?' Kevin touched his throat, looking from his sticky red fingers to my – my not-claw (it couldn't be a claw). 'Sure felt real. How'd you control it like that?'

What? 'No. I – I didn't.' My head pounded. 'It's not real.'

Something about the way Kevin laughed sent a bolt of pain straight through me.

I tried to breathe, like Kate always said, but my heart was racing and my eyes were white-hot. Kevin looked straight into them and tilted his head.

'Nightmare eyes,' he mused. 'Cool!'

Rom's terrifying, black-rimmed, yellow demon's eyes flashed through my mind. I'd imagined them, Kate said. So how come, when I stumbled to the mirror, they stared back at me from my own face?

Another surge of pain hit. I had to grab the bed to steady myself.

'Kate!' I gasped. 'Kevin, get Kate.'

'What, and miss the show?' Kevin laughed. 'Nuh-uh.'

My vision blurred. My muscles jolted again, and I had to grit my teeth to not scream. Kevin sat down cross-legged on the floor.

'You're *so* good at this, pup. I shoulda brought popcorn.' Then he leaned forward, all serious. 'Look at that control. You're not like the others, eh?'

'Others? *Ow!*'

My head was splintering again. I grabbed my scalp, trying to resist the urge to rip it open. Pain-tears seeped onto my cheeks. This death-ache was going to kill me.

'Kevin, *please –*'

But his nasty smirk said he wasn't going anywhere. I needed to stop myself, somehow, so I squeezed my eyes shut and imagined Katie.

Breathe! she said. *Come on, Evie. In, out. In, out. Calm. Peaceful.*

Kevin sniggered.

'Calm' gave way to white-hot, all-consuming agony. This wasn't working. I needed something else. 'My insulin!'

'Your …. insulin?' Kevin laughed.

The bags were by the door; my insulin had to be in one of them. The muscles in my legs pulsed. I just needed to hold off this seizure long enough to find it.

But Kevin jumped up, right in my way.

'Move!' I snarled

'Why? Got somewhere to be?' He grabbed my arm.

I shoved him away, ignoring the crash and his surprised 'HEY!' as I staggered to the bags and dropped to the ground.

36

Heat throbbed through my arms. I grabbed the closest back-pack and tried to unzip it, but my claw-hand ripped through the canvas.

Except, no, it didn't! I didn't have a claw.

I held my not-claw up and glared at it. *You're not real, go away.*

And it did! Just like that, my hand was right back to normal. But still covered in creepy Kevin's blood ...

'Holy super-powers, Red!' muttered Kevin.

I spun around. He was right behind me, staring at my hand.

'Wolf on, wolf off, eh? How –?'

He was cut short by a bang as the door swung open, and Katie appeared.

'What the hell?' She took half a second to absorb the scene, then stormed in, grabbed Kevin and shoved him towards the door. 'What did you do, freak?'

Kevin laughed. 'Me? She nearly ripped my throat open!'

Kate must have known that; she'd seen the blood. Still, she just glowered and yelled, 'Get. Out!' Kevin didn't budge. Kate pulled the dart gun from her pocket. 'Now!'

'Whoa!' Kevin grinned. 'You're scary, huh? Although, that's a dart gun so ...'

'So either you leave,' said Kate. 'Or I'll tranq your skinny nerd butt and slide you down the stairs like a freaking tobog-gan. Clear?'

She helped me up, one-handed, as she kept the gun on Kevin.

'Skinny nerd butt?' he repeated. 'Harsh! But I still don't wanna leave you alone with that *thing*.'

37

Kate pressed the tranq gun against his chest. 'Go!'

'OK!' Kevin raised his hands and backed away. 'Your stupid choice, I'm gone. Later, Little Red.'

He winked at me, then wheeled around and made it as far as the door before turning back – looking softer, somehow. 'Kate, wait. I can't just …'

'You can.' She shoved him out. 'Now fudge off!' (All right, that's *not* what she yelled, as she slammed the door and locked it – but it's close enough.)

Kate slid the gun into the waistband of her jeans, then turned around. 'You all right, Evie?'

Was I?

My body had relaxed, with Kate here. The twitches and aches felt less urgent. and my skull seemed less likely to shatter into my brain. But: 'Katie, I hurt him! I thought he said something homophobic. I wanted to rip his throat out – and then I almost did.'

'Did you?' Kate pulled a face. 'He looked fine to me.'

'He was bleeding!' I showed her my hand, still covered in Kevin's blood. 'And I hallucinated again, Katie. I –'

I'd barely thought about the claw-hand, when it sprang back up.

Kate jumped.

She didn't mean to, and she only needed half a second more to go from freaked out to fine. But that split-second of terror was enough.

Oh. My. God! 'It's real?'

'Evie.' Katie touched my arm.

I pulled away. 'No!'

My body was flooding with white-hot, muscle-twitching

38

energy again, as my head and heart began to pound. No, I didn't have a claw!

I was still seeing things. I had to be. 'I need my insulin!'

I dived for the bags. Kate pulled me back.

'Evie, stop,' she said. 'You've had enough today. You just need to calm down.'

Calm down? '*I HAVE A CLAW!*'

'I know.'

She knew? It was real?

I'd really almost killed Kevin. 'SO WHY CAN'T I FREAK OUT?'

Kate sighed. 'It'll make it worse.'

'Worse how?' I said. 'What, two claws?'

My left hand burned. Kate's eyes widened. Oh no.

'I've got *two claws*, Katie. Two giant, evil, freaking Freddy Krueger monster things. I am not calm.'

Kate chuckled. *She* would have been the poster-girl for calm right now, if I couldn't somehow hear her frantic pulse. What the hell?

'Look,' she said. 'Obviously, it's weird. But –'

'But *what*? How can you possibly be planning to finish that sentence?'

'But it's going to be OK,' she said. 'I promise.'

'You promise? How? I don't even know what's real any more. Was Rom real? Monster Rom, I mean? With the eyes and the claw?'

Kate chewed her lip, then nodded.

'And he really stabbed me with his claw-hand, and now I have claw-hands and yellow demon eyes too? Is that real?'

Kate hesitated. 'Evie, listen –'

'Is it real, Kate?'

'Yes!' said Kate. 'It's all real. But you need to breathe.'

'I am breathing!' If I was breathing any faster, I'd be hyperventilating. Stalker Rom clawed my arm, and now ... 'Am *I* a monster now?'

'Evie –' said Kate. But she actually 'said' it. Not 'gasped' or 'scoffed' or, you know, anything suitably 'that's ridiculous' sounding. She wasn't denying it. Oh God!

'I'm a monster.' Every joint in my body burned again. 'You said I imagined it all. I thought I was going crazy! You lied.'

Rom had said that. He'd said they were lying, and I hadn't believed him, because Kate and Mom would *never* lie to me.

'Evie, I'm sorry, I just –' She couldn't finish her sentence. That's how bad things were. Kate Wilder couldn't finish a sentence. Nothing made sense any more. We were runaways; monsters were real; Kate had lied – I couldn't even unzip my bag.

'I want my hands back,' I groaned.

Just like that, they tingled and came back. I laughed. It wasn't funny, but I laughed anyway. 'What the hell?'

'I don't know. But ...' Kate rubbed her temples. 'We need to talk. Come here.' She guided me to the bed and handed me a bar of chocolate. 'Open this.'

'Um, OK.' I did. 'What's this? Like, a metaphor or a science thingy ...'

'It's chocolate.' Kate smiled, but her hands shook as she broke some off and held it out. 'Have some.'

'But I'm diabetic!'

Kate winced apologetically.

Oh, what? 'I'm not diabetic?'

Kate shook her head.

'But I take insulin! I watch my blood sugar. Mom spends her life in the basement trying to cure me. Right?'

'Kind of,' said Kate. 'I mean, she's definitely trying to cure you.'

Cure me of *what*?

'Katie, if I'm not diabetic – what am I?'

8. Kate

I wanted to lie.

Evie looked so wide-eyed and worried. And terrifying.

Last time I'd seen those black-rimmed, flickering-yellow eyes, Not-Evie had swiped me down the stairs. My ankle still hurt.

'You're my sister,' I said.

'Right, but what else?' said Evie. 'And don't lie. I'll know.'

She wouldn't; she never did. We hadn't meant to keep the truth from her this long. Mom was always on the verge of finding a cure, and then it wouldn't matter. But the cures never worked, and Evie was so happy not knowing. What was the point of the truth if it would ruin her life?

Now, though? Our lives were a horrifying mess anyway.

'All right, no lies. But we'll need to start *waaay* back.'

'Like, when my parents died?' said Evie.

Oh, boy. 'Let's just start, OK?'

* * *

Evie's story actually started with *my* dad.

He'd been a folklore lecturer in Ireland, until Mom was offered her own lab in Toronto. Dad couldn't let her pass that up, even if it meant a few years of random bar jobs for him when they moved. Once I was born, Dad did the stay-at-home-parent thing like a pro. Sure, I got my bedtime stories from huge tomes of Irish mythology and world legends instead of squishy animal books, but we'd had fun. I had thousands of photos and videos to prove it.

Still, I wasn't always the greatest conversationalist, and Dad got a bit bored, sometimes. So he found new challenges – like monster-hunting.

Not actual hunting, obviously. But I was a terrible sleeper and Dad was a horror fanatic. So when the animal attacks started in our area, Dad spiced up our late-night drive-until-Katie-passes-out excursions with a bit of make-believe.

And it *was* make-believe; he wasn't genuinely hunting werewolves with a toddler. Imagine if he'd found one! No, this was just something to keep his poor, sleep-deprived brain from switching off with me in the back seat.

But, one night, it didn't work. Dad dozed off at the wheel, and never woke up. I got away without a scratch – but Mom spiralled a bit after that. I guess she needed something of Dad to hold on to and, for some reason, that something was his wolf game. Only Mom wasn't playing.

She asked her PhD student, Robert Rose, to help develop a tranquilliser dart that could take out a werewolf. And Robert was so nice. He just wanted to be there for his grieving boss – even if that meant inventing monster-strength tranqs and going 'hunting' together to make sure no-one got hurt.

He never thought they'd find anything, until they discovered that poor student who'd taken the wrong shortcut on the wrong night. The bloody pawprints leading away from his body definitely weren't human. And then, suddenly, they *were*.

Robert and Mom found Madison in a parking lot, sobbing and covered in blood. Mom might've gone full-slayer if Robert hadn't stepped in.

He'd whipped off his coat and wrapped it around Madison, before she spotted his gun and begged him to use it on her. She didn't know it was just for tranqs.

That's what broke Mom. She couldn't hate this sobbing, terrified young woman – she had to help her. She promised she would, somehow.

Which is how we wound up with a not-person, an unregulated lab and a silver-plated cage/bedroom/playroom in the basement – and Robert in the guestroom, because friends don't let friends house monsters alone.

We became this odd little family unit. And Robert and Madison became this other little unit, too. Mom always said they were madly in love.

Love definitely made Robert a bit mad.

He decided a fresh infectee might help them spot a weakness in Madison's virus. They had tried with mice, but mice aren't human. So one night, while Madison and Mom watched a movie, Robert snuck into the lab. He stole a blood vial, locked himself in Madison's room and injected it into his veins. Classic mad-scientist stuff.

But it worked! Or it seemed to.

Robert's blood helped them find a formula to stave off his episodes, they increased the dosage for Madison, and that was it. The transformations stopped, Madison moved out of the lab and into Robert's room, and everything was good.

Better than good, actually. Because then Mom detected elevated levels of hCG (aka the pregnancy hormone) in Madison's bloodwork and everyone sat me down to ask how I'd feel about a new baby in the house. It was all perfect.

Until it wasn't.

The contractions woke Madison, and she panicked. I'm sure it's always scary but, when you're planning a home birth in a silver-coated cage with just a couple of immunologists as your midwives … well, between that and the pain, Madison slipped.

Robert and Mom had to take off around town to find her.

Unfortunately, that didn't go so well. Mom wound up with two unconscious not-people in her basement and – when Madison's waters broke – a scalpel in her hand trying to wing an emergency C-section.

Luckily infectees heal fast. Madison survived, but that didn't mean she was OK. Nobody was. Evie's crazy-in-love parents had nearly killed each other; they couldn't trust themselves with a baby. But they could trust us.

There's a video hidden on my laptop (in a file called 'Early Stage Non-Consanguineous Sororal Bonding' – too boring for Evie to snoop). I've watched it so many times I don't know how much I really remember, and how much my brain has filled in over the years. But I do know this: the look on my little two-year-old face when I met Baby Evie was pure love.

Robert had sat me down, with a cushion on my lap. Madison laid this teeny bundle across my arms and asked, 'Do you like her?'

Like her? Little Video-Kate said, 'Yes.' But she meant so much more.

Baby Evie was the most wonderful thing. I know I was fascinated by her little nose. And those chubby baby fingers, because I reached out to touch them – and she wrapped her entire teensy fist around my finger, holding my hand.

I grinned up at the camera and you could see it in my face: I was besotted. And I was never letting her go.

'Would you like to keep her?' asked Madison.

I couldn't say 'yes!' fast enough. But I didn't realise what she meant. Not even when she started sobbing, and I tried to kiss her tears away and make her happy again.

Only, I couldn't. Just like I couldn't always kiss Mom happy, and she couldn't always fix me. I was only two; I shouldn't have known sadness like that.

But I did. And Baby Evie didn't. She was pink and perfect, with no idea how much life could hurt. She never would, I decided. She'd be happy. Always.

I'd protect her from the rest.

* * *

I turned the video off, and looked at Evie. I'd really thought ending with that would help. We were so adorable. But that wasn't Evie's key take-away.

'My parents are alive?' she said. 'And they're *werewolves*?'

'Well, we don't say …'

Evie stared at her hands. '*I'm* a werewolf?'

'No! Evie, we – we don't say "werewolf".'

I'm not sure that helped either.

46

9. Evie

They don't say 'werewolf'? My head was spinning.

My parents were alive. My parents were monsters. My parents turned into big scary nightmares and ate people. So did I. But Kate and Mom didn't say 'werewolf'?

'No!' I said. 'You're wrong. I'm not ... I don't have crazy memory gaps, or wake up covered in other people's blood.' My muscles were twitching. 'Or just flip and hurt people, or ...'

Except I had, hadn't I? I'd nearly ripped Kevin apart with my monster claw. And Kate was beautiful and badass, but boy was she clumsy. She'd broken her arm twice falling downstairs in the middle of the night. She'd cracked two ribs knocking a bookcase on herself in the middle of the night. She had a thin white scar through her left eyebrow and a longer one across her jaw, and I'd never been able to figure out how she'd sleepwalked into a mirror *that* hard.

The twitching in my muscles got stronger.

'Evie –' Kate tried to take my hand.

I yanked it away and stood up.

I didn't want to listen. I'm not proud of this, but I jammed my hands over my ears, screwed my eyes shut and hummed loudly, trying to block out my own thoughts.

Kate put her hand on my shoulder. 'Evie, please –'

'DON'T TOUCH ME, I'M DANGEROUS!' My arm jolted as I shoved her away.

Something went crash.

I spun around to see Kate pushing herself up from the floor. By the door. On the other side of the room. Her lip was bleeding, and there was a gash above her scarred eyebrow. I'd done that. I'd hurt my big sister.

'Oh my God, Kate!'

I raced over, faster than I meant to, somehow. Kate fell backwards again, then scrambled to her feet and reached back to her waistband. But the gun had fallen on the ground. I picked it up.

'KATE?' The door handle moved urgently. 'KATE! Are you OK?' Kevin sounded ready to smash the door down.

Kate's heart was pounding. I could hear it. But somehow she sounded pissed off, not scared, as she yelled: 'I tripped on your stupid carpet! By the stupid bathroom.'

She paused to steady herself against the nightstand.

'Oh, no,' said Kevin, totally unconvinced. 'I should fix that. Let me in.'

Kate lowered herself onto the bed, flinching, as she dabbed the cut with a Kleenex. 'No. But if you leave us alone, we won't sue for negligence.'

'Kate, let me in!' yelled Kevin. 'Please.'

We should *let him in*, I thought. *Kate shouldn't be alone with me*. I moved to unlock the door, but Kate shook her head.

'If you wanna help,' she called to Kevin, 'get ice, then get lost.'

There was a pause, then: 'All right.'

Kevin didn't sound happy, but he didn't say anything else. After a few seconds, Kate nodded towards the door. I unlocked and opened it.

Kevin was gone.

'That's better,' said Kate. 'Dork needs to mind his own business, eh?'

She laughed. I didn't. Kate sighed. 'Don't freak out. It was an accident; we're fine. I've had way worse.'

Well, that was less comforting than she probably thought.

I glanced down at the tranq gun in my hand.

'Don't!' said Katie. 'Come on, sit down. Let's talk.'

I shook my head and moved away.

Kate groaned. 'Evie, don't make me stand up.'

'No, stay there,' I said, 'away from me. I'm not safe to be around.'

'I've been around you my whole life, silly,' said Katie, laughing. 'You were just panicking. You didn't know you could do that. It's fine.'

Fine? 'I could have killed you. How was that fine?'

'Room service!' called Kevin.

That was oddly quick!

The door swung open. Kate turned to glare.

The split-second glance away was all I needed. By the time she looked back – 'Evie, *NO!*' – I'd shot myself.

As the world fuzzed up, I couldn't help noticing she looked a bit less annoyed than I'd expected. And a lot more horrified.

10. Kate

'*Evie, NO!*'

She'd tranqed herself!

Kevin dropped the ice and spun around. I don't know what he was expecting to see, but that wasn't the body language of someone turning to catch an unconscious teenager mid-fall. He did, though. That annoyed me even more.

'Hands. *Off*.' The world swam a little as I stood up.

Kevin looked worried.

'Are you supposed to be wobbling?' he asked. 'Sit down. I've got this.'

He lowered Evie on to the bed, then reached for the covers.

'You are *not* tucking her in!' I yanked the quilt from his hand. 'Move.'

Kevin shrugged, then plucked the empty dart out of Evie's shoulder to examine it.

'Is this her "insulin"? It knocked her straight out, eh?'

'Yeah.' I swiped it out of his hand. 'Wanna see what it'll do to you?'

I knew what it would do. We'd adjusted Evie's dose so many times in the past few months that this much could take an elephant out. It would kill Kevin.

He passed me the gun and held his arms out.

'Sure.' He smirked. 'Fire ahead.'

Asshole.

I tucked the gun away and sat down.

Kevin shrugged, and repacked the ice into the tea-towel.

'So, what *is* she, exactly?' he asked. 'She's not like other wolves, eh? The way she grew her claw into my neck and then just … stopped, without changing? I've never seen control like that before. It's awesome!'

He was using a lot of words I didn't think applied to this situation, like 'control' and 'awesome'. But the one I focused on was:

'*Wolves?* Seriously? Do you even hear yourself, Kev?'

'It's Kevin.' He handed me the ice. 'And, yes, I hear myself, accurately describing what just happened. Wait, are you trying to gaslight me? Make me doubt being attacked by a dangerous monster? That's adorable!'

All right, so he knew stuff. That didn't mean he knew Evie.

'She's not dangerous!' I pressed the ice against my forehead and winced.

Kevin raised an eyebrow. 'Exhibit A would like to disagree with Exhibit B.'

He pulled a packet of painkillers from his pocket and held them out. I wanted to glare until he put them away again, but I knew from experience I'd need them, so I glared and took them instead.

'She thought she was defending me,' I said.

'What, from me?' Kevin shrugged, like: *fair enough*. 'So who was she defending from you, then?'

He indicated my bruises, face full of patronising fake concern.

'This was an accident,' I said. 'Stop acting like I'm so naïve. I've met four not-people, lived with three and fought two. Including the one who mauled Evie in our house today, then tried to kill me.'

'Wait, it attacked *her*?' said Kevin.

'Yeah. So I threw him across the room, tranqed him and got us out of there. 'Cos that's what I do, Kev.'

'Wow.' Kevin must have been impressed; he'd forgotten to correct me on his name. 'So, you think it's still after her?' he asked. 'Is that why you're here?'

'We came here to be safe,' I said. 'And then *you* attacked her too, didn't you? You must've scared the crap out of her. She's never done anything like this before. All that control you think she has –' I stopped.

My voice was rising again, along with my temper. Kevin didn't deserve that much of my energy, so I took a beat and centred myself.

'Evie had no idea what she was before tonight. And you stole my chance to tell her in a way she could handle. Instead, she found out while she was sobbing and shaking, and covered in your blood. And you think *she's* the monster?'

Kevin turned from me to Evie. 'A monster, not *the* monster.'

But there was something different in the way he was looking at her now. A little less angry, and a little more … sympathetic? Or fascinated, maybe?

He touched his neck. 'So that control's innate? She didn't learn it? Could your others do that too?'

'Just the one today,' I said. 'But he definitely knew what he was doing.'

'Which was trying to kill you?' Kevin chewed his lip for a moment, then looked back at me. 'Why don't you leave, Kate? Just you.'

'Excuse me?'

Kevin sighed. 'Look, I can see the scars under your make-up. Maybe she's never done this before, but she's clearly gone full-wolf on you. A lot.'

'She's not a –'

'Whatever you want to call her,' said Kevin, 'she hurts you. And now this other one's out there too? Kate, you're in so much danger. And you don't have to be. You could hit the road at dawn and go – go anywhere. It's all safer than here.'

So, just abandon my baby sister with him? Was he serious?

'*OUT!*' I snapped.

'You're no good to Evie dead,' he said. 'And if she loves you like you clearly love her, she'd agree with me.'

She would, that was definitely an argument we'd have tomorrow morning. But *not* one she was winning. I whipped the gun off the bed and pointed it at him.

'I'm not leaving. You are, now go!'

Kevin didn't budge and my finger was aching to pull the trigger, so I dropped the gun, stood up and shoved him through the doorway. My head only barely swam.

'How about your own room, then?' said Kevin. 'So I know you're safe tonight?'

And so Evie would be all alone?

'My sister poisoned herself to keep from hurting me,' I snapped. 'She's not dangerous. But if anything happens to her, I will be. Understand?'

Kevin nodded.

'Good. Now, fudge off.' (I didn't say 'fudge'. But he did leave.)

I flexed out my fist and pressed the ice pack to it, soothing the ache of being clenched so long. Beside me, Evie shivered under her quilt.

I threw mine over her too, then tucked it around her.

Poor Evie. She'd feel like hell when she woke, hopefully. As long as silver made her feel ill, it was still working, at least a bit. Although she'd barely been out at all earlier. And as for channelling Not-Evie? That wasn't good.

If that *thing* could make daytime appearances through Evie – what was stopping it from swallowing her whole some day?

'It's OK,' I told Evie. 'We'll find Mom. She'll have something.'

She had to. Her last text before she went quiet had mentioned a breakthrough. Maybe she'd found Robert and Madison? Maybe Robert had a way to help Evie? Maybe they were burrowed away in a lab somewhere, working on it right now.

'This is just a glitch,' I told Evie. 'That's all.'

I sat there a moment longer, then found my laptop in the mess of bags and got started on Mom's 'missing person' poster. 'Fun freaking night,' I muttered.

11. Evie

I woke up, and wished I hadn't.

I was shivery all over. My brain was on fire, my joints felt like I'd spent the day lifting elephants and my stomach churned like one wrong move would be a fast-track to puke-central. I deserved all of it.

There was a blue glow from across the room.

I got up, slowly, to investigate. Kate's laptop was open on the desk, and she was fast asleep in front of it. The glow from her screensaver highlighted her face – bruises, swelling and all. The dart gun was beside her.

My stomach gave a sick twist. Kate shouldn't be passing out, beat-up and exhausted, at a desk in some weirdo guest-house. She shouldn't have to sleep with a gun in case she woke up to a monster. And she should be able to hug her sister without being thrown across the room. Or worse. Because it could have been worse.

Kate knew how to defend herself, but she hadn't. She hadn't expected me to hurt her. Even though I'd clearly done it before. Fifteen years living with something like me, and she still saw her sister before she saw a monster. But I *was* a monster.

Being around me put Kate in danger, and not just from me. Stalker Rom literally would have killed her. Even through all the achy coldness and the waves of nausea, I could feel my muscles pulse at the thought. I remembered the warmth as Kate put her arms around me and told me it was OK. It wasn't; it never had been. But still, I longed to wake her so she could hug me and tell me that again. Kate was done having to pretend for me, though.

Rom had implied she didn't love me. I was just some lab-rat, and she and Mom were ruining my life. But he'd had it backwards.

Kate did love me. Of course she did.

And I loved her. But I'd ruined her life anyway.

* * *

The stairs creaked. I kept going. This house was huge, and it was after 3AM. Everyone was definitely asleep. One grouchy step wouldn't wake them.

My head was still pounding. I couldn't stop shivering.

I buttoned my coat as I reached the door, took a deep breath and –

'Oh, don't run away. It's such a cliché.' Kevin flicked on the hall light.

He was right in front of me, arms crossed like I'd better have a good explanation for this, young lady. I'd swear he hadn't been there a moment ago, but he must have been – right?

'Well, clichés in … dark houses … something, *ugh!*' What I wanted to say was that creeps lurking in the shadows

57

shouldn't talk about clichés, but my brain was too fried to quip. 'Just move.'

Kevin didn't budge. 'You look awful, Red. You really did poison yourself, eh? You can't leave – you'll be too weak to do anything except lie in the snow and cry.'

'Sounds like a perfect plan. Bye.'

I reached to push him aside, but he caught my hand. Then his eyes widened. 'Holy cow, you're freezing! I thought you guys ran hot.'

I yanked free and hugged my arms around me. 'It's winter.'

'Yeah, and you've made yourself sick with that dart,' he said. 'You're not leaving, Red. Ashton would have you drained and hanging on a trophy wall before I finish my next chapter.' He held up the book he'd been reading, like I'd care what it was.

'A trophy wall?' My skin prickled. 'Is that a joke?'

'Why? Was it funny?' said Kevin. 'Look, I get it. You're protecting your sister, you'll sacrifice yourself, blah blah blah hero speech. But we both know if Kate wakes up and you're gone, she'll be right out after you. Straight into Ashton's guys.'

Crap, he was right. I sighed, defeated, and Kevin smiled.

'I know, sisters, right?' he said. 'OK, since you're staying, how about a nice warm drink and – what do you eat? Cat? Raccoon? Squirrel?' He paused, like he was waiting for a reaction. Then he gave up. 'That actually was a joke.'

'Yeah?' I said. 'Was it funny?'

'Ouch!' Kevin laughed. 'You really *are* her sister, eh?'

The promise of food made my tummy grumble, then lurch, as we headed for the kitchen. I stopped to clamp my hand over my mouth but the nausea passed, and I was left with Kevin looking worried while I tried not to think about my belly pangs.

'Uh, do I need to carry you?' he asked.

'Do I need to bite you?'

'Fair enough. You're sure you can walk?'

'I'm fine,' I said. 'I just need a steak.'

Kevin stopped dead. He looked alarmed, then seemed to re-run the sentence in his head. 'You meant, like, meat. Right?'

'Yes,' I said. 'Like meat.'

In case it's unclear, there was something a little different about Kevin. Let's see if you can figure it out faster than I did.

* * *

Kevin was an amazing cook. By which I mean he put a pile of raw steak in front of me like a pro and didn't even flinch as I devoured four in three minutes. Total Top Chef.

'You look better,' he said, as I finished the last steak. 'Here, drink this.'

He handed me a huge steaming mug of hot chocolate piled with whipped cream and mini marshmallows. He'd even added sprinkles.

'Dude, you know I'm *not* diabetic, right?'

Kevin looked confused.

'You're not trying to murder me with sugar?'

'Oh, right!' Kevin chuckled. 'Nah, wouldn't be my go-to wolf-weapon. But if you don't want it ...' He reached for the mug.

'Don't you dare!' I slapped his hand away. 'This might be more sugar than I've had in my entire life, but I *am* having it.'

I took a sip. It was amazing. All creamy sweet cocoa-y bliss with … something else. I scooped up a spoon of cream and marshmallows. The chocolate underneath was redder than I'd expected. Maroon – or mahogany, maybe? Kate would've known; she was the artist. But it definitely wasn't chocolate-coloured.

'Kevin,' I said. 'Is this …?'

'Don't freak out.'

'Red velvet?'

'Yes!' said Kevin, too quickly. 'You like it?'

Silly question. I'd already gulped down half the mug.

'Why you being so nice?' I asked. 'Three hours ago you wanted to murder me; now you're making me fancy cocoa and steak?'

'Yeah, sorry about that.' Kevin smiled. It was much nicer than his smirk. 'It's just – most wolves aren't like you. They don't have your control. You're the first one I haven't had to, you know …'

I waited for him to explain, but he just shifted awkwardly, expecting me to get it.

'You don't mean *kill*?' I asked eventually.

Kevin chewed his lip and didn't look up. Well, that was a 'yes' then.

'You kill werewolves?' My heart was starting to pound again. 'People do that, in real life? You're a … a hunter?'

If Kevin was going for casual as he shrugged, he missed.

'Retired, mostly,' he said.

'Retired? Aren't you, like, fifteen?'

'Sixteen,' he said, 'and a bit.'

'Dude, *I'm* almost sixteen. The only thing I've had time to retire from is the school book club.'

'Book club? Why?' He looked horrified.

'You're gonna judge me for dropping book club? You just admitted to killing people.'

'I admitted to killing wolves,' he corrected me.

'That's different?'

He looked like I'd slapped him. '*Most* wolves lose control when they change. So, it's either them or everyone around them. What would you choose?'

That wasn't rhetorical, I realised. He actually cared what I thought. He seemed weirdly vulnerable, suddenly, for a guy still talking about murder.

But he was making sense.

'I'm not in control either,' I said. 'I nearly killed you, and Kate. And I've done other stuff. Things I don't remember. Kate's covered in scars and –'

Oh God, my eyes were hot with tears. Hold it together, me. Do not cry in front of the confusingly friendly, semi-retired, dorky-hot teen monster-hunter.

'Yeah, I saw,' said Kevin. 'But I also saw you channel that thing. And if you can channel it, you can control it. Like the wolf at your house did.'

What, control claws? And demon eyes? And super-strength and speed and whatever else Stalker Rom could do? No. I'd seen enough horror movies to know what happened if I tried. It would take me over or – or drive me mad, or I'd flip out and burn down the gym or …

'I don't want to control it. I want it gone.'

'It can't go. It's you.'

'Then I want me gone!' I said. 'That's what you do, right? To things like me?'

Kevin sat back. The excitement drained from his face.

'What? No!' he said. 'Look, I talked too much. I made you scared again. Let's –'

'I'm not scared *again*,' I said. 'I never stopped being scared. I hurt people. I don't want to, but I do. And Kate –'

Kevin sighed. 'OK, so I kill you. Then that wolf shows up looking for you and finds Kate, the teenager who kicked his ass, all alone. Then … what? She had the element of surprise last time. She won't next time.'

He leaned forward with a slightly wicked smile.

'But he could have her big, scary little sister.'

He waggled his eyebrows, like he was suggesting a practical joke, not telling me to channel a killer monster. My head pounded.

'No! I *can't* control this. I –'

'You already have,' said Kevin. 'You just need to learn to do it on purpose. I can help.' His eyes locked with mine. I felt a weird chill. 'And if I'm wrong, if this really is more than you can handle and it looks like someone might get hurt –'

He didn't want to finish that sentence, and I didn't need him to.

The thud in my head died down. 'You promise?'

Our eyes were still locked as Kevin nodded. It was scary and reassuring all at once.

'But I won't let it come to that,' he said, ''cos if I tell Kate I've killed you –'

'She'll rip your head off?'

'Exactly!' Kevin grinned. 'See? I can train you. We're in sync already.'

He was so adorably excited about this. It was hard to believe he'd ever killed anyone, wolf or not.

He bounced to his feet, grinning. 'All right, let's go, Red. Let's get your wolf on!'

12. Still Evie

My wolf was decidedly *not* on.

I'd spent ten minutes staring at my hand, willing it to claw up, but – nothing! Picturing my inner Fido hadn't help either. And sitting in front of another steak only made me hungry again.

'This isn't working.' I said. 'Just do it now.'

'I'm not killing you; it's only been half an hour,' said Kevin. 'Are you always this impatient? Let's try something else. How did you *feel* last time?'

'Last time? When I nearly ripped your throat out?'

'And didn't, yes.'

He was so calm. Like: I hadn't, so it didn't matter. I shoved my hands in my pockets and stood up. 'I can't do this. I'm going to my –'

I stopped. I couldn't go back to my room, could I? Kate was there. God, this place was full of people I'd nearly murdered. I paced over to the wall, away from Kevin.

He followed. 'Evie, are you still scared of hurting me?'

'Yes!' Obviously.

And now I was thinking about it – how angry I'd been, how I'd wanted to rip his throat out, and how warm his blood had felt on my skin. My heart thumped.

Kevin put his hand on my shoulder.

I pulled away, but there was nowhere to go. I was stuck between him and the wall.

'Leave me alone,' I said.

'Make me.' He sounded different.

The muscles in my hand twitched. 'Kevin, I don't want to –'

'Oh but *I* do. Come on, mutt. We were interrupted last time. Let's do this.'

My head prickled as I turned around.

Kevin's eyes were glowing again. He looked taller somehow. And scary.

'Kevin …?'

'Nah, it's Kev.' He smirked, moving almost right against me.

The death-prickle spread across my skull.

'Stop!' I said. 'This isn't a game.'

'But it's so much fun,' said Kevin. 'Do you know how hard it's been, waiting till you were well enough to play, Red? Now do your thing and Wolf. On.'

'Kevin, stop!'

He didn't mean that. He'd been helping me. Hadn't he? My heart raced as my muscles twisted and burned. I gritted my teeth against the urge to scream.

Kevin laughed. 'Stop fighting it, you dumb mutt. At least with Fido out you stand a chance.' He paused, before adding, 'And so does Kate.'

'Kate?' My stomach twisted again.

'You know, when I tell her? And she tries to avenge you? I mean, she thinks she's badass.' He leaned in. 'But I'm just plain bad.'

I didn't realise I'd moved until Kevin went flying backwards – smashing against the pan-rack above the breakfast bar, before colliding with the fridge.

I was on him before he'd even had a chance to sit up.

My hand muscles stretched. By the time I pulled Kevin to his feet – and then off them – I'd clawed giant holes in his stupid shirt.

'DON'T touch my sister.'

'What? You're gonna stop me?' said Kevin.

His glasses had fallen off, so I could really see his eyes. They were glowing amber. But mine were burning too. I knew how they looked – huge and yellow and scarier than his. I was scarier than him.

'I'm gonna do whatever it takes,' I snarled.

Kevin grinned. 'Yeah, ya are!'

He wriggled out of my grip, like I wasn't holding him with a giant claw, then examined his top. 'Nice work, Red! You're terrifying.'

He didn't seem terrified. Last time I'd felt like this, I'd heard Kate's heart racing from across the room. I couldn't hear his at all.

'OK, that's claws,' he said. 'You wanna try fangs? Go on, go for the jugular.'

He tilted his head, exposing his Band-Aid-patched neck.

My gums tingled. Kevin's face lit up. 'Holy – fangs! You did it! You're *so* good.'

'And you're just plain bad.' I took a step forward. 'I'm not falling for the nice-guy thing again. You threatened my sister, psycho.'

Kevin held his hands up. 'Well, I didn't mean it. I like Kate!' He said it like I was being unreasonable. 'I just needed you to stop holding back.'

'I'm meant to believe that?' I said. 'I just met you and already you're, like, three people. How can I trust you if I don't know who you are?'

Kevin gave an almost naughty grin. 'Do you have to trust me to throw me across the room? Or hit me? Or see what else those claws and fangs can do?' He held his arms out wide, in a 'you know you want to' gesture.

Seriously? 'Dude, do you want to die?'

'That's not the point. The point is –' He peeled away the Band Aids to show me his neck. His smooth, perfectly un-savaged neck. 'You couldn't kill me if you tried. Well, you could but there's only, like, two or three really specific ways. I'm safe to practise on. I promise.'

He gave another impish smile, as if this was some cute quirk he'd just revealed instead of, you know, what the hell?

'What are you?' I asked. 'Are you ... like me?'

Kevin's smile vanished. He almost shook his head, then didn't.

'I'm not a wolf,' he said. 'But my whole life was destroyed by a monster. I know what it's like being scared of yourself. Being terrified of hurting someone. Freaking out. Begging the world to go back to normal, even though it can't. So ...'

He trailed off, not quite answering my question.

'So we're not *un*alike?' I said.

'Basically.' Kevin's smile was endearingly vulnerable.

'And I really can't accidentally kill you?'

Kevin's eyebrows rose. 'Oh. So you *do* like me?'

Did I? 'Don't get ahead of yourself, you still threatened my sister.'

'And yet …' That smile got a little naughtier. 'You don't want to kill me.'

'Dude, you know it's not a binary,' I said. 'There are other ways to feel about someone, besides "liking" or "actively murdering" them.'

Kevin snorted. 'Sure if you wanna overcomplicate things.' He picked up his glasses and put them aside. ''K, enough mushy stuff. Let's take that you-threatened-my-sister rage, figure out what you're capable of and do it to me. It'll be fun.'

Talk about a sales pitch.

'OK,' I said. 'What do I do?'

Kevin grinned. 'Well, I've never been on this side of a training montage but – ever hit anyone?'

'Not yet.' *CRUNCH!* Kevin fell back, his nose suddenly bloodied as his head whacked against the ground. 'Oh my God! I'm so sorry, that was harder than I'd planned. Are you OK?'

Kevin sat up, laughing. 'I think I'm in love.'

'You're bleeding! Did I just break your nose?'

'Not *just*.' He chuckled again. 'You also cracked my skull. You've really never hit anyone before?' He was looking at me like he was still dazed. 'You're awesome. I mean, that was awesome.' He jumped up. 'Do it again!'

My fist tingled. I think my inner Fido was ready to come out and play. Outer Evie wasn't so sure. 'But you're hurt!'

'Nah!' He wiped the blood away on a tea-towel. 'See? All healed. I'm unbreakable, Red. Now, *come on*! Hit me.'

I curled my fist uncertainly. Kevin's excited grin softened.

'Evie, your wolf-stalker tried to kill Kate. He's not playing around. If you want to protect her, you need to be able to hurt him. So you *can't* go easy on me, OK?' He waited until I nodded, then continued: 'Good. 'Cos I won't go easy on you either. Three more warm-up hits, then I start fighting back.'

His eyes flashed amber, and he grinned very wickedly.

My inner Fido turned a full-on somersault. Maybe this would be fun.

13. Kate

Ow, my neck!

I checked my laptop clock. Six thirty-eight. No wonder my spine was killing me, I'd been slumped on the desk for almost five hours. Still, at least I'd gotten the poster done.

I clicked it open. Maybe 'done' was an overstatement. The only words I hadn't mis-spelled were ones I'd left out completely. I fixed all that, hit 'save' before my inner art student could start reformatting everything, then sat back and groaned.

I'd have to tell Evie about Mom today. She'd notice the posters. It's not like I could tranq her again while I went to stick them up, tempting as it was. Tranqs were a last resort, not for avoiding awkward conversations. Besides, she was adjusting so fast the next tranq mightn't even buy time to print the posters out. That would be irresponsible *and* pointless.

Still, at least I could grab a few more hours' sleep before ripping Evie's world apart even more. I flopped down onto my bed, then rolled over to look at her.

Her bed was empty.

'Evie?' I jumped up and ran to the bathroom. 'Evie?' No sign. And her bag was gone too. 'EVIE!'

I yanked the door open and raced down the stairs.

This couldn't be happening. She couldn't be gone. It was sub-zero outside. She didn't have any money. And she was only fifteen. 'EVIE!'

'Ssssh!'

The light flicked on. I didn't mean to yelp, but Kevin startled me. He *sssh*ed again, and nodded towards the sitting room.

Through the dark, I could see Evie on the sofa, under a fluffy blanket. Her bag was beside her, and I could just make out two mugs on the table.

I felt a rush of relief, followed by annoyed confusion. 'What the hell?'

'She's just dozed off,' whispered Kevin.

'So you're watching her sleep?'

'What? No!' He thought about it. 'OK, yeah. But not the way you said it. You made it creepy.'

'Says the guy sitting in the dark watching a little girl nap?'

'Little girl? She's *my* age!' said Kevin. 'And it's not like that! She was scared to sleep in case she wolfed out again –'

'Not a wolf.'

'Whatever. Point is, she was terrified of herself. So I said I'd sit with her. Then if anything happened, I could ...' He trailed off, adjusting his stupid lopsided glasses like that would change the subject.

'No, keep going,' I said. 'What *would* you do if she transformed?'

Kevin shifted awkwardly, and didn't answer.

'Yeah, that's what I thought.' Mr Wolf-Pro had no idea what he'd do face-to-face with an actual Not-Evie. 'Next time my sister's freaking out, maybe get me instead of skulking in the shadows like a creep. OK?'

'I wasn't skulking,' said Kevin. 'I was reading. And without me, she would've Littlest Hobo'd it outta here into the freezing cold. I'm trying to help.'

He fixed his glasses again. They really weren't sitting right. Had they been that bad earlier? Then I noticed his shirt, covered in claw marks, and …

'Is that blood?'

'Uh –' Kevin's eyes followed mine to his ripped sleeve. 'Oh, right. Yeah. Don't freak out.'

'Why would I freak out?'

'You wouldn't,' he said. 'Shouldn't, I mean.'

He glanced over at Evie. My blood went cold.

'What the hell did you do?'

'Nothing!' he yelped, as I shoved him aside and raced to the sofa.

'EVIE?' I skidded to my knees beside her. 'EVIE! I swear, if he's so much as touched you …'

'Hmmm?' Evie opened her eyes groggily. Then something clicked and she jumped back. 'Katie! What's wrong – did I – is someone hurt?'

'It's OK.' Kevin was suddenly beside us with his hand on her shoulder. *Comforting* her. I shoved him away and sat up beside Evie.

'Everyone's fine, come here.' I reached for a hug, but she shrank back, still clearly terrified. 'Evie, I know this is new

72

and scary to you, but I've been doing this my whole life. I know how to hug you.'

I put my arms around her again and, this time, she leaned in.

'Good, now how about a few more hours' sleep before –'

'What? No!' Evie was back out of my arms, shaking her head. 'I can't share a room with you. What if I go all beast mode and hurt you before you can tranq me? I've done it before. Clearly.'

Her eyes fixed on my bruises from last night, then fell to the older scars on my jaw and eyebrow. They did look bad without make-up, but they were no big deal – just a reminder not to forget to up her dose again during a full moon.

She probably wouldn't see it that way, though. So much for sleep.

'I meant, *you* rest,' I lied. 'I've got errands to run. There are two keys, so I'll lock the door while you're asleep and you can let yourself out later. Everyone'll be safe, I promise. Now, come on.'

I headed to the stairs. Evie followed me, but paused at the first step – then turned back to Kevin.

'Hey, um, thanks,' she said. 'For, y'know ...'

'Any time.' Kevin grinned.

He kept grinning, even as Evie turned and started upstairs. Then he clocked my glare and looked away, flushing.

'We're not done,' I told him. 'Stay here.'

Kevin saluted, then went back to his book like this was all normal. I could not wait to check out, and get as far from him as possible.

*   *   *

I got Evie to bed, then showered and did the usual con-
ceal-don't-heal make-up job on my bruises before turning
to leave.

'Wait!' called Evie. 'Don't go out in the dark. It's not
safe.'

She was right. The second time I'd broken my right
wrist, it'd had nothing to do with Not-Evie and everything to do with over-eager twelve-year-old me racing out
before dawn on an icy morning to answer a Science Fair
SOS from Zoe. (She'd brought guilt-flowers, though, so
no regrets.)

'Don't worry,' I said. 'I'm not going anywhere until I'm
caffeinated.'

I slipped the dart gun into my waistband, then kissed
Evie on the forehead and ruffled her hair. 'Sleep tight, missus.
Love you.'

'Love you too.' She yawned again. 'Oh, and Katie?
Kevin's actually –'

'Awful?' I didn't want to hear anything else. 'I know.
Bye.'

I found Kevin sitting at reception, trying to bend his
glasses back into shape. He popped them on when he
saw me.

'How does that look?' he asked.

I shrugged. 'I mean, they're straight. But I can still see
you, so ...'

'Yep, I'm solid like that.' Kevin chuckled, until I didn't.
Then he stopped and cleared his throat. 'Ah, I see. You're still

74

mad at me for bleeding. I get hurt and you get angry, that's our dynamic, eh?'

'Wanna switch it up?' I said. 'I get angry, *then* you get hurt. How's that sound?'

Kevin gave a nervous half-smile. 'Um, likely? Although, hopefully not right now because – if you could drop the murder-glare and give me a drum-roll ...'

'Nope.'

'All right.' Kevin pounded on the desk himself. 'Your sister can control her powers. Yay!' He self-applauded, and waited for my reaction.

Which was, 'No, she can't.'

'She can!' Kevin hopped over the desk, landing proudly beside me. 'She's amazing. I mean, it's amazing. What she can do. She's so strong and fast. She threw me clear across the room, then caught me before I hit the wall.'

She did *what*? 'No!' I said. 'That's not – these aren't powers. It's a monster.'

'Then it's one she can control,' said Kevin. 'She's even got the claw down, she ...' He trailed off as I shook my head.

That thing had thrown me down the stairs. It had broken my arm, dislocated my shoulder, almost clawed my eye out. Evie would never hurt me like that.

'I thought you'd be happy,' said Kevin. 'She's taking charge.'

'She's *not*,' I said. 'She can't handle this. I *saw* her stalker. He was violent and angry and a ... a human-shaped monster. If that thing's coming out during the day now, that's not Evie taking control. That's *it* controlling *her*.'

75

'It's not!' said Kevin. 'I've seen enough wolves. There's no conflict inside Evie like there is in the rest: it's not *it* versus *her*. It's just her!'

'You don't know what you're talking about.'

'I do, actually,' he said. 'The same way I knew she was a wolf the second I saw her, I know she's not like the rest of them. Trust me.'

A few hours alone with Evie, and suddenly he knew her better than I did? The temptation to re-break those oversized glasses was *very* strong.

'Dude, I wouldn't trust you with my breakfast order,' I said. 'Evie needs to manage this thing, not channel it. And *I* can teach her that.'

I could. Breathing, meditation, meds – same as always, just more.

'And what about when this stalker, Rom, shows up?' said Kevin. 'Will you "manage" him too?'

He said it like I hadn't, already, just yesterday.

'You're not the only one with monster experience, Kev,' I snapped. 'I've survived just fine without your input for the last fifteen years. I don't suddenly need it now just 'cos you're here.'

I pushed past him, towards the dining room. The sun was almost up, and Chris had promised to leave a stash of mocha pods by the coffee maker. That sounded like a way better option than continuing this conversation.

Suddenly Kevin was at the door. *How?*

'I *am* here, though,' he said. 'I know you think you don't need me but there are so many towns between Brightside and Toronto, yet you wound up with me the night you were attacked by a werewolf? You don't think that means something?'

'Something' as in 'fate', he meant. His expression was so earnest I almost felt bad laughing. But only almost.

'No power in the universe could convince me you're destined to be part of our lives,' I said. 'I've got things to do in Brightside, and you were open. That's why we're here.' I jerked my head in a 'move' gesture. Kevin sighed and stepped aside. 'At least, until I get back and we check out,' I added, slamming the door.

'Wait, check out?' Kevin sounded startled. He yanked the door open and followed me to the coffee machine. 'You can't! Evie's still ... glitchy, and you've got a monster stalker, remember? If you leave and go somewhere else, someone's gonna get hurt.'

I opened my mouth to argue, but I couldn't. He was right.

And he was still talking. 'Look, we'll turn off the sign outside. It'll just be you and us, and I'll back off. I promise. You try things your way for as long as you need. Just don't leave until you know she's safe. Please.'

He looked so sincere and intense, and I had no comeback

'Fine,' I said. 'But if you so much as *look* at Evie wrong ...'

'Colourful and graphic violence will ensue?' said Kevin. 'Yeah, I got that.'

'Good.' I grabbed a coffee pod, and turned to the machine.

Kevin whipped the pod out of my hand. 'Lemme make you a real one. And a proper breakfast. Come on, sit down.'

I hesitated.

'Kate,' said Kevin. 'You don't have to like me, but you *do* need to eat. And rest. You're no good to anyone if you're burned out. Take a few minutes.'

I nodded reluctantly. He was right, again. He sucked, but food was good. And I did have a long day ahead of me. Although if I'd known how bad the day would be, I would have lost my appetite completely.

14. Kate again

I felt ill. I'd made the mistake of trying a quick post-breakfast Google search for printing places in Brightside. Instead, I'd wound up down a horrifying rabbit hole of stories about 'animal attacks' in the area.

Of course, why else would Mom have come here?

The attacks could easily have been Evie's bio-parents. Not that *that* was particularly comforting. Especially once I hit the frozen streets of Brightside and saw those 'missing person' posters. All these young, strong-looking guys from Brightside and its surrounding towns. I'd seen them before, scrolling past tiny portraits on my phone alongside photos of dozens of people whose bodies had already been found.

But it was different watching their weather-faded faces flap in the breeze, as I scrutinised every spot, trying to decide if I could squeeze Mom in amongst them.

The girl at Prints Charming attempted some early-morning chat as their machine spat out my posters, but she went quiet when she saw the image.

'You've got her eyes,' she muttered, ringing up half the number of prints I'd done, charging for black and white instead of colour, then throwing in some rolls of tape for free.

'Won't you get in trouble?' I asked.

'With who?' she said. 'My manager's missing and the owners' daughter was killed last week. Even if they notice, they won't mind. Sorry, you don't want to hear that.'

'No, it's OK.' I felt like I'd been punched in the gut. 'I'm sorry. Thanks.'

The wind cut through me as I postered. Every once in a while, a powdery gust of snow would whip around my face into my eyes. When I started shivering too hard to tape straight, I ducked into a little pink coffee shop to ask about leaving some flyers.

The old lady behind the counter – Miriam – nodded sympathetically, then insisted I stop for a free mocha to warm up. I was too cold to argue, so I stuffed five dollars into the tip jar when she wasn't looking.

'Here you are, dear.' Miriam handed me my coffee, then picked up a flyer curiously. Her eyes widened. 'Oh, no. Sinéad!'

My heart jumped. 'You know her?'

'She was in every day for a while. Caramel latte and a toasted sandwich. She asked all sorts of questions. But then …' Miriam paused guiltily. 'My little grandson Linc vanished. And your mom came right back with more questions. I'm afraid I wasn't very nice to her that day.'

That sounded like Mom all right. 'I'm sorry. She gets so laser-focused sometimes, she can forget other people have their own thing going on.'

'No, *I'm* sorry.' Miriam handed me a muffin from the pastry display. 'She really was lovely, it's just … There's no-one here who hasn't lost someone, you know? And some outsider, poking around in our tragedies – I'm afraid I was quite relieved when she didn't come back in.'

She looked ashamed, which wasn't fair. I could absolutely see Mom pissing people off to try to help Evie. I could see her doing anything if she thought it was best for us.

I thanked Miriam, took my things and sat at a table near the notice board. It was empty aside from a poster of her 'little' grandson, Lincoln Wells – a 6'2" seventeen-year-old who looked like he could smash a brick wall. Another missing giant, like the rest of them.

Mom didn't exactly fit amongst all that testosterone. Plus, she'd come armed with dart guns, tranqs and sixteen years' experience. All any of these guys had was their bulk. I'm sure they'd fought well but, even if they'd escaped, it only took one bite.

Was that what happened? Not to Mom, obviously, she knew how to protect herself. But if she'd come across a bunch of scared new infectees, that might be worth going off-grid for. Studying Robert's blood *had* helped, after all, and we knew a lot more than we had then. If this was her breakthrough, it was a dangerous one.

She wouldn't want us around, especially if she was worried about Not-Evie's monster-radar. But we couldn't leave without Mom. As long as Evie kept taking her meds and stayed indoors with wolf-pro Kevin on guard, she was still safer here than at home with the stalker we knew was after her. And I could help her meditate, focus on keeping Not-Evie at bay now she knew. That should help.

I just wished Mom would let me know she was OK. Because we weren't.

*   *   *

Mid-way through my mocha, Miriam came over with a couple of regulars who'd met Mom and wanted to see if they could help. They couldn't, but they were very nice. Just like the next couple, and the one after that and ... I must have spoken to half the town that morning. And no-one could tell me anything except they'd loved Mom's Irish accent, and hadn't seen her in a while, now they thought about it. Which at least confirmed that twenty-four dollars at Ray's Diner ten days ago was the last real record of her. But surely someone knew more.

Eventually, I headed back out to poster my way across town towards Ray's. It was lunch-time when I arrived and, between the cold and the free coffees, I was shaking again as I held Mom's picture to the lamp-post outside, trying to tear the tape with my chattering teeth.

'Need a hand?' asked a girl's voice.

'Thanks!' I said with a grin, turning around.

The girl was really pretty; all curvy-blonde cuteness wrapped in goth make-up and a velvety purple coat. Like a vampire Harley Quinn – with dimples.

I liked dimples. The short, skinny, equally gothic-looking boy holding her hand probably did too. I hadn't noticed him until he took the poster from me.

'Dr Sinéad Wilder?' he read. 'She looks like you. Is she your mom?' I nodded, and he gave a sympathetic grimace. 'That sucks! Sorry.'

He had nice eyes – big and green, with a smudge of eyeliner – and floppy, definitely dyed black hair poking out under his toque-hat. He pursed his lips awkwardly to one side, like he didn't quite know what to say next. It was very endearing.

'You OK?' asked the girl.

I nodded, but I don't think any of us believed me. Then the girl's face changed.

She yanked the poster from her boyfriend. 'Holy cow, we *saw* her. Remember, Felix? With Bruce Wayne? On my birthday? That's the day she went missing, look!'

Felix re-examined the poster, then pulled his phone out and started scrolling.

'Bruce Wayne?' I said. 'Like, Batman?'

'He looked like Bruce Wayne,' said Felix. 'Or our friend Amy thought he did. He was all, y'know, suave and slick.'

'With perfect hair and skin,' added the girl. 'And these cheekbones.'

'Everyone's got cheekbones, Cass,' said Felix. '*I've* got cheekbones.'

'Oh, she knows what I mean,' said Cass.

I did, annoyingly. 'And he was with my mom? You're sure?'

Felix nodded, holding out his phone – where Cass and another girl were posing adorably. Then he zoomed in, behind their heads.

'That's her, right?'

I grabbed his phone. 'Yes!'

Mom looked happy, for someone about to disappear. She was holding a big glass of red wine and laughing at someone I couldn't see, behind Cass and her friend.

'Do you have any with Bruce Wayne in them?' I asked.

Felix shook his head. 'Sorry, I only got that one by accident.'

'Amy might, though.' Cass pointed to the girl in the photo. 'She was soooo jealous of your mom, on a date with *him*.'

'Wait – date?'

Mom didn't date. Mom still wore her wedding ring. And Dad's.

'I don't know if it was –' started Felix.

'No, it definitely was,' said Cass. 'Remember, Amy nearly spontaneously combusted when he held her hand?'

'He what?'

'And he had his arm around her when they were leaving, remember? Amy –'

'They left together?'

'CASS!'

'What?' said Cass.

'That's her mom,' said Felix.

'It's OK,' I lied. 'I just need to find him. I wonder who served them? Maybe they … What?'

They'd exchanged glances. Neither of them answered.

'What?' I said again.

Felix sighed. 'We know who served them. My stepmom's friend, Sage.'

Sage? My stomach clenched. That was an unusual name and I'd already seen it once this morning, as I'd scrolled through news reports on my phone. The picture had shown a vibrant-looking twenty-something with blue braids and a cool pentacle necklace. The article said they'd found her body.

'I just read about her,' I said. 'Animal attack, right?'

They nodded in sad unison.

'Just after that shift,' said Felix. 'Right by her car.'

'Like something was waiting,' added Cass. 'Felix's stepmom, Heather, thinks Sage was targeted! She says there's a dark presence in this town, doesn't she?'

'CASS!'

'What? She does.'

'Yeah, but –' Felix glanced at Mom's poster before shooting me an apologetic look. 'Heather's just upset. I'm sure your mom's OK. Right, Cass?'

'Oh!' Cass squeaked, realising her tactlessness. 'Oh, totally. Yeah. Everything's fine, I'm sure. Hey, it's cold, eh?'

Felix winced, embarrassed. But his stepmom wasn't wrong.

'OK,' I said. 'So Sage was possibly the last person to see my mom, aside from Batman. And now she's dead and Mom's missing.'

I didn't say *hell of a coincidence*, but Felix caught it anyway.

'Sage was killed by wild animals,' he said. 'You can't fake that.'

'Ooh, unless you're the killer on that TV show!' said Cass. 'With the monster suit? And metal beast jaws? And –' Her brow knit up as she looked from me to Felix. 'But that's not what happened here, obviously.'

85

Felix smiled. 'It's unlikely.'

'What about a trained wolf, then? Or, like, a really big dog or ...' She trailed off again. 'Is that crazy too?'

Felix's mouth did that sideways purse thing again. 'Maybe a bit Sherlocky for Brightside?'

Cass nodded. But she still wasn't done thinking, judging by the way her brow-knot intensified. 'Well, even if Batman's not murdering people with wolves, we still saw him with Dr Wilder right before she vanished. That's something, right?' She looked at us. 'Like, to tell the police? He might even be a lead on these missing giants. Or are they blaming animals for those too? What did they say when you spoke to them?'

I glanced at Felix, until I realised she meant me.

'Oh, um ...' I was too cold to lie. 'I haven't. Yet.'

Cass's eyes widened. 'You haven't told the police about your missing mom? Why? You're telling everyone else.' She gestured to the posters.

Felix grimaced again. 'Cass.'

'It's OK,' I said. 'She's right. I should report it, but ...'

I trailed off and shrugged sadly, hoping they'd interpret that in a way that made sense, but wasn't *I need a cover story that won't accidentally drag my little sister into all this if the scary not-people ever come to light.*

Felix gave a sympathetic nod. 'It'd make it real, eh?'

He looked like he really understood. And, even though he didn't, it still helped.

'You do need to talk to them, though,' he said. 'So do we, now, I guess. Hey, how about we get this over with together? Come on.'

Now? 'Shouldn't you get back to school?'

Cass pulled a face. 'To double alge-*bleeeeh*? We can totally skip for this.' She grabbed my hand urgently. 'Let's go!'

I hesitated. I'd barely decided to do this at all, never mind in company. Still, it wouldn't hurt to test drive my lies on the way, I guessed. Plus, some moral support would be nice. I smiled at Cass and Felix.

'OK. But can we take a quick selfie? To reassure my little sister I'm all right?'

Otherwise she'd wake up, panic and come looking for me – and I did *not* want her seeing Mom's posters before we had a chance to talk.

'Ooh, yes!' said Cass. 'If Batman did do anything, this'll be our "before-reporting-the-murderer" shot! That's, like, historic. Can we use a puppy-filter?'

* * *

We spoke to Officer Jonson, a kind-faced middle-aged white guy with a 'brunette Santa' vibe. I'd decided to stick to Mom's golden rule: Stay as close to the truth as you can without mentioning monsters. (It's a pretty specific-to-my-life rule.)

Also, when in doubt, play dumb.

'So,' said Officer Jonson, 'she's been missing for ten days, but you're only reporting it now? Why?'

'She's my mom,' I said. 'I knew she was working, and when she's working sometimes she just … loses track of time.'

'For ten days?' said Officer Jonson.

He was certainly buying the 'dumb', and all I'd told so far was the truth.

'No, but there are weeks where she basically sleeps in her lab and wouldn't eat if I didn't cook for her and my little sister.'

That got a sympathetic head-tilt. I wondered if I should try welling up for some proper emotional manipulation – then my eyes did prickle and suddenly I was fighting back actual tears. Cass squeezed my arm, as I continued.

'I didn't want there to be anything wrong. I know her research's dangerous, but she'd said not to panic if she lost contact. I should have panicked, huh?'

Officer Jonson scribbled something in his notebook, then looked up. 'Let's not go jumping to conclusions, sweetheart.' He poured a glass of water and slid it over to me. 'What kind of "dangerous research" does she do, do you know?'

'Some sort of infection,' I said. 'I don't know the name, but it makes people a bit … Jekyll and Hyde-ish, I guess? She must've thought it was behind these "animal" attacks around town. I know she spoke to Miriam who runs that pink coffee shop?'

'All's Wells,' said Felix and Officer Jonson together.

Officer Jonson laughed. 'OK, I'll pop by. Anything else?'

'About the infection?' I shook my head, then looked at Cass and Felix. 'But we know something about the last time she was seen.'

We spoke for about another hour. Officer Jonson was kind and thorough. He didn't even laugh when Felix got grouchy at Cass gushing over Bruce Wayne's teeth, just steered them back on track and kept going.

'OK.' Officer Jonson closed his notepad finally. 'I think I've got enough. How about I get you two back for the last hour of school and see about chatting with your buddy Amy? She seems like she'd have some thoughts.'

'Amy's gonna flip,' said Cass.

He offered to drop me back to the guesthouse, but I wasn't sure Evie seeing me get out of a police car was how I wanted to open the conversation about Mom, so I declined. She'd texted back, a photo of a plate of bacon and a message telling me to have fun, so I knew she was OK. I was starving, though.

'Hey, before you go,' I said, 'does anywhere here do a good veggie burger?'

Cass shook her head. 'Ray's do a terrible one, though.'

I laughed. 'Maybe I'll just grab a salad.'

15. Evie

Kate's text-bing woke me up.

Wow! She'd been busy, hanging out with the cutest Monster High-looking pair ever. Not quite what I'd expected after yesterday's drama but she might as well make friends here, because I wasn't leaving the guesthouse any time soon.

Stay indoors.

Practise.

Try not to claw anyone's face off.

That was my three-point plan, at least until I got on top of my ... what had Kevin said? 'Impulse control issues'? Like what I'd done to his arm when he made me picture Stalker Rom cornering Kate.

I was getting better, though. And it was fun training with Kevin. *He* was fun. And funny, in a dorky way. My tummy swirled as I remembered a quip he'd made about lycanthropy changing you, and how pink he'd gone when I pretended not to get it. Would he be up, if I went downstairs now?

He'd been awake all night but then so had I, and I was – *oooh!* The most amazing scent-combo hit my nose: bacon, hot chocolate and ... Kevin? OK, that last one was a bit weird. Still, the whiff of yum got closer. I yanked the door open, racing into the hall so fast I almost knocked Kevin over.

'Wow, hungry?' He laughed.

My stomach growled. He was holding a tray packed with bacon, toast, fruit, more bacon, so much bacon and two giant mugs of cream-and-sprinkle-topped hot chocolate. *Two?* I bit back a grin.

'I could eat. Might need help with that second drink, though.' I smiled, then backed away, towards the room.

Kevin hesitated. 'Well, anything for a guest, obviously. But, um, are your curtains closed? I get these ... headaches. From the sun.'

Headaches from the sun. Yep, he seriously said that, and I still didn't figure it out. Although, even if I had, he'd brought hot chocolate and bacon. He probably could've been carrying a human head and I still would've been racing to close the curtains.

'So,' said Kevin, as I swooped in on the tray, 'heck of a workout last night, Red. You did amazing.'

I was too bacon-stuffed to speak, so I pointed to him and gave a thumbs-up.

'*I'm* amazing? At teaching?' He looked so happy. 'Thanks! I've never done this before, but I do think we work well together. And you want to keep going, right?'

'Yefffff!' I took a glug of hot chocolate, then tried again. 'Ahem, yes. Obviously! I don't wanna accidentally hurt anyone. And I need to be able to protect Kate. And it's fun.'

'It is?' Kevin grinned. 'I mean, it is! Yes. Glad you agree.'

His cheeks flushed a little, which made mine pinkify as my tummy turned another cartwheel. Then Kevin cleared his throat. 'Um, if we are gonna keep going, we need to talk. About Kate.'

My mug shattered as my hand clawed up. 'What's wrong with Kate?'

'Nothing. She's fine.' Kevin watched me pull my claw back to regular-hand mode, then smiled. 'That's still so badass. But, yeah, Kate just hates me, that's all.'

'What?' I said. 'No, she –'

'She does, it's fine. If someone treated my little sister the way I treated you, I'd do far worse than threaten violence.' He knelt down to clean up my mess. 'I don't blame her, it's just gonna make training awkward since she's threatened to check you both out unless I stay away from you.'

'She said that?' I knelt down to help pick up the pieces.

'Of course she did,' said Kevin. 'I was horrible to you.'

'But you're not horrible!' I felt an irritated pinprickle. 'And you're helping me. Have you told her that? Does she know what I can do?'

Kevin pulled a face. 'Sorta. But she's not happy. I got this whole lecture on what her little sister can and can't handle.'

Seriously? 'Ow!' That pin-prick in my head jabbed harder. 'How would she even know? She's never given me a chance to find out!'

I stopped and rubbed between my eyes.

'Red?' asked Kevin. 'What's going on?'

'I don't – ow – know!' I mean, I was annoyed at Kate, but it was hardly Defcon death-ache. 'I think I need my insul...'

No, I didn't. Because it wasn't insulin, and I was *not* jabbing myself with placebos for fun. (Spoiler alert: not a placebo! I'd have realised that if I'd thought a bit harder. But I didn't. Oh, well.)

I closed my eyes and tried *breathing,* catching a yummy whiff of chocolate, Kevin and that familiar, sweet-metallic-y tang. Which I recognised suddenly.

My eyes flew open – focused on the maroon splodge on the carpet – and the ground shot up into my face. I hadn't fallen, but I could see the tiny shards of mug nestled amongst the red-soaked fibres, like I was down on the floor peering at them.

I jumped back, tripped over my own feet and landed safe in Kevin's arms. His warm, strong arms.

'You OK? What happened?'

'I – I, uh …' Wow, words, Evie. Come on! 'Sorry. I … my eyes. Everything just sort of zoomed in at once.'

Then zapped back to normal, when you caught me. But for some reason my cheeks burned at the thought of saying that out loud.

'Like a new super-power?' Kevin asked, helping me to my feet.

'I dunno,' I said. 'It's not just my vision, everything's crazy today. My head's pounding over nothing, I can smell everything and the world's all … *more, y'*know?'

Kevin nodded. 'Sure.'

'*Sure?*'

'Absolutely. You've been tapping into skills you didn't know you had. Your body's adjusting, that's all.' Kevin smiled. 'I went through the same thing when … well, when I went through the same thing. It's trippy, but you've got this.'

Had I? 'But what if I don't? What if this is me losing control? What if –?'

The image of Kate's face, all bashed up and scarred, flashed through my mind. My head streaked with pain.

'Hey, it's OK.' Kevin touched my arm. 'You're not gonna hurt anyone you shouldn't. I promise.'

Our eyes met and, despite everything, my stomach flipped.

'But I'm dangerous.'

Kevin gave a kind of bad-boy smile. 'Yeah, me too.'

Then the smile wavered and, for a sec, he looked nervous. But he kept eye contact as he moved his hand down my arm 'til his fingers laced with mine.

My hand tingled in a way that had nothing to do with claws.

'I know you're scared, Red,' he said. 'This *feels* new, but it's not.'

'What?'

'You weren't bitten, you're not infected,' he said. 'You were born to do this.'

Oh! The wolf thing, right.

'And you have been,' said Kevin. 'You weren't awake to control it before, but your body *knows* what it's doing. Your head just needs help catching up.'

He squeezed my hand, then started to let go. I held tight. My heart was still threatening to slam out of my chest, but my head was calming down.

'Is it OK if I hold on a little longer?' I asked. 'Until I'm done freaking out?'

'Oh! Uh, yeah,' Kevin gulped. 'Don't – don't let go on my account.' He cleared his throat awkwardly. 'So, what about Kate? I don't want to make you lie.'

I didn't want to lie either, but the truth would only cause arguments, and I still couldn't risk getting upset around her. Just like I couldn't risk staying away from Kevin, no matter how much Kate disliked him.

And *not* just because of the tingles. Maybe not even to help with claw control, if he was right about me adjusting. No, I needed Kevin because, if Stalker Rom found us again, Kate would get between him and me without a second thought.

And Rom would go straight through her, unless I stopped him. Unless Kevin taught me to do the things my pacifist big sister wouldn't dream of.

'Kate's lied to protect me her whole life,' I said. 'Time to return the favour. Now, how about I text and find out when she'll be back? Then, once we're finished cleaning up my mess, maybe we can squeeze in some illicit training?'

'Ooh, illicit?' Kevin winced immediately, regretting repeating that. 'I mean, yeah. Cool. I'll grab cleaning supplies.'

As he left, I picked up his now-lukewarm chocolate to move it somewhere it wouldn't get knocked over. That familiar scent hit again.

'Hey,' I called. 'This isn't *human* blood, is it?'

Kevin froze, then turned back. 'It's pig's. But it perked you up, right? And you like it?' He was almost pleading, like he was scared guzzling blood together might've been too much monster, too fast.

But I *was* a monster. And it certainly wasn't the worst thing I was going to do. So I knocked back the rest, then grinned.

'Yeah, I really do.'

16. Still Evie

I really liked Kevin too.

And, no, *not* because he was so dorky-hot when he smiled, or got super-serious, or went all heroic monster-hunt-ery with the jaw-clench that made his eyes smoulder and my tummy … wait, what was I saying?

Oh, yeah. *Not* because of that, but because he was fun.

And he made all of this fun. I wasn't scared around him. I know I should have been – he was a wolf-killer – but that was easy to forget as he grinned playfully, daring me to pick the desk up and fling it at him. Or as we sat on the bed together, while he explained how to tune in to one 'super-sense' at a time without the rest overwhelming me.

'It's like focusing on a book,' he said. 'Everything else is still there, it's just not right here.'

He poked me on the forehead, and I blushed and giggled like a full-blown idiot. Who'd have thought monster-powers would be easier to get a handle on than these Kevin-jitters? Good thing he didn't seem to mind.

* * *

Katie wasn't back until nearly four. But she brought me a steamed milk with caramel, so I couldn't be mad. Also, I'd just spent the afternoon secret-training with the guy she'd banned from seeing me. So, really, not mad.

She was, though, when she caught Kevin leaving our room.

'What are you doing here?' she demanded.

'My job?' Kevin held up the tray, still piled with untouched fruit.

'Fine, job done,' said Kate. 'Now get lost.'

'Uh, *you* stopped *me*. Hey, want an apple or –?'

Kate slammed the door in his face.

'No? Nothing?' he called through the door. ''K. Good talk, Kate!'

I tried not to feel too sad as he left. In fact, I tried not to think about him at all, now Kate was here. I did have other thoughts, after all. Other non-boy thoughts. I was usually very good at them.

'Hey, don't let Creepy Dork in when I'm not around,' said Kate.

'He's not –'

'He is.' Kate dumped her bag and opened the curtains. '*Super* creepy. Like, have you noticed how dark this place is? Serial-killer dark?'

'He's *not* a serial killer.' Technically. As far as I knew.

'That's what they always say about serial killers.'

'And non-serial killers,' I said. 'They say it about most people.'

97

'Yeah? Name one perfectly non-creepy person you've ever heard described as "not a serial killer".' She raised her eyebrows cheekily and I laughed.

I couldn't be mad at her when she was being goofy. Well, I could, but the whole point was not to get into an argument. So I changed the subject. Or at least, I pulled a face and stuck my tongue out. Same thing.

'Oooh, *touché*, Evie,' said Kate. 'Solid rebuttal.' She chuckled and sipped her coffee, flinching as it touched her lip.

I felt a twist of guilt – and the lid popped off my paper cup as my hand clawed.

Katie jumped back, but I'd already willed it away.

'Whoa, Evie!'

'Cool, eh?' I grinned. 'Wanna see what else I –?'

'NO!'

Course not. 'You sure? I got mad skillz.' (OK, she couldn't hear the *'z'* but it was implied.)

Kate put her coffee on the desk, then stole mine and put that down too.

'Evie.' She took my hand between both of hers, gently. 'That was amazing! You *willed* not-you into submission. A little belly breathing and meditating, and you'll have it so whipped it'll be hiding and whimpering in your pinkie toe. Total beast-masterdom achieved!'

She grinned, trying to get me excited, but – *hiding-and-whimpering*? Boring Fido to death on a yoga mat, instead of fighting and tingling with Kevin? That was the exact opposite of what I wanted. Kate wouldn't want to hear that, though. So –

'Can't wait.' Well, that could have been more convincing.

'Evie, please,' said Kate. 'I know Kevin thinks he can help. But he doesn't understand this thing. It's not some mutant super-power you can control; it's a monster. And it's been itching to control *you* for ages. Look –'

She grabbed her duffel bag from the corner and rifled through until she came up with a tranq dart and a test tube of 'insulin'. 'These are your meds, right?'

'You mean the tranq and that placebo?'

'It's not a placebo,' said Kate. 'It's a sedative mixed with wolfsbane and silver nitrate. It's super-poisonous, and you take three a day just to stay you.'

So I'd been poisoning myself my whole life? 'Do I even know what normal feels like, then?'

Kate shrugged. 'You know what it's like to go to school, and have friends, and not live in a cage. That's pretty normal. But it's not working any more. We've gone from having to add a little extra silver once or twice a year to upping it every few days. Your bloodwork's a mess. That's why you're getting those headaches. That *thing* is getting stronger.'

I felt a shiver, and couldn't tell if it was fear or excitement. 'Stronger how?'

'The silver's not working like it used to,' said Kate. 'These days, every hit your body takes just makes it stronger for the next time.' She held up the tranq. 'This is a mega-dose of silver nitrate and sedative. Used to keep you out all night and leave you flu-y the whole next day, using a lot less silver. Yesterday you took two, slept a couple hours and then went battling Geekboy in the kitchen, right?'

99

Kevin's blood-spiked hot chocolate might've had something to do with that quick recovery, but basically ...

'Right,' I agreed. 'So, I'm becoming immune to silver?'

Kate nodded. 'And without the silver, nothing else works. That thing's too strong to sedate with tranqs alone.'

And no tranqs meant no way to stop me if I lost control – which could still happen, no matter how much fun I was having with Kevin. I felt a cold jolt.

Kate must've noticed. She'd looked like she was about to say something else, her face was still in serious mode, but instead she put her arm around me and squeezed.

'Hey, don't worry,' she said. 'Mom's working on alternatives. We'll figure this out. For right now, though, let's limit your silver exposure to only what's necessary, OK? Keep taking your meds, but no more shooting yourself.'

I nodded, like my brain wasn't already somewhere else. Namely, with the silver-packed 'insulin' in my bag. I'd skipped my morning dose completely, so I'd been meds-free when I'd learned to keep my senses from overwhelming me.

In fact, I'd felt more like me than ever: strong and clear-minded and mostly focused (even if that focus was a bit more Kevin-centric than it should have been).

And I know Kate thought my inner Fido was trying to erase my outer Evie, or whatever, but I wasn't even sure there were two of us in here. I think I'd just found a bigger, scarier side to me – and I'd happily limit my silver exposure all the way to zero if it meant I'd learn to control it. Of course, there was no way I'd get Kate on board with *that*. But maybe Kate didn't have to know.

'All right,' I said. 'Teach me the power of "ommmm",
Sensei Kate.'

* * *

Well, this felt stupid. Sitting on my bed, listening to Kate's
'calm guru' voice telling me to 'focus on my breath' and
'think about every part of my body in turn'.

I knew where my body parts were, they were here,
begging to fight again.

'All right, try to be aware –'

'– wolf.'

'What?'

I opened one eye. 'Aware ... wolf? Werewolf? Get it?'

'Evie,' Kate groaned. 'Close your eyes. Focus!'

'OK, OK.' I tried to settle myself again. 'It was funny,
though.'

'Maybe a little,' said Kate. 'But you'd better not do that
every time I say "aware", because I'll be saying it a lot. Now,
ready?'

I nodded, then sat still and tried. Eventually, I did manage
to start feeling something, although probably not what Kate
wanted.

I thought about my hands, and they pulsed with power.

I brought my focus to my arms. The energy swelled into
my chest, flooding my stomach and radiating out until the
warm flow of strength enveloped me like a hug. Fido buzzed
in every part of my body, wide-awake and itching to play.

'Evie?'

'Huh?'

'I said: open your eyes.' Kate laughed as I blinked. 'Wow, you were miles away.'

Was I? My mind felt clearer, like Kate said it would, but my body was fizzing. I wanted to get up and run laps, but then I heard voices downstairs.

'I'll give it to her.' That was Kevin. 'You should go home, it's nearly dark.'

'Oh, lighten up!' said a bouncy-sounding girl. 'We'll be five minutes.'

And a boy: ' I'll try her cell again.' Kate's phone lit up on the desk. She'd put it on silent, so I was able to dive and grab it before she realised it was ringing.

'Katie Wilder's phone! This is her secretary, who's calling?'

There was a pause, then: 'Uh, Felix Maxwell?'

'Felix! I love that name,' I said. 'Are you the cute goth boy?'

'The ...?' There was a pause, then: 'Sorry, um, is Kate there?'

Kate whipped the phone out of my hand, apologised to Felix and said she'd be right down. Then she hung up and gave a very Mom-like headshake.

'Oh, stop grumping!' I said. 'I wanna meet your new Monster High friends.'

'Fine,' sighed Kate. 'But don't call them that. And try to act normal.'

'You mean like I'm not a werewolf?'

'You're *not* a werewolf. I meant don't be a crazypants.'

'Oh.' Yeah, I couldn't promise that. Fido was still itching to play.

* * *

'KATE!' The adorable blonde literally bounced when she saw us. Felix didn't, but he did smile and wave. He had a nice smile.

'Hi, Kate,' he said, then turned to me. 'Madam Secretary.'

I grinned back, but Kevin shot me a meaningful head-shake, then darted his eyes towards the window. Dusk was settling in, which meant it wasn't safe to be out. But Cass didn't seem to care. She bounded over, gave Kate a giant hug, then shoved a huge plastic container at her and turned to me.

'OMG!' she squealed. 'You're Evie!'

Ooffff! Cass packed a surprisingly tight squeeze for someone so soft. My 'Hi!' got lost in the velvetiness of her coat.

'Sorry!' She let go, giggling. 'Kate's just talked so much about you, and you're so Princess Anna adorable and I LOVE THOSE MOVIES! How are you both so pretty? It's not fair!' She nodded at the container in Kate's hands. 'Well, open it! I felt awful about our town's lousy Kate-friendly food situation …' Kate lifted the lid. The scent of beans and onions flooded the room. 'So I made burgers! They're mush-room and butterbean!'

Not burgers then. I wanted to barf.

'Yummy!' Kate closed the lid, smiling politely.

'Right? Ooh, and I made snacks, look!'

As Cass raced back to her backpack, I threw a questioning glance in Kate's direction. She didn't respond, but that was probably just politeness. Kate *hated* vegetables. The way she talked about salad, you'd swear her dad had been run off the road by a rogue carrot. Poor Cass had clearly misread some vegan-related sarcasm at lunchtime.

'Protein on the go!' Cass held up a bunch of plastic baggies, almost bursting with seeds. 'I've got salted, plain, sweet and salty – I even made chocolate-covered ones. They're so good! Here, try one.'

She struggled to open one of the bags, her hands still full with the others.

Kevin shifted nervously. 'Um, maybe don't do that here? You might –'

Cass yanked the twisty tie off, lost her grip and spilled the entire bag everywhere.

'Oops.'

'Move!' Kevin leapt over the reception desk, shoving Felix aside before dropping to his knees in front of the seeds.

'Ouch,' said Felix.

'Sorry! Just – I need to clean these up. And you need to leave.'

Kevin looked at me helplessly. He was actually twitching. I wasn't sure what was happening, but he clearly needed some alone time with those seeds.

'We're *not* leaving,' said Cass. 'We need to talk to Kate.'

'Common room's comfier!' I said, grabbing Kate's arm to usher her in.

Cass and Felix followed – happy, I think, to get away from Kevin, who was picking the seeds up one at a time, dropping them into his left hand while his right hand moved so fast it practically blurred. He was also muttering something under his breath. I focused my ears and ... was he *counting*?

'Freak,' muttered Felix.

'Can't believe he pushed you!' Cass put her arm around Felix. 'You OK, babe?'

Felix pfff'd. 'He's not that strong!'

Yes he was. So at least I knew he'd made an effort not to hurt anyone. Still – what?

'Anyway, enough about that weirdness!' Cass pulled her phone out. 'We've got a way more important weirdness here. See, Officer Jonson spoke to Amy, then Amy spoke to us, then we all dug around our videos until ... hang on.'

Something flashed across Katie's face. Panic – or guilt, maybe? She looked at me, then back at Cass, who was tapping at her phone irritably.

'Sorry, stupid screen acts up.'

'How about you send it to me?' said Kate all of a rush.

'No, I've got it too. Here!' Felix held up his phone, showing a video of Cass lit up by birthday candles. 'Amy hadn't watched it, 'cos Sage is in it and she didn't want to cry, but watch this.' He pressed play and a chorus of 'Happy Birthday' kicked in, led by a cool-looking waitress with blue braids.

Felix zoomed in behind Cass's head, where ... 'Is that Mom?' She was with someone I couldn't see – and she was laughing. 'Mom's here? I thought she was at the Burnaby lab?'

'Evie, um, listen.' OK, Kate was definitely panicking.

I wasn't the only one who noticed. Felix stopped the video and slipped his phone into his back pocket. 'Actually, we've gotta go. We've got a – a thing, right, Cass? A game thing, we –'

'No, that's tomorrow,' said Cass. 'And we're just at the best part, look.' She jabbed her phone screen again, then zoomed as it finally started playing. Video-Cass leaned forward to blow out the candles, revealing the full booth behind her. Or rather, the *entire* booth. It definitely wasn't full.

'Mom's on a date with … no-one?' I said.

'Except it *wasn't* no-one! It was literally the hottest …' Cass looked at Felix. 'The second hottest guy you've ever seen. Right, Felix?'

Felix groaned. 'Let's just go.'

'What? No, this is important. Bruce Wayne was there! But he's not in the video, and –'

Wait! 'Bruce Wayne? Like, Batman?'

'Kate didn't tell you about him?' said Cass.

I shook my head. 'I think there's a *lot* Kate didn't tell me.'

'Oh.' Cass frowned, briefly. Then her eyes widened. 'Oh! *That* game thing. Yep. I remember now. We should go. But we're treating you two to shakes in Ray's tomorrow after school. No excuses.'

Felix shot me an awkward half-smile. 'Hope you'll join us, Madam Secretary?'

'Sure,' I said and smiled. It wasn't their fault Kate had lied.

They said goodbye, and vanished out into the dark.

My head prickled as I turned to Kate. 'Mom's *here*?'

'I … um … I'm not sure,' Kate admitted.

She wasn't sure? My head thumped. 'We don't know where Mom is?'

'I know where she *was*,' said Kate. 'I haven't heard from her in a while. But she'll show up, she's just –'

'Missing?' I said. 'After a date with Invisible Batman?'

'It wasn't a date!'

'That's not the point!' And she bloody knew it. 'Who's Officer Jonson? Why's he talking to random girls about Mom? And what were you doing in town all day? It must have been important, to leave me here with him!'

My hand clawed as I waved it in Kevin's direction. He jumped to his feet and Kate stepped back, but I pulled it in. Just about.

'Evie, breathe!' said Kate. 'We'll talk about all this, just –'

That's as far as she got. Or at least, it's as much as I heard. Because then, somewhere in the not-too-distant distance, somebody screamed.

A horrible, blood-curdling, nightmarish scream.

Only not *any* someone. Cass. And the scream stopped way too abruptly.

17. Still Evie

'Evie?' Kate followed me to the door. 'Wait!'

I didn't wait. I stopped, but only because Kevin was blocking my way.

'MOVE,' I said.

Kevin shook his head. 'You can't go out there, Red. I – I can't leave the house, and you're not –'

I didn't have time for this. 'Fine, don't come! Katie, stay here. Call the police.'

'The police? Why?'

'Kevin'll tell you,' I said. 'Once he *moves*.'

I shoved him aside, yanked the door open and raced out – ignoring their yells. The scream had come from towards town, so that's where I headed, following Cass and Felix's scents until I caught a sickeningly familiar smell. *Nonono*.

I quickened my pace. Fear mixed with adrenaline, churning inside my stomach and pounding inside my head.

'Evie!'

Kate, crap! She sounded pretty far behind – and getting further, judging by her footsteps. But she was supposed to be in the nice safe guesthouse.

I tried yelling at her to go back, but it caught in my throat and came out raspy. The smell of blood was so strong now I thought I might throw up.

I knew what I was going to see before I turned down the alleyway, but that didn't make it any easier. The sight of Cass's torn-up body sent pain ripping along my spine, into my skull – then out, into every tiny corner of me. I tried to take a deep breath, but my heart was racing too fast.

Fido, stop!

Kate was nearly here. Inner Fido didn't care.

My muscles spasmed – jerking me backwards, then forward so fast the bones cracked as my knees hit the ground beside Cass.

After that, there was no stopping it. If my smashed knees hurt, that was lost among the waves of white-hot pain. My joints twisted, yanking at my bones as my skeleton burst open. I was almost glad when my vision blurred so I couldn't see Cass any more, but her blood-scent was everywhere. I felt one last, horrible full-body spasm – then something clicked inside and it was over.

Except it wasn't. My body was still pulsing as the world swirled back into focus. Everything looked different. Brighter. More terribly vivid. Poor, dead Cass was the centre of the universe, brought into nightmarish high-def focus by my new wolfy-vision. There was a spine-chilling howl, coming from *me*. If I *was* still me. I felt different. Bigger, and stronger. A rush of energy hit my veins: white-hot, like the pain I'd just felt. Only not, because this felt good. My muscles tensed and rippled against my skin. It felt ... right.

Then I glanced back at Cass, and something else surged through me. Because *that* was wrong. My muscles clenched again. All that energy rushed to my head and joints.

Where's Felix?

I sniffed the air. The smell of Cass's blood hit so hard I could taste it. Still, I forced myself to do it again, and again. Because Felix had either escaped or been taken. If he'd been taken, maybe I could save him. If he'd escaped and left Cass ... Another rage-surge hit. My Freddy Krueger claws curled into the snow as I found Felix's scent, and ... something else. Something slightly musty and half-familiar.

Then I caught a scent I definitely knew.

I spun around as Kate turned the corner. She gave a horrified gasp, then threw up on the pavement as she spotted Cass. I started back down the alleyway towards her, until she snapped her head up and I saw the terror on her face.

Her hand flew to the tranq gun in her waistband.

'Don't!' I yelled. Or tried to. But that's not how it came out.

Kate paused, confused, then pulled the gun out anyway. 'Evie?'

I barked again. Kate frowned. 'OK. Now bark twice.'

So I did. Kate lowered the gun. 'Evie, you're *you*? I mean, you're not ...'

I gave another bark. She almost smiled. Then she caught another glimpse of Cass, and threw up again. I whimpered. Kate wasn't able for this. She needed to go home.

Then something changed. Kate shook her head, inhaled deeply and pulled herself upright, into Mom-mode.

'You didn't do this, right, Evie?'

I shook my head and barked twice, for no, like in those clever-animal movies we'd loved before we discovered horror.

'OK,' said Kate. 'What about Felix? Can you smell him?'

I barked once, for yes, took a couple of steps down the alleyway.

Kate nodded. 'Is he alone?'

I sniffed the air again, then barked twice. Whoever that musty scent belonged to, they'd either left with him or followed him, I was certain.

'Cool.' Kate held the gun up again. 'Now go home.'

Me? Hell no! Two huge barks.

Kate frowned and stepped forward. I moved in front of her, growling.

'What, you're going and I'm not?' said Kate.

One bark. It was far too dangerous for her. I turned and started down the alley.

'Evie, don't you dare!' yelled Kate. 'Evie!' She sighed. 'Fine, but I know you're not leaving me here alone, with whatever did *that*.'

I stopped, then turned back grumbling.

'Thought not. OK.' Kate pulled a scrunched-up plastic bag from her jacket and stuffed my ripped clothes inside. 'Let's go.'

We'd followed the trail through the alleyway, down the street and off behind a row of shops, when I caught another scent. Musty, like the last one, but different. I stopped dead. The hairs on my back stood up. There was something I didn't like, and I didn't know what it was.

'Evie?' Kate stroked my head with one hand, and raised the tranq gun in the other. 'What's wrong?'

I spun around as a tall blond man blurred to a halt in front of us.

'Fee fi fo fum, little wolf,' he said with a leer.

'Wrong story, idiot!' Kate pressed the gun to his temple.

The guy blurred again. In one movement, the gun was skidding across the ground and Kate was slammed into the wall, her head pulled to one side.

I reacted without thinking, lunging and snapping my teeth around the guy's throat. We fell to the ground and I tore back, taking a chunk of his neck with me.

He should've been dead, but I didn't have time to think about that as he tried to shove me off him. I caught his arm in my jaws, and bit down.

The bones cracked, but I kept going. I had to buy Kate time to get away.

I'd just slashed into his chest, when there was a soft *fffdun*. The guy raised his head, weak and slightly cross-eyed, then passed out.

'Well, that worked!' said Kate, tucking the tranq gun away before turning to scan the dark. Her gaze landed on a big yard-brush beside a dumpster.

'Perfect!'

She rushed over, snapped it across her knee like that was easy, then tossed the brush-end aside and race back to me – dropping down beside me and the body, broken handle poised like a makeshift stake.

She wouldn't actually ...

The guy's eyes flicked open. He was on his way to bolt-uprightness when Kate punched him with her left fist, then rammed the stake through his heart with her right.

He exploded. A cloud of guts and gore hit the air, transforming into thick red dust-mist before starting to fall. Katie jumped back, coughing.

'Do you still have Felix's scent?' she asked.

I took a deep sniff, almost choking on a lungful of powdered corpse. Then I barked twice and shook my head.

'Crap,' said Kate.

We looked at each other a couple of seconds longer. My pulse was starting to slow. My muscles were relaxing, like a tightly wound spring releasing in slo-mo. Not far away, a car pulled to a halt. A door slammed, and there was the sound of footsteps, before –

'Evie? Kate?'

Then Kevin was there. He saw me and froze, his brow furrowed half-way between confusion and action-scowl.

'Oh, look, Evie,' said Kate. 'The hero has arrived! Surprised you even found us, you lagged so far behind.'

'We found Cass,' said Kevin. 'Then I followed your footprints through the snow.' The car sounded too close for that to be true. He must have followed our scents. He kept talking. 'The police are on their way to my house. And Chris brought the car. Is she …?' He nodded towards me.

'She's fine,' said Kate. 'She's Evie.'

Was I, though? *Evie* didn't usually rip bits off strangers and not stop until her sister tranqed them. I could still taste his blood in my mouth.

Still, my body was relaxing – my skin tingled as the world blurred up again.

Kevin gave a yelp of 'Oh! Sorry!' and then something soft hit me.

When everything came back, he was facing the other way, his coat flung over my clothes-free body. I didn't really want anything from him right now – I was still pissed off that he'd tried to stop me leaving. But being naked in public wasn't a great plan, and I wasn't taking Kate's coat, she'd freeze. So I pulled Kevin's coat on and stood up.

I was surprisingly not-cold, even without shoes, but I still let Kate wrap her arm around me. We both needed the hug.

'Let's get to the car before –' Kevin stopped and looked around. 'Let's just go.'

I caught that smell again, as we started back down the alley. That odd, musty … I lifted my shoulder and sniffed Kevin's coat.

'Kate,' I said. 'That thing you just staked. Was that a –?'

'A vampire? Yup! Fangs and all.' Despite everything, she couldn't help shooting a smug glance at Kevin. 'Guess I'm officially a vampire slayer, eh?'

'Very impressive,' muttered Kevin.

But he didn't sound impressed. No wonder, really.

I breathed his scent from his coat again, and our eyes met behind Kate's back. I think he could see me figuring out that thing *you* probably guessed ages ago, Reader. He swallowed nervously, like he was worried I'd blurt it out.

But of course I wouldn't!

I might've been a bit pissed off right then, but Kate full-on hated him.

I don't know what she'd have done if she'd found out he was a vampire.

18. Kate

A vampire.

My mind raced as we climbed into the car.

I staked a vampire. Vampires are real. And I killed someone.

Evie had changed, but stayed herself. Kevin was all talk. I was a killer, and Cass ...

Don't think about Cass. I couldn't help it. My mind was a mess of thoughts and images. Cass's pale, petrified face merged with the vampire's – her glassy, unseeing eyes fading into his flashing amber ones. Cass must've seen those eyes too, right before he killed her. I imagined her earnestly explaining to the vampire how things like this didn't happen in towns like Brightside, before he sank his teeth into –

Stop!

I couldn't. I was seasick from the grotesque tableaux swirling through my brain, but I couldn't stop them. I saw Felix's big friendly eyes turn dull and lifeless, like Cass's; his tiny frame bloodied and broken and dumped somewhere. It had to be. He wouldn't have left Cass, so he wouldn't have stood a chance.

Tears burned my eyes. I felt weak and shivery, but I couldn't break down. Evie was right beside me. I took a deep breath and forced my feelings back.

It's fine. We're going to be fine.

As the car pulled up in front of the guesthouse, I grabbed Evie for the longest hug we've ever had. I couldn't even tell her it was all OK; she knew it wasn't. So I held her and *wished*, until the wail of police sirens tore us back to – reality? Was that really the right word for all this?

Officer Jonson spoke to Chris and Kevin as Evie and I cleaned ourselves up.

Too soon, Chris knocked on the door. 'Your turn, sweethearts.'

We'd barely gotten our story straight. Not that we were suspects: the attacks had been happening long before we arrived, but still.

'Wait, attack*s*?' said Evie. 'Plural?'

I hadn't quite gotten to that bit yet.

Evie moved closer to me as Officer Jonson kept going, telling her everything I hadn't about savaged bodies and missing people. A couple of times she rubbed her forehead, wincing and making tiny circles as she inhaled, deep and slow, trying to calm herself. Officer Jonson stopped and offered to let us take a break.

Evie shook her head. 'It's just a stress headache. Keep going.'

Kevin brought us hot drinks, then lingered by the doorway shooting uneasy glances in Evie's direction. I think he was waiting for something to happen, but it didn't.

Eventually, Officer Jonson snapped his notebook shut on our mostly true statement and sighed. 'I still don't know what you were thinking! What if you'd gotten there in time to face whatever did this? You think I wouldn't have two more bodies to deal with right now? Because I would. And you –' He pointed his pen at me. 'You ought to know better, especially after our chat today.'

'Yes, sir,' I said.

'Yes, sir?' Evie glared at Officer Jonson. 'She didn't do anything! *I* ran out in the dark. I found Cass and went looking for Felix. All Kate did was try to stop me. So if you're gonna be mad at anyone –'

'Whoa, sweetheart!' Officer Jonson gave a 'calm down' smile. 'I'm not mad, I'm just –' He took his glasses off to massage the bridge of his nose. He looked exhausted. 'I don't want anyone else getting hurt. So, just promise, if you hear anything like that again, you'll run *away* from it. And call me, OK?'

Evie shrugged, so unconvincingly that Officer Jonson pulled me aside before leaving. 'You think she'll be all right? She gonna stay out of trouble?'

I glanced back at Evie, who was somehow sipping her drink in a way that implied she wanted to murder it. She did not look ready to stay out of trouble.

'I'll make sure of it, sir,' I said.

Officer Jonson nodded, then frowned, concerned. 'And what about you, sweetheart? Are *you* gonna be OK?'

'Me?' I almost laughed. 'Always, sir.'

I really thought I meant that.

* * *

After Officer Jonson left, Chris suggested dinner.

Evie said she wasn't hungry.

I wasn't either, especially not for meat, although that was nothing new. I would've gone vegetarian years ago if Mom hadn't worried Evie would try to copy me, which could be bad for everyone. So I told Chris we'd have as much bloody steak as possible, please, and ignored the churning in my stomach as she left.

'You all right?' I said, sitting down beside Evie.

'Nope. You?'

'No,' I said. 'But, hey! That meditation worked, you stayed totally in control – even in Not-Evie's body. Beast-masterdom achieved!'

'Beast-master?' said Evie. 'I mauled that guy. I didn't even know he was a vampire. I just ripped his throat out. Isn't that … bad?'

Obviously, it wasn't perfect. But compared to racing around clawing madly at Mom and me, I'd take it. Though maybe Evie didn't need to hear that.

'I didn't know he was a vampire when I almost tranq'd him in the brain,' I said. 'Probably not great either.'

'You kidding? That's awesome!' Kevin's voice seemed to come out of nowhere, but when I looked – there he was, collecting mugs and eavesdropping. 'Vampire or not, he jumped you in an alleyway in creepy-murder central – and you both went full-slayer mode to protect each other! He must've been terrified.'

My stomach twisted.

Terrified was right. He'd been looking into my eyes when he realised I was going to kill him – and he'd been petrified.

He wasn't much older than us; he hadn't wanted to die. And Kevin thought I should be proud?

'What would you know about slayer mode?' I snapped. 'Hanging around the house while the girls save your town?'

'Wait, you think you saved us?' Kevin looked at Evie, who shook her head.

I felt a creeping cold. 'What?'

'Our guy didn't kill Cass,' Evie told me. 'Or take Felix. He smelt similar, but it wasn't him. There's more of them. Right, Kevin?'

Kevin nodded.

The cold feeling spread out, until my whole body shivered. More vampires. In the town where Mom was missing. I grabbed my drink back off Kevin's tray and took a long gulp before replying: 'OK, you're never leaving this house again, Evie. And Dean Wimpchester clearly doesn't leave anyway, just mopes about letting the bloodsuckers terrorise the town, eh? Freaking badass!'

Kevin's jaw flexed angrily. 'If I could take these psychos down, I'd have done it already. But there's *one* of me, and they keep recruiting. This time tomorrow, there'll be another giant asshole on another missing-person poster, to replace the one you killed. There's no stopping them. There's just surviving.'

'And letting everyone else get hurt while you stay home, right?'

The light must have hit Kevin's eyes oddly. For a second, they seemed to blaze.

'That,' he said too calmly, 'is not what happened. Sure, I didn't just race into the dark like a reckless idiot, but I did go.

Me and Chris got you *out* of that vampire-infested craphole, remember? What happened tonight sucked, but it wasn't my fault.'

He started to leave, then stopped. 'We've got your backs, Kate. Now, if you'll excuse me, I'm gonna go chop potatoes so you can have proper fries with dinner.'

'Im'a gonna chop you some proper fries,' I muttered as he left. 'Jerk!'

Evie gave a half chuckle, which was my plan.

Then she sighed. 'He's not wrong, though. I was stupid – he *did* come after us. And you were awesome, Katie.'

'Ooh, high praise from the beast-master!' I grinned.

Evie grinned back. 'Just trying to keep up with the slayer.'

I almost laughed. Things almost felt nice. For a second.

'Look,' said Evie. 'I get why you didn't want to tell me Mom had gone missing in a freaking hellmouth. But I'm really sick of being lied to.'

She didn't look angry. It was worse – she looked hurt.

'Evie, I never wanted –'

'But you did,' she said. 'And I know you were just trying to protect me, but you don't have to do that any more. I can handle things, even the bad bits.'

That vampire's face flashed through my mind again. When he hadn't looked scared, he'd been horrifying. I'd honestly thought I was about to die.

Evie had saved me, in Not-Evie's body.

'You can,' I admitted. To both of us.

'Then no more lies,' said Evie. 'I want to know everything.'

So, as dinner cooked and Kevin pretended *not* to eavesdrop nearby, that's almost exactly what I told her.

* * *

'So, Mom thought Robert and Madison might be *here*? Doing all this?' Evie flexed her fingers, agitated, then rubbed that spot between her eyes again.

'You OK?' I asked.

'Yeah.' She took a slow breath, released it, then took a few more. 'No. I dunno! You told me what they were, I just – I don't think I really got it before. They left 'cos they were scared of hurting me, and – and instead they're running around hurting, y'know, whoever?' She gripped her head. 'Kevin's right. They're not good people. They're not people at all. *I'm* not –'

'Hey, no!' I grabbed her into a giant hug. 'Robert and Madison are brilliant people; they're just not always themselves. And *you* are my favourite person. Fangs and claws and all. You know that!'

Evie nodded, and let me keep hugging her until her breathing and her heartrate slowed to normal. She was getting really good at that.

'So,' she said, finally. 'Mom arrived looking for werewolves, and wound up on a date with Vampire Batman?'

'It wasn't a date!'

'You sure? 'Cos it really looked like –'

'Mom *doesn't* date,' I said. 'And if she was gonna start, it wouldn't be with some overly handsome vampire sleazeball. She was clearly using her, you know, feminine wiles. To ... charm him. Find out what he knew. Etcetera.'

'Oh, yeah. Etcetera. Totally.' Evie agreed, too earnestly. 'So, do we know where she was staying? Did she check out, or just not come back?'

It was a good question, for an awkward segue.

'No idea,' I said. 'Officer Jonson's looking into it. There's nothing on her credit card, so he thinks she used a secret second card, under a fake name, so I couldn't use her paper statement to follow her.'

'Ooh, criminal!' Evie sounded impressed. 'Well, at least we know she's not using a fake second face. Your posters helped.'

'That's true,' I said. 'Um, I'm doing more tomorrow, if you wanna come?'

It would be a terrible idea. Actually coming face-to-face with all those missing giants might seriously upset Evie. But I couldn't keep telling her what to do, and that monster-radar I'd chickened out of mentioning earlier wasn't such a huge problem if we were dealing with vampires, not not-people. So she didn't need to stay indoors, I guess.

Still, she shook her head. 'You go. I'll do some vampire research here.'

'Vampire research?' I said. 'Evie, you heard Kevin. There's too many –'

'I'm not planning anything.' Evie laughed. 'But they're real, and they're here. It'd be dumb *not* to prepare for a possible next time, right?'

'Right,' I said, and sighed.

Only next time would come way too soon. And we wouldn't be prepared at all.

19. Kate again

'You OK?' asked Evie.

'Me?' I poked the bloody flesh on my plate. 'Yup, fine.'

I sawed off a chunk, trying not to picture Cass's ripped-up throat and wide-open stomach.

'Katie?' said Evie. 'You've gone green!'

Cold sweat popped along my skin. I jumped up. 'I'm fine. Just gotta go to the bathroom.'

I'd almost made it to our room when my legs gave way. This time, I couldn't stop the tears, so I sat in the hallway and sobbed into my arm. I was vaguely aware of the sound of a door opening, but I didn't look up until I felt a hand on my shoulder.

Kevin passed me a Kleenex, then helped me to my feet and had to half-carry me to my bathroom. He turned on both taps and the shower, full blast.

'She won't hear you over this,' he said. 'Not from downstairs.'

I tried to say 'thanks' but it came out as one long sob.

Kevin shifted, uncertainly. 'Um, do you need a hu...' he started, then changed his mind. 'Need to punch me or something?'

I couldn't help laughing, through the tears. 'Not right now, thanks.'

'No rush,' he said. 'You can cash it in later.'

'Cool.' I laughed again.

Kevin smiled, then passed me another tissue, as I slipped back into sobs. 'Should I stick around or what?'

I shook my head. 'Just keep Evie out. Tell her I need another shower; there's still dead guy lodged in my sinuses anyway.'

Kevin hesitated. 'You know, Chris is used to … feelingsy stuff, if …'

'I'm fine,' I said. 'Really, I do all my best crying alone.'

Kevin gave me one last worried smile, then left. The moment the door shut, I collapsed back onto the closed toilet. And howled.

Everything was wrong, and I couldn't fix any of it. But what I *could* do was puke into the bath until I dry-heaved, then shower-steam the vampowder from my lungs.

Not the most heroic plan, but it's what I went with.

* * *

I did eat, eventually.

Chris reheated one of Cass's burgers. It stuck horribly in my throat for the first few bites, but the thought of it being thrown out was worse, so I finished it, while Evie went and chose a movie to keep our brains from replaying the night on a loop.

'Ooh, they have all the Disney!' she called.

'Perfect!' Singing princesses was about as dark as I could manage right now.

We snuggled under a fluffy blanket.

Kevin stood by the door, waiting for an invitation to join us. When he didn't get it, he sat at the desk with his book and definitely watched through the doorway. But poor Evie was wiped. Half an hour into the movie, she curled up against me.

Maybe twenty minutes later, she was out. I turned the movie off, scooped her up like I'd done hundreds of times over the years, and headed for the stairs.

'Do you think maybe she'd be happier down here again?' asked Kevin.

'She can't avoid room-sharing with me for ever,' I said. 'Besides, I'm not worried; she shouldn't be.'

'Because you saw her control it tonight?' Kevin asked.

His tone was innocent, but his words still grated.

'No!' I snapped. 'Because I've been doing this my whole life! That thing's still inside her, but I can handle it. I always have.'

Kevin clearly wanted to argue, but he sighed and went back to his book. 'OK.'

'*What?*'

'I didn't say anything,' said Kevin.

'No, but you want to. Go on, what am I wrong about now?'

'I – I didn't say you were wrong,' said Kevin. 'You've got this.'

He didn't believe that. He hadn't since the moment we arrived, and he'd never had any problem telling me before now. Before seeing me cry.

'I'm *not* weak, you know!'

'Whoa, what?' Kevin looked up, surprised. 'How did you get –?'

'I know you saw a vague moment of weakness earlier,' I said. 'But that was a glitch. I'm fine. I don't need to be humoured or coddled. Especially not by you.'

'Who's coddling? You're badass!' said Kevin. 'I'm just stepping back like we said. You know what you're doing.'

'Yeah, I do.'

'I know,' said Kevin. Then, as I turned to leave, he added, 'But crying doesn't make you weak, Kate. We're supposed to feel stuff.'

'I know,' I said.

'OK, good,' said Kevin. 'Just – you called it weakness. But it's not. Wasn't that the whole point of that movie? Bottling stuff up doesn't make it go away, it just shoves it down until it festers and comes out.'

Festers? 'There's nothing festering inside Evie!'

'What?'

'That's where you're going with this, right?' I said. 'We've been lying to Evie, using meds to suppress the monster – but it's never really *been* a monster? Just a huge, repressed part of Evie, "festering" away until it bursts out, every few weeks, in some – some violent somnambulist nightmare?'

'*What?*'

'It means sleepwalker, idiot.'

'Yeah, I know what somnambulist means,' said Kevin. 'And that's hardly the craziest idea I've ever heard, but I wasn't talking about Evie. I meant you.'

'Me?'

Kevin nodded. 'Kate, I know you're brave, and awesome, and I *know* you don't want to put any of this on Evie. I get wanting to be the strong older sibling, but –'

'Oh, so now you're psychoanalysing me?'

'No!' Kevin groaned. 'I'm relating, or trying to. Look, I just mean, next time you need to have a – a wobbly moment, I'm here. Or Chris is, maybe that's better. She's way less irritating.'

He laughed, and I felt that angry knot inside me unwind. Slightly.

'You're really just being nice?'

'I know, weird, eh?' Kevin pulled an awkward face, and I smiled, then shifted a bit under Evie's weight. I carried her all the time, but usually just from the upstairs hallway to her room. Holding her this long was a little harder.

'I'd better get her to bed,' I said. 'But, um, thanks, Kev.'

'Kevin.'

'I like Kev.'

Kevin shook his head. 'Nah, I don't think you do.'

* * *

I tucked Evie in before plopping onto my own bed and opening the text I'd gotten from Zoe earlier:

Missed you at school today, hun. You OK? X

I felt a little flutter as I re-read. If I'd stopped and thought for a moment, I might have realised Zoe never called me 'hun'. And her single 'X' was way more restrained than her usual seven-smiley-face-emojis-and-dancing-cat-GIFs.

But I was too busy wondering if I'd ever see her again. I lied back:

```
All good, just family stuff. Miss you too
xx.
```

I hesitated, then deleted everything after 'family stuff' and hit 'send'. I hated lying to Zoe, but what was I supposed to tell her? The truth?

I opened the photo I'd taken with Cass and Felix earlier, and my stomach churned. They were so happy. So alive. How had that only been this afternoon?

I had Felix's number from when he called me, so I saved it, then opened a new message and typed:

```
Are you there?
```

He didn't reply. I hadn't expected him to. I typed again:

```
I'm so sorry, It's all my fault. I dragged
you into this.
```

I hit 'send' again, then watched the screen a moment longer before adding:

```
Please be alive. Please be OK.
```

He couldn't be, of course. Even if he *was* alive, there was no way he was OK.

I'm not sure what time I eventually dozed off, but I was fast asleep by the time Felix texted back:

```
You awake? Need to talk. ASAP!
```

20. Evie

Kate was in the shower when I woke up.

Or at least, the shower was running. But so were the taps and I could hear her whispering through the gushing water. Whoever she was talking to, she didn't want me to know. So, obviously, I tiptoed over and pressed my ear against the door.

'OK, bye!'

The water stopped. Dang it!

I superwolf-dashed back to bed, but the bedsprings were still creaking as Kate came out, wrapped in a big towel and scrubbing her wet hair with a smaller one.

'Morning, nosypants. Hear anything exciting?'

'Me?' I tried to smile innocently, then gave up. 'No, I missed everything. Who were you talking to?'

Kate attempted a casual shrug, then grinned. 'Zoe.'

'Zoe?' Zoe-from-Next-Door Zoe? Zoe-Kate-had-been-pretending-she-wasn't-crushing-on-for-years Zoe? 'Zoe King?'

'Yep!'

I glanced at my phone. Ten-thirty on a school morning. 'Doesn't she have class?'

'Don't *you* have class, stinky?' Katie flung her wet hair-towel in my face. 'Go shower, you still smell of dead vampire.'

I sniffed my hair. Ugh, those guys really lingered.

'Fine. Shower, then breakfast and more Zoe gossip. Deal?'

'Just *go*!'

* * *

Breakfast was delicious. Or mine was anyway.

Chris had been into town to stock up on meat and, I swear, she stacked an entire pig's worth of bacon and sausages onto my plate. Kate had some distinctly non-meaty smelling 'fauxsages' but – she seemed to enjoy them? Somehow? I did not get it.

There was no Zoe-chat, because Chris sat down to update us on what she'd heard around town. 'Nobody blames you two, obviously. They're just worried for you, Kate. You made quite the impression. Miriam Wells practically wants to adopt you.'

'Miriam?' said Kate. 'Oh, Linc's gran, right?'

'Who?' I said. 'Kate, you were in town half a day and you're friends with some dude's granny already?'

Kate shrugged. 'It's a nice place. Any word on Felix?'

'Oh, plenty of words about Felix.' Chris sounded annoyed. 'It's a lovely place. If they like you.'

'They don't like Felix?' I asked. What was wrong with Felix?

'They don't like his family,' said Chris. 'They're quite … alternatively spiritual. Plus, apparently Felix went through a rough patch after his mom died. That was a few years ago, before we moved here. But Miriam and her ilk have *not* gotten over it.'

'Why? What happened?' asked Kate.

Chris shook her head. 'Nothing, basically. He was only twelve. I think he dyed his hair, stopped smiling and maybe stole from Miriam's tip jar a couple of times. Hardly a master criminal. But he's still a boy in eyeliner with a weird family so, you know, all the hallmarks of a serial killer.'

I laughed, because it was ridiculous. Kate didn't.

'They don't actually think he's a serial killer, do they?' she asked.

'Oh, they definitely do,' said Chris.

What – *Felix*?

'But he's so nice!' I said. 'And his girlfriend's dead. He's missing, not evil.'

'Yeah, but he wears black and plays games down the back of Ray's once a week with other black-clad, eye-make-up-wearing teenagers. So ...'

'Ugh!' I rage-ate some bacon and tried not to punch the table.

I'd known Felix about three seconds, but his adorably lopsided smile as he quipped 'Madam Secretary' had stuck in my head along with Cass's hug.

What would they think if he showed up dead? Would they still manage to blame him? Or would he be guilt-elevated to sainthood?

'Don't worry,' said Chris. 'The police don't suspect him. But Miriam and her gang are talking and the rest of the town's scared enough to be listening.'

The whole town?

'Is everyone here an idiot?' snapped Kate. 'If nothing else, he's half the size of those missing giants. How do they think he's doing this?'

'I don't think they care about logistics,' said Chris. 'They just want someone to blame. To hear them tell it, every death, every missing person, it's all part of his devil-worshipping satanic something-or-other.'

'Oh, a *satanic* serial killer?' said Kate. 'Of course! Jeez, I'm tempted to buzzcut half my head, pierce my septum and spray-paint a Pride skull on the back of Dad's jacket, just to see what happens next time I go out. But I need people to talk to me.'

'No, they'd talk to you,' said Chris. 'You're new. Plus, Miriam's already told everyone you snuck her a big tip on a free coffee. So *you'd* be "going through a phase".'

Kate groaned, buried her face in her hands and took a few deep breaths before looking up with an over-the-top smile. 'Yay, phases! Freaking love this place.'

* * *

After breakfast, Kate headed into town, and I settled down on the sofa with my laptop to wait for Ke– uh, to research. I was researching. Not waiting for Kevin to come downstairs. Although he *was* an actual vampire – because of course he was.

Of course the first guy to give me proper, real-life tummy jitters turned out to be an ageless immortal. Made about as much sense as the rest of my life.

Oh, something else that made no sense? The Internet! Shocking, I know, but how was I supposed to figure out vampires when no-one agreed on anything?

134

I mean, stakes worked. We'd seen that. And silver, maybe? Kate's tranq had knocked that dude out – briefly – but was that down to the silver or the sedative?

Any talk about holy water and religious symbols got nasty way too fast to be helpful, and as for sunlight, reflections, running water, garlic ... I found, like, a zillion different answers with nothing concrete. I think the only thing everyone agreed on was that vampires and werewolves were natural enemies.

And that vampires would kick our asses.

'Evie?'

'Kevin!' I nearly knocked the laptop over as I jumped up and spun around. 'Uh, hi. Good morn– um ... day!' *Good day?* 'No, I mean, uh –' *What's the word again?* 'Morrow!' *MORROW?!?* 'Good morrow to you? Sir?'

Oh, God, Evie, stop talking!

'Uh, yea verily?' Kevin laughed. 'I come bearing cookies and blood?'

Oh, food! Good. Something to do with my mouth other than talk.

I glanced at his empty hands. 'Invisiblood?'

'All right, news of cookies and blood.' Kevin laughed again. 'In the kitchen. Don't want Kate freaking out if she gets back early. Plus, um, Chris is meeting our blood-supplier, Jim. She'll be a few hours, so ...'

My breath caught in my chest. 'It's just us? On our own?'

Kevin obviously heard my heart start to race. He glanced at my computer screen (and the words 'WEREWOLVES VS VAMPIRES: THE ULTIMATE DEATHMATCH' in giant flashing letters).

His face fell. 'Are you scared of me now, Red?'

'What? No!' But I could see why he thought I was – the pounding pulse, the nerviness, my words being straight-up broken? 'I'm just, um, a little on edge after last night.' Oh, look, a full sentence. 'Let's go drink some blood, eh?'

* * *

He'd meant *blood* blood. Straight, no chocolate.

And it was good. Who knew? Well, Kevin, obviously. And all the other scary vampires and – oh, I don't know. I had no idea what was real or not any more. Although according to Kevin: 'Basically, everything.'

'What – ghosts? Wendigos? Demons? Zombies?'

'Probably,' said Kevin. 'Once you get down the magic rabbit hole, it just keeps going. Although, I don't think there are actual magic rabbit holes. But there *is* magic. It's all magic. We're magic.'

'We're magic?' Ten-year-old Evie would've flipped.

'Sure! I mean, look.' Kevin rested his hand against my face. It felt warm and nice. 'See? My heart doesn't beat. But my blood flows anyway. I'm warm. I can bleed and blush. I can pass for human.' He slipped his hand onto mine. 'And obviously you're magical. So pretty and terrifying all at once.'

'Pretty?' *Oh my God, Evie! Out loud?*

I yanked my hand away and gulped some blood as an excuse to hide behind my mug. Where was a werewolf-specific floor portal when I needed one?

Kevin blushed. 'Sorry, should I not have said that?'

136

'What? No, I – um – thank you, just …' *Seriously, portal. Any time.* 'Sorry, I'm just malfunctioning. Tell me more about monsters.' *So I can stop talking.*

Kevin nodded, looking as relieved as I felt.

'I don't really know much. I've been trying to stay out of it for the last …' He stopped. 'Well, longer than I was ever *in* it. But I know Jim supplies all sorts of blood to different customers. Even human blood, ethically. He's got suppliers too.'

'So, if there's monsters, are there hunters too? Aside from you?'

'Of course,' said Kevin. 'Fewer now, though. Jim says the good ones are either getting old, killed, or they're spread too thin trying to protect their own territories. A couple did show up here, but I didn't realise until Jim spotted their pictures in the paper, after Ashton's guys had … y'know.'

Ah, I see. 'So it's not like on TV?'

'No.' Kevin shook his head. 'No Chosen Ones, just a bunch of humans trying to save people. But none of them can handle Ashton's army.'

He looked sad again. I wanted to hug him – but the thought also terrified me, so I put my hand on his arm instead. 'What if some non-humans tried?'

Kevin's eyebrows shot up. If his heart could beat I knew it would be pounding.

'I'm just saying,' I said. 'We're stronger, and faster, and harder to kill. And we make a good team.'

'No.'

'But –'

'They'd *kill* us,' said Kevin. 'Then Chris and Kate would come looking and –' He sighed. 'We're not looking for a fight,

137

Red. But we *can* try to be ready if they bring the fight to us.' He gulped down the rest of his blood and looked at me. 'Whaddya say? Wanna learn how to rip their heads off?'

My right claw popped by itself. I drained the contents of my mug, licked my lips and stood up.

'Hell, yeah!'

* * *

We lost track of time. That happened a lot when I was with Kevin.

I mean, fighting. With Kevin. When I was … oh, who am I kidding?

You know what I mean. (I swear, he got cuter the longer I spent with him.) Anyway, around the time I accidentally bit into his bicep, Kevin decided we were overdue for lunch. We'd just sat down in the living room when Katie returned.

She looked freezing and she kept eyeing my hot chocolate, so Kevin went to get her one (minus the secret ingredient) as she dropped her bag angrily to the ground.

'No-one cares that Felix is missing,' she said. 'Miriam literally offered me free apple pie, then told me he was a serial killer *in the same breath*. Do you know how hard it is to stay angry at someone while you're eating free pie?'

'Oh, so you took the pie?'

'I'm angry, not stupid. I also got a free grilled cheese on the way back.'

'Seriously?'

'What?' said Kate. 'If she's gonna call my friend a psycho, I'm gonna steal her food. *Quid pro quo*, Evie.'

'You didn't tip, then?'

Kate hesitated. 'Well, her grandson's missing. I can't be a total bitch.'

'No,' I said. 'You never can.'

'Whatever.' Kate unzipped her snowy coat and hung it on the rack by the door. She had this odd expression when she turned back, but just for a second. 'Hey, you want a judo lesson?'

'Really?'

'Sure! You're always asking, and you do need to be able to defend yourself.'

'Can she teach you to decapitate a vampire?' Kevin whispered from the kitchen.

That wasn't fair. I'd wanted to do judo like Kate for ever.

Mom had always said too much exercise was bad for my blood sugar, which, I now realise, was definitely a ruse to keep Not-Evie from learning what Kate could do. Not-Evie had her own skills now, but …

'I'd LOVE that!'

Katie grinned. 'Yay! This'll be fun.'

* * *

It was fun!

Even Kevin got involved. Sure, that was mostly so Kate could show me how to punch him, or sweep his leg, or flip him onto the floor, but he liked that.

I swear we'd only been at it five minutes when Chris returned, lugging two giant plastic blood-containers. Kevin rushed over to help.

'Thanks,' she said. 'I'll get the rest later – we need to start dinner. It's six-fifteen.'

'Six-fifteen?' Kate's eyes widened. 'Already?'

'Time flies with a fun teacher, eh?' I said. 'Wanna keep going?'

Kate hesitated. Then she grabbed me into a giant bear hug and squeezed.

'I love you so much, Evie.' Was she tearing up?

'Katie,' I said. 'What's wrong?'

'Nothing.' Kate let go and forced a chuckle. 'Just a sucky day in a sucky town. Oh, I got you something, though.'

She grabbed her bag and flipped it open.

'A present?' I said. 'From Hallowe'en Town?'

'Don't get too excited, it's just your first non-Diet Coke.' She opened it and passed it to me. 'Enjoy!'

I took a swig. Something was … strange. I gulped again.

'This tastes weird. Like, different?'

'Yeah, sugary,' said Kate, grinning. 'Yum!'

Right, of course. I took another glug and – wait, was the room swaying?

'Am *I* swaying?'

'You're just tired.' Kate led me to the sofa and sat me down. 'Drink some more; the sugar will help.'

''K.' I swigged again. The room started to fade. 'Why's e'ryting all … all … where's t' world goin'?'

'Sorry, Evie.' Kate took the bottle and stood up.

And then everything was cushions.

21. Kate

Evie fell face-first into the cushions.

I rolled her over, covered her with a blanket and kissed her cheek.

'Stay,' I whispered. 'I mean it.'

'Evie?'

I spun around. Kevin was right behind me.

I shoved the Coke into his hands before he could say anything else. 'If she wakes up, give her this. Make sure she finishes it.' I pushed past him. 'But don't drink it – it's packed with silver nitrate and sedatives.'

'Whoawhoawhoa.' Suddenly he was back in front of me. 'Where are you going?'

'Out.'

'After last night? I can't let you –'

'You don't have to let me,' I said, flinging my bag over my shoulder. 'You're not responsible for my stupid decisions. Just keep Evie here.'

'Kate, no!' He was blocking the doorway now. How did he keep doing that? 'Whatever you think you're doing, there's another way. There has to be. Evie says you're a genius. Don't be an idiot too.'

'I'm not a genius. Now, move.'

'Make me.'

'Fine.' I swung the world's least committed punch.

He dodged and caught my arm at the elbow, predictably. I twisted my arm, grabbing his wrist to yank him forward, then punched him in the jaw with my left fist. That always took people by surprise, the ambidextrous switcheroo, and it stunned Kevin long enough for me to flip him off his feet and into the front desk.

'Sorry!' I yelled, slamming the door behind me.

I reached the car and jumped in. The stakes I'd carved this afternoon spilled off the passenger seat and onto the floor as I sped away.

* * *

Felix was right where he'd said he would be, by the dumpster behind Ray's – hood covering his face, like a very short grim reaper.

'Dude, everyone already thinks you're a serial killer,' I said. 'You're not exactly helping your cause.'

Felix laughed, halfheartedly, and craned his neck to look past me. 'Where's your secretary?'

'I gave her the night off,' I said. 'Can't afford the overtime. Are you OK?'

'Should I be?' said Felix. 'Come on, we shouldn't stand in one spot too long.'

I nodded, reaching to pull the tranq gun from my waist-band as we left Ray's. Then I changed my mind. The streets were basically empty but we were still in public, and people were jumpy enough already. A gun-toting, bisexual vampire slayer hanging out with Brightside's most wanted outcast might just push them over the edge.

All Felix had managed to tell me this morning – before I'd heard Evie moving around and had to rush to hang up – was that he'd spotted Mom in an old abandoned church with some 'maybe-vampires', and that she'd looked like she needed help.

Just the thought of Mom in danger had twisted my gut so hard I'd had to invoke my own inner Mom to keep from racing out there and then. I'd needed to prep: make the stakes; practise fighting with stakes in a side-alley; and get those few precious moments in with Evie, just in case.

Besides, Brightside was one giant hunting-ground at night. And if the monsters were out hunting, maybe they wouldn't be at the church, guarding Mom.

Assuming they were monsters.

'What did you mean "maybe-vampires"?' I asked, as we slipped along a side street, away from the town centre.

Felix shrugged. 'I just meant maybe vampires, maybe not. They weren't the gang I escaped from, but they looked weird and creepy. And, I dunno, maybe they're just regular creepy weirdos. Hard to tell the difference until it's too late, isn't it?'

His voice wobbled at that last bit, so I nodded and didn't push it.

143

So, maybe vampires. Maybe humans. Maybe not-people or zombies or homesick banshees looking for company or who knew? My life had exploded into a supernatural mess; anything was possible. But that was fine. After years of Not-Evie, I was ready for anything.

The path we were on was steep and twisty, and seemed to fork off into new paths every couple of metres. It was horror-movie creepy, too. No streetlights or houselights; just stars, thousands more than you'd see in Toronto. I found myself staring at them, wondering how many had died years ago, and we just didn't realise yet. Even the sky was undead in Brightside.

'Felix,' I whispered, 'if something goes wrong in there, you run – OK?'

Felix frowned. 'What?'

'I'm serious. Last night was my fault. If you hadn't tried to help –' I stopped. He didn't need to be reminded, he'd seen his life ripped apart. 'This is my family. My mess. So if we get there and those maybe-vampires aren't off hunting, if it even looks like things are about to go wrong – run. Or hide. Whichever. Just lie low until it's done. I've got this.'

Felix's eyes were huge as he looked sadly at me. 'It's not your fault. We could've texted that video. But Cass wanted to make burgers. That's why she's dead, because she's *nice* and I –' He stopped as his voice cracked, then pulled away when I touched his arm. 'I'm fine. Let's just keep going, OK?'

I nodded, ignoring the twinge in my heart. Talking probably wasn't the smartest idea, anyway, in a night full of super-powered fiends.

The stake in my back pocket chafed against my butt. I thought about giving it to Felix but, if I armed him, I wasn't sure he'd stay back and let me do the protecting. Of course, not arming him had its own risks, but I could worry about that if I had to.

We reached a tall metal gate. It creaked with rust as Felix opened it, letting me through first. Then I spotted the rows of headstones.

'Wait, a graveyard?' I whispered 'You said *church*!'

'Church*yard*.' Felix nodded to a small building in the distance. 'With graves.'

And tombs, I realised, as we wove our way amongst the headstones. And neglected, once-grand monuments and a crumbling mausoleum right at the back – which we were headed straight for. One door hung open.

The lock looked like it'd been smashed, and it wasn't as dark inside as it should've been, which wasn't remotely comforting.

'We're not actually going in there, are we?' I asked.

Felix didn't say anything. He just stopped outside, then jerked his head at the entrance like: you first. Something uncomfortable twisted in my stomach.

'Mom's really in there?' I asked, before finding the question that was actually nagging me. 'This is where you came? After escaping the vampires who murdered Cass? Not the church, the mausoleum?'

Felix shrugged, and didn't look at me.

I stepped back. 'How did you escape last night, Felix?'

'I told you,' he muttered. 'You don't spend four years playing *Vampiremageddon* without –'

'Learning a few tricks, yeah. I remember. That's not an explanation.'

It'd felt like an explanation, whispered hurriedly over the phone with spotty reception and Evie about to wake up at any minute. It'd seemed like enough, when the next thing he'd said was he'd seen my mom. But it wasn't. It wasn't anything at all.

I took another step back.

'Kate,' Felix said anxiously. Or guiltily maybe.

I'd barely grabbed my tranq gun before Felix somehow snatched it, flung it aside and lifted me straight into the air. His eyes were glowing, like the vampire's last night.

'Just get in the frakking crypt, Kate!'

He hurled me through into the not-quite-dark of the mausoleum. I hit a large tomb, with a crack that shot along my entire body. *Mother-fudger!*

I inhaled, trying to breathe through the pain. Someone had set up a few cheap battery-lamps along the floor, just enough for me to make out the three orange-eyed vampiric freaks lurking in the shadows.

And the complete lack of my mom.

'Felix, you lying wimp! I'm gonna – *AAAH*!' I tried to stand up, but a jagged bolt of pain shot through me and I landed back down on the ground.

He'd fractured my tailbone.

A huge red-bearded vampire blurred forward and pulled me roughly to my feet. I didn't *mean* to whimper, but maybe my sobbing would distract them, as I reached for my –

'Donnie!' yelled a voice from the shadows. 'Stake!'

Crap. I lunged anyway, but Donnie caught the stake and flung it out into the snow. It clunked off a headstone, then landed uselessly beside my gun.

I had a few more stakes hidden around me, but I had no idea how I'd get to them without being noticed. Donnie leaned forward and sniffed my hair.

'Uh, boundaries?' I said.

He sneered, then glared at Felix. 'You were bluffing, eh, runt?'

'What? N-no! That's her. Tell them, Kate!' He looked at me hopefully. 'Tell them you're a werewolf!'

'I'm a *what*?' I turned to Donnie. 'Did he say werewolf? Ooh, is this one of those LARPy things – can I be a mage instead?'

'You can be a corpse.' Donnie looked to the other glowing eyes. 'Kill them both.'

'No! NO ,WAIT!' cried Felix.

Donnie didn't wait.

He shoved me back into a giant frat-boy-looking vampire, who flicked his fangs down and slammed me against the wall. The crack through my lower back was so intense I almost puked – but they'd have enjoyed that. So I gritted against the pain, like always, and focused on faking fine instead.

'She has a sister!' yelled Felix.

He'd been backed into the other wall by the most Ken-doll-looking giant I'd ever seen. Donnie held his hand up. The two hench-vamps paused.

'A little sister, Evie! If it's not Kate, it's her. Right?' Felix said, desperately willing me to – what? Sell Evie out?

'Sure,' I said. 'My character could have a sister. Can we call her Emma May, though? I feel like that's more me.'

147

'Kate, stop!' Felix sounded like he was going to cry. 'This is serious.'

'So's Emma May's medical condition. Mixed Martial Arts-eritis. Every full moon she's all roundhouse-kicks and double-leg takedowns.'

'Oh, I get it,' said Frat Boy. He was blond and looked like he got punched in the face a lot. 'Emma May ...'

'MMA!' said Ken Doll. 'Heh, that's good.'

'Thanks, I knew you guys had to have *one* functioning brain between ya – *ow*!'

Frat Boy grabbed my wrist as I tried to slide it behind me.

'We're not *that* dumb, princess.' He pulled the stake from my waistband, tossed it outside with the first, then leaned in until I felt his breath on my skin.

His fangs grazed my neck and ....

'STOP!' yelled Felix again. 'Kate, listen. Ashton doesn't wanna hurt Evie, but they *will* hurt us if we don't get her for them. They'll stake me and drain you, and we'll be dead, Kate! *Dead* dead.'

'We're already dead dead, you idiot,' I said. 'You really think they're about to welcome *you* to the buff bloodsuckers brigade? You don't exactly fit the profile!'

Felix swallowed, then looked from me to Donnie, who shrugged and said, 'She has a point. Maybe not a sister, but a point.'

'But – but you promised,' stammered Felix. 'You said –'

'Holy crap, seriously?' I said. '*I* can't trust *you*. What makes you think you can trust the evil vampires who've killed half the town?' I looked from Frat Boy to Ken Doll, then back

148

to Felix. 'I don't know what to say, guys. I don't have a sister. Oh, yeah, and one more thing. Go f–'

I stopped. Donnie had his hand up again, but something else must have happened too. Everyone had reacted at the same time, turning towards the open doorway, where – wait, where was the tranq gun? And the stakes?

Oh, no. Evie!

I glanced at Felix, and I knew he saw me edge my hand back toward my next stake, because he gave a tiny nod. We weren't friends, not after this, but neither of us wanted to die either, so – allies? Allies worked.

If I grabbed the third stake from my back pocket, I could slam it into Frat Boy while everyone was distracted, then toss Felix the stake from inside my jacket and take out Donnie while he hit Ken Doll.

It wasn't an awful plan, but Donnie moved forward and my mouth made a unilateral decision to screw everything up.

'EVIE, RUN!'

I grabbed my stake, but it was too late.

Evie had run, just not in the direction I wanted.

22. Evie

'Where's Kate?' I'd barely been out twenty minutes this time. I really was getting stronger. 'Where'd she go?'

Kevin shook his head. 'Dunno. But she said to keep you here.' He held up the Coke bottle. 'Thirsty?'

'I'm not touching that! Why didn't you stop her?'

'I tried. She threw me into the front desk and ran.'

'And you couldn't run after her?'

Kevin's jaw flexed. 'No! If I left, and Ashton was waiting –'

'ASHTON? Kate's out there right now 'cos you're scared of the vampire bogeyman?'

Images of Cass's body, all ripped up, flashed through my head.

Then Cass turned into Kate. My stomach lurched. My hands tingled. My joints burned. *To hell with Kevin!* I started towards the door, but he blocked me.

'It's not about me, Red. But Chris –' He paused, then dropped his voice. 'Look, let's just move away from the door. I'll make hot chocolate and –'

'I don't want your freaking hot chocolate!'

I tried to shove him aside, but he blocked me and managed to spin me into the stairs.

'No fighting in the hall,' called Chris from the kitchen. 'You'll knock the Christmas tree down.'

'We're not fighting,' said Kevin.

No, we weren't. I didn't have time. 'I'm going to my room. Don't try to talk to me.'

I turned and stalked upstairs.

It only took him a couple of seconds to realise I wasn't going to stay there, but by then I was already trying to yank the window up. He'd nailed it shut.

OK, fine.

'Red, listen –'

He'd just reached the doorway when I flung myself at the window.

'RED!'

The glass shattered, burying into my skin as I hurtled downwards. *Holy cow, that hurt!* But not as much as landing.

'EVIE!'

I think Kevin was at the window, but I was in far too much pain to look up.

Come on, Fido, I thought. *Do your thing.*

And she did.

My head pounded and my eyes burned but my body, so used to twisting and changing by itself, pulled back together like it was the most normal thing in the world. I was up on my feet and running in seconds.

'Evie, come back!'

I ignored him, obviously, and sniffed the air as I ran.

Come on, nose. Come on … I caught Kate's scent, but only for a moment. Her car wasn't in the parking lot. My body pulsed with adrenaline.

She'd gone into town. She must have.

Everything inside me wanted to change, so I took that energy and forced it downwards. The muscles twisted and tightened, until I thought my jeans might burst.

Then I *really* ran.

I sped past rows of houses and shops, fighting the urge to change because, sure, a speedster would raise eyebrows – but a werewolf would cause mass hysteria.

Besides, even on two legs, it didn't take long to catch her scent from the carpark behind the diner. And someone else's. Felix?

He smelt different, though. He smelled like – *No!*

Fido was desperate to turn now, but I held her back and followed their trail, up a twisty road and into a – derelict old graveyard? Seriously?

Way to trope, vampires.

I could *just* pick up their voices, drifting across from the giant run-down mausoleum. Because of course that's where they were.

'Ashton doesn't wanna hurt Evie.' Felix sounded terrified. 'But they *will* hurt us if we don't get her for them. They'll stake me and drain you, and we'll be dead, Kate! *Dead* dead.'

My whole body burned as I picked my way across the snow, setting my feet in Kate's footprints to avoid any icy crunching. My heart was racing, but Kate's was too, so maybe it wouldn't stand out that much. I clamped my hand over my mouth, trying not to breathe as I reached the building.

'We're already dead dead, you idiot.' Kate's voice was way calmer than her pulse. I sniffed as she kept talking. All that vampire mustiness blended together, but I thought I could pick out, like, four separate scents? That was a lot!

I snuck closer. The tranq gun was lying in the snow, beside two stakes. Kate brought stakes? Wow, she'd really prepped for this.

I darted across the doorway, grabbed the weapons, and flattened back into the dark.

'... evil vampires who've killed half the town?' she was saying.

I'd done it! I was armed.

Fido wasn't the only one burning to fight now. I slid one stake into my waistband with the gun and held the other up, ready for vamp-dusting.

'Oh, yeah, and one more thing. Go f–'

Wait, that wasn't like Kate, stopping before the best part.

Panic threatened to surge, but it didn't sound like anyone was hurt. There was just too much silence. Like a lot of noise very deliberately NOT being made.

And then, ripping through that: 'EVIE, RUN!'

So I did.

Every muscle and impulse in my body flung me into that oversized grave, straight into the scariest-looking anything I'd ever seen: all fangs, muscles and orange hair. His glowing eyes seemed way freakier than Kevin's ever had.

Or maybe I just hated him already.

Behind him, I spotted Kate, pinned to the wall by an obnoxious jock.

She looked terrified.

My vamp blurred towards me, faster than I could move. Or than I thought I could, but my body didn't care what I thought. Suddenly, I'd dropped the stake and grabbed the monster's head – twisting like Kevin had shown me. My hands throbbed, clawing up as I ripped through his neck, then yanked back to tear his head clear off.

His body exploded.

'Holy ...' whimpered Felix.

My sentiments exactly. The stupid-looking pretty boy flanking Felix seemed to forget about him completely as he stepped forward to watch the red mist fall.

Kate's jock was hypnotised too. She didn't miss her chance.

She stomped down hard, crushing his foot under her boot. The guy yelled, but so did Kate. She was hurt.

'Felix, help her!' I cried, as Pretty Boy blurred towards me.

I growled, launching myself into him, until I heard his skull crack against the wall. He snarled and snapped his head forward, straight into my mouth.

I staggered back, the taste of my blood on my tongue as his fangs clenched into my shoulder. 'OWWW!'

'Evie!' cried Kate – but the grunt that followed told me she was in the middle of her own fight. Felix had better be helping.

Fido begged to transform again, but I wrenched the gun from my waistband, pressed it against Pretty Boy's chest and pulled the trigger.

At that range, the force sent the dart tearing through his body, but it still worked.

'Bitch,' he muttered.

Then he was out. I thought about leaving him like that, but last night's vampire hadn't stayed out long. And, besides, they'd started it. So, I drove the stake through his chest, and the shower of innards told me I'd actually found his heart. Somehow.

I held up my stake again and turned around. Suddenly, it seemed far too quiet.

'Kate?' I waved the vampire dust out of my face. 'Katie.'

There was a low, gurgled whimper from behind the tomb. *NO!*

I must've moved without realising, because, by the time my brain knew what was happening, my body had already grabbed the freak drinking from my sister and slammed a stake through his heart too.

'Kate!' I caught her right before she hit the ground and – *OH GOD!*

She was so pale. There was so much blood and she wasn't moving.

'Katie?' I dropped to my knees, still holding her. 'Come on. Wake up!'

Something shifted in the shadows. 'Evie? Evie, I'm so sorry.'

'Go away, Felix.' I didn't even trust myself to look at him.

My body throbbed with anger. My hands tingled eagerly. My jaw tensed.

Nobody would know, I could just do it.

'I didn't want her to get hurt, but I was scared.' He sniffled.

Was he crying? HIM?

I spun around, roaring so loud it knocked Felix clean to the ground. 'GET LOST!'

He scrambled to his feet, backing into the tomb behind him, before turning and racing out the door. I looked back at Kate.

This wasn't real. It couldn't be. Her heart was still beating, I think. It was faint, but I could hear it. I could. Right?

'Katie, wake up!'

It felt like someone had thrust their fist into my chest and was squeezing tighter and tighter. I didn't even realise tears were pouring down my cheeks until I saw them land on Kate's face. She moaned and tried to move her head.

'Katie!' I hugged her. She gave a sharp whimper, so I loosened my hold. 'It's OK. You're all right, I promise.'

She was; she had to be. My arms were already soaked with her blood, but she was still here. I pulled my phone from my pocket. Two reception bars.

That should work, but who could I even call? The police? Paramedics? No, they'd take too long. I needed someone *supernaturally* fast.

My hands were slippy with Kate's blood. I wiped them off, then opened a browser and typed until – Goodman's Guesthouse, Brightside. Got it!

I pressed 'call'. *Come on, come on, come on.*

'Hello?' Kevin! Oh thank God.

'Kate's hurt. I got here too late. I – I couldn't …'

'OK,' said Kevin. 'All right. I'll get Chris, we'll drive –'

'There's no time to drive. I need *you*, super-vamp speed! Please.'

Kevin was too quiet for a moment. Then: 'Evie. I told you, I can't …'

'Kevin, please. She's so pale, I don't know what to do.'

'If Chris sees me leave, she'll come after me.'

And she could get hurt too. I didn't want that.

'Sneak out, then! Use the open window in my room. We both know you can jump. Please! Kevin, it's – this is Katie. She's not supposed to –' I couldn't finish, because suddenly I started sobbing.

I think that's what did it.

'Don't cry. I'll be right there. Stay where you are. I'll find you.'

He hung up, and Kate murmured vaguely. I honestly think she might've been trying to comfort me. I lifted her head into my lap, stroking her hair with one hand as I clamped the other over her neck to slow the bleeding.

'It's OK,' I said. 'You're OK, Katie. I've got you.'

She gave another muted groan and I had to force myself not to lose it completely. She looked worse, even since I'd called Kevin. Her gorgeous face was all clammy, her bangs were sticking to her forehead. I tried to brush them away but just wound up wiping blood all over her. I'd gotten it in her hair, too, I realised.

My strong, perfect sister was lying there, covered in her own blood, and I couldn't do anything but wait.

'You're not going anywhere,' I promised her.

But she was so pale. How much blood did people have in them? How much more could she lose? I could still feel it oozing between my fingers.

We couldn't really have been waiting that long, but it felt like for ever until –

'Evie!' Kevin stopped dead at the mausoleum entrance. 'Oh. That's – that's a lot of blood.'

'I know! Come on, help her.'

Kevin shook his head and bit down on his fist. 'I can't. I'm sorry, I thought I could but …' He moved back anxiously. 'I can't come down there. It smells delicious.'

He looked so ashamed, but Katie's lips were blue and I really wasn't sure I could hear her heart any more. This was no time to come over all ethically squeamish.

'Kevin, she's dying! You need to save her.'

'Save her?' Kevin's eyes widened as he realised what I meant. 'No. No no, you don't – I can't – Evie, no.'

'YES! Please, I can't lose her.'

He took a deep breath and stepped forward. A strange mix of craving and guilt crept across his face, as his eyes fixed on Kate.

'Kevin, she's my *sister*!'

That worked. He was on his knees beside us before I could blink.

'I – I've never done this before,' he said. 'Or even seen it done. I know the theory, but if I mess up –'

'Oh my GOD! It's not like you can make it worse. She's *dying*.'

'All right, but you're really not going to like it.' Kevin was trying to look at me, but his gaze kept being drawn back to the blood pumping between my fingers. 'I need to kill her first. I need to drink until her heart stops, then bring her back before her brain catches up.' He gulped. 'I don't even know how long that is, but if my timing's off, or – or if I can't stop, I –'

'Dude, shut up and do it, or I will stake you!' I don't think I meant that, but my eyes flashed angrily enough to convince Kevin.

In one motion, his fangs were out and deep in Katie's throat. She gave a tiny, pained cry. Her eyes flickered open. Something inside me started to growl.

Kevin was right, I didn't like this. But I held her hand and watched anyway.

After about thirty seconds, Kevin raised his head and pulled back the sleeve on his left arm. Katie was staring up, lifeless, just like Cass.

Oh God. I bunched my fingers into fists, trying to resist the urge to claw up as my head pounded. My sister was dead.

Kevin bit into his wrist and tore back, wincing. Then he jammed his thumb in the wound to keep it open, and squeezed it over Katie's mouth.

The blood landed on her lips in thick, heavy drops.

She didn't move.

He squeezed more, and more. Nothing.

'Is it working?' I asked, like I didn't already know the answer.

'I ... I don't ...' Kevin gulped. 'Maybe I'm doing it wrong?'

He bit again, tearing away a huge chunk this time, then pressed down hard and brushed the open cut over Kate's mouth. *Come on, Katie! Drink.*

But she didn't.

He tried again, and again, until her face was covered in his blood. Still nothing.

No, this wasn't right. This couldn't be right.

'Red,' said Kevin. 'I don't think it's gonna –'

'It will. SHUT UP! You killed her. Now, bring her back!'

Kevin shook his head. 'I can't. I don't – maybe I didn't stop in time. Or maybe she'd lost too much blood already, or maybe I'm just doing it wrong, but it's … it's not working, Red.'

No, this wasn't it. It couldn't be, there had to be … wait!

'She can't swallow! She needs to swallow it, that's all!'

'Evie,' said Kevin.

'That's *all*!' I grabbed his wrist. It was already healing again so I tore it with my teeth and let his blood flow into my mouth.

'Ow, Red! What –?

I leaned towards Katie.

'Wait!' Kevin pulled me back. I tried not to gag on his blood. 'You're not bleeding, are you? 'Cos if our blood mixes in her veins …'

I spat out on the floor. 'You do it then!'

Kevin nodded, then sucked a mouthful from his wrist and pressed his lips against Katie's before sitting back. Nothing.

'Do it again!'

So he did. Again, and again – and Kate was so still, and pale, covered in her and Kevin's blood. Kevin leaned in a fourth time and – 'Kevin, stop.'

He looked at me, his mouth still full.

'It's been too long, hasn't it?' I said. 'She's not – we can't …'

The rest of the sentence was lost in tears. I lifted her up, pulling her head to my chest in a way that would have made her cry out a few minutes earlier.

But it couldn't hurt her now. Kate was gone. That huge, wonderful brain of hers had stopped along with her giant heart, and there was nothing Kevin or I could do.

Kate was dead. *Dead* dead.

I held her close, and howled.

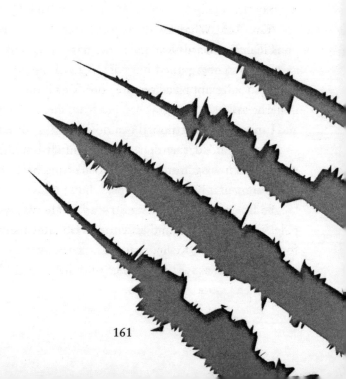

23. Still Evie

Pain crushed my chest.

I was vaguely aware of Kevin saying, 'Evie'. Putting his arm around me, I think. I dunno. Maybe not. It didn't matter, nothing mattered. I just –

Something gasped. No, wait! *Kate* gasped.

My heart leapt, as the world snapped back together.

'Katie!' I pulled away to look at her, and regretted it immediately. She was so pale and glassy-eyed. So dead. She gasped again and gagged horribly.

'Katie? Kevin, what've we done? She's –'

'She's fine!' Kevin grabbed her from me, ripping his wrist and putting it back to her mouth. 'She just needs more.'

He couldn't know that, but he sounded confident; that was good enough. Katie seized Kevin's arm with both hands and crammed it between her lips. I didn't know if I wanted to laugh, cry or throw up as she guzzled Kevin's blood.

'Sure, *now* she can't get enough of you,' I sobbed.

Kevin chuckled, then winced, then tried to smile. 'Not exactly how I wanted to win her over but – ouch! Whatever it takes, eh? Good work, Red.'

'It's your blood.'

'But she couldn't swallow, like you said. Then you pulled her upright and – OW!'

Kate pushed herself up on one elbow, leaning in to drink even deeper. Kevin flinched, and I guess I looked concerned because he smiled again.

'It's OK. She just – ow – needs a lot. Wow, she's strong, though!'

She was starting to look better too. My hi-def vision could make out some colour returning to her cheeks. Still, I couldn't help wondering how many toothbrushes it would take to scrub tonight's imagery out of my brain.

'She's gonna be OK, right?'

Kevin nodded. 'I mean, she'll have to call me Dad, but ...'

He stopped and blinked hard.

'Are *you* OK?' I said.

'Uh-huh, just – ow! – woozy. Don't think I've lost this much blood since *I* died. OUCH! OK, Kate, we're done.' He reached over to prise his wrist from Katie's mouth, but she didn't want to let go, so he loosened her grip with his fingers and slid his hand free. 'Kate, that's enough!'

She sat up and giggled. 'I feel funny.' She looked at me drowsily and giggled again. 'Heeeeey, Evie!' She booped my nose. 'I love you. Did you know that, Kevin? I do, I love her. She's the cutest –'

She stopped. Her stomach gurgled loudly. For a second she looked like she might throw up, but she didn't. She did turn slightly green, though.

'Is that normal?' I asked.

163

'Probably?' Kevin really did look groggy. 'There's a lot going on in there – she just chugged a few pints of magic blood.' He blinked hard again, then smiled. 'Come on, let's get her home.'

He tried to stand, lifting Kate with him, and didn't quite manage it.

'Pfft! Can't even walk,' snorted Katie. ''S easy, look!'

She wriggled out of his arms, leapt to her feet, then crumpled. I caught her just before she hit the floor.

She chuckled. 'Oops! OK, not like that.'

Kevin pushed himself up, steadied himself on the lid of the tomb, then glanced at me. 'Don't worry, I'm fine. Just recovering. Now, let's get to Kate's car. I'm OK to drive, but I do *not* want to fight anyone tonight. Not even you, Red.'

* * *

Chris was pacing frantically by the back door when we got home.

She'd called as we reached Ray's and Kevin had assured her we were on our way, but that was all he'd said. So the sight of the three of us covered in blood and vomit (yep, it'd happened) ... well, it was a lot.

'Kevin!' she cried, then took in the full scene. 'Oh my God, Kate! Kevin, what did you do?'

'It wasn't him,' I said. 'Well, it was-*ish*, but ...'

Chris didn't even look at me. 'Is that her blood? Around your mouth, Kevin? Is that Kate's blood?'

She looked horrified. And Kevin looked so ashamed.

'It's – it's not what …' He stopped, exhausted. The journey back had wiped him completely. 'I – I need to sit down. Chris, could you get some – what's the word? You just said it –'

'Blood?' said Chris.

Kevin nodded, then leaned against the wall and slid to the floor. 'That's it. Thanks. I'll just … I'll, um, floor chair. Floor's good.'

Chris looked at me. 'Evie, what's wrong? What happened out there?'

'Pfft, he's fine,' giggled Kate. 'Just being a baby 'cos I drank all his blood and he only got a *liiiittle* bit of mine.' She snorted a laugh, then retched and vomited on the countertop. 'Oooh! Sorry.'

'*You* drank *his* …' Chris looked equal parts angry and confused. Then the realisation dawned. 'Wait! Kevin, you didn't … is she …?'

Kevin nodded, weakly. 'It's a girl, yay! Can – can I get that blood now?'

Chris's jaw flexed, like Kevin's did when he was trying not to say something.

'Sure.' She stormed to the fridge, while I sat Katie down at the table before going to pull cleaning supplies from the cupboard under the sink. Chris took a huge carton of blood from the fridge and started towards the hob, but Kevin held his hand out.

'Cold's fine. I'm not feeling, um, fussy,' he said. 'Just – I need to refuel.'

'Oh, you're not fussy about your blood today? Cool!' She shoved the carton into his hands, then rolled her sleeves up and came over to help me clean.

'It's OK, I can –' I started, but Chris got stuck in, furiously. I leaned forward. 'Please don't be mad at Kevin. This is my fault.'

'Your fault?' Chris glanced up at me. 'For not letting your sister die? Yeah, selfish!' She raised an eyebrow.

I wasn't sure if I should smile or not. I mean, she was joking. Obviously. She just ... didn't sound it?

Chris sighed. 'Look, I get it, sweetie. Two sets of bite-marks, two vampires. It's not like you had a choice, it's just –' She glanced back at Kevin, who was trying not to gag as he glugged his way through the cold blood. 'You look like crap, Kev.'

'It's still Kevin,' muttered Kevin.

'You sure?' said Chris.

Kevin groaned, gesturing along his puke-soaked, exhausted self. 'Do I *look* like I'm about to go on a – a murder buffet thingy? She was dying!'

'Yeah, 'cos Felix is a grade-A poophole,' Kate yelled, before stopping to snigger 'poophole' again. And again. This was gonna be a long night.

'Felix?' Chris looked at me. 'Felix *Maxwell*?'

I nodded. 'I know. Should've listened to Miriam.'

Chris went back to scrubbing, even harder and angrier, as we filled her in on everything. Or I did, mostly, Kevin was busy chugging that blood and Kate mainly drowsy-giggled 'poophole' in the corner – although she did stop long enough to add that Kevin was her hero, which was nice. Until she laughed so hard she fell off her chair and I had to pick her up. Still, though, he was a hero.

166

And Chris got that. It's not like she wanted him *not* to have saved Kate. She just wasn't delighted he'd had to drink her blood. Which, I mean, yeah. Me neither.

Eventually, Kevin finished the blood.

He wasn't totally recovered, but he felt well enough to go take a shower – which was good because we all stank right now. Especially Kate. She also kept alternating between dozing off at the table and jolting awake insisting she wasn't tired.

'Of course you're not, sweetheart,' said Chris, helping me get her to her feet. 'Now, let's head upstairs, eh? Evie's gonna help me clean you up, then she can shower and I'll come back down for a whole lot of rosé.' She paused, then added, 'In a sensible grown-up way.'

Kate nodded, woozily, and snuggled her face into my neck.

'Mmm, you smell yummy, Evie. Yummy li'l sister-wolf.'

* * *

Kate was barely conscious by the time we got her into the bath. I'd expected that. Kevin had said he'd been out for hours after he was turned. I actually thought she'd drifted off, until she drowsy-groaned and half-opened her eyes.

'Shush,' I whispered. 'It's OK, we've got you.'

'I know.' She flopped her hand out of the tub to grab mine. 'Y'got all this, Evie. You can do anything. An' I'm sorry I ...' She laughed weakly. 'I'm sorry Kevin's right. 'S just, if there's no monster, if you're *all* you, what am I? Y'know?'

'What're you? Kate? What does that even –?'

Her eyes drooped closed again, and her hold loosened on my hand. She was out. My stomach twisted with the urge to cry or scream or punch someone.

'Hey.' Chris nudged me gently. 'She's right, you have got this.'

'How? I can't fix this. All I ever do is screw things up for her!'

Chris sat back, one eyebrow arched like I'd just told a bad joke.

'Hun, you jumped through a closed window and took out three vampires to save her,' said Chris. 'Love like that's worth more than any "normal" life. She doesn't need you to fix anything. Just be there, like you already are. All right?'

I nodded, fighting back the impulse to run into the dark and keep running until none of this was real. Chris's sympathetic smile said she knew the feeling.

We finished cleaning Kate, wrapped her in a towel and laid her on the bed to dress her. She looked so young without all her make-up.

'So is this it now?' I said. 'She's just seventeen for ever? Or will she grow up and be, like, forty-three in a teenager's body?'

'Why?' Chris looked hurt. 'Is forty-three terribly old?'

Crap, how old was she? 'No, I didn't mean it like ...'

'Relax! I'm teasing.' Chris laughed, then grew serious. 'And no, she won't be a pensioner in a teenage body. She'll stay seventeen, like Kevin's always sixteen.'

Kevin. My heart jumped. She'd answered the question I hadn't realised I'd been too scared to ask him.

'He is?' I said. ''Cos he doesn't always talk or act like a regular sixteen-year-old.'

'Well, he's not a regular sixteen-year-old,' said Chris. 'He's been through some horrible things, kinda lost himself for a while. And now he's shut himself off from everyone but me. And you, apparently.'

She paused to smile, and I felt a flutter.

'But, honey,' she said, 'I've known Kevin my whole life and, in that time, I've gotten *terribly old*. And he's stayed him. Sadder and angrier, and a lot more scared of himself, sure. But still sixteen. I promise.'

I felt a little stab. Kevin's impish grin flashed through my mind. He joked about being 'dangerous' and shrugged off not being liked, saying he deserved it.

But after what Chris just said, it didn't feel quippy. It felt awful.

'Did you know him before, then?' I asked.

Chris nodded. 'Yep. He wasn't that different, really. Just … softer, I guess? But still kind and funny. And shy. Always reading and writing.'

Her eyes lit up. 'He'd make up these worlds where we could fight dragons or be pirates or whatever I wanted. He was too old for all that, but I loved it and he looked out for me. He was my whole world. I guess he still is, eh?'

Her smile faltered, and she looked down at Kate.

'She's gonna be OK,' she said. 'Kevin didn't have an Evie to keep him grounded, like she does. But … maybe he's got one now?'

The way she said that made my stomach flip.

'Of course. We're friends.'

'Good,' said Chris. 'He needs friends. He really tries, you know. Even those giant glasses are just his way of seeing himself like he used to be.'

Wait! 'Kevin doesn't need glasses?'

'He's a vampire!' Chris laughed. 'And I know he'll never be the old Kevin again, but he seems happier with you here. Although –' She leaned in. 'Maybe you could work in some movie nights or something? Alongside all the secret throwing-each-other-across-the-kitchen?'

She raised an eyebrow, and suddenly my cheeks were burning .

'I … it's not …' Words again, Evie. 'We're training, that's all.'

'It's OK,' said Chris. 'I'm all for you figuring out that side of yourself. But this monster world's easy to get sucked into. We need a good dose of normal to balance out the crazy. It keeps us human, you know?'

I nodded, and Chris pulled me into a little side-hug before standing up.

'Good,' she said. 'Now, go wash off all that blood, vomit and vampire dust. I need my wine.'

*   *   *

After I'd showered, I lay down beside Kate. Her chest rose and fell under my arm. She didn't technically have to breathe, Kevin said. It was a reflex, to help them blend in. Which sounded innocent enough until you realised blending in let them get away with literal murder.

Kate wasn't a killer, though (aside from that one time last night, which barely counted). So the warmth of her skin and the slow rhythm of her chest felt soothing. Like everything really could still be OK.

'Room service!'

I jumped up as Kevin came in. He looked better. I wouldn't say he had colour in his cheeks; he never did unless he was flushed from fighting (or too much eye contact). But he was smiling, and he could walk without wobbling. That was good.

He handed me a mug, then nodded to Kate. 'How's my new daughter?'

'Ew! Don't call her that.'

'But it'll annoy her so much!' He chuckled. 'Fine, how's my progeny?'

'Ick, dude, no!'

Kevin laughed again. 'Katiekins it is.'

'Oh, she'll punch you so hard!'

'Again?' Kevin rubbed his jaw, grinning as he sat beside me.

Up close, I could see the dark circles under his eyes. 'You're still not better.'

'I'm getting there.' Kevin took a sip from his mug. 'This is helping. It's just, like Kate said, she took a lot of my blood. I didn't get much from her. And pig's blood's an OK proxy for human, but it's not the same. I'll be fine. Magic blood regenerates like the regular stuff. It just takes time.'

That wasn't fair. He'd saved my sister; he shouldn't have to feel so crappy.

'Ooh, I've an idea, come on!' I grabbed his hand and pulled him into the bathroom, ignoring the sloshes of hot chocolate on the carpet. I could clean that up later, but I didn't want to leave a bloody mess on Chris's nice white bedsheets.

Kevin smiled quizzically. 'What're we doing?'

'Getting rid of this, for a start.' I took his mug and placed it on the window-ledge, then held my left arm out. 'I've got something better. Here –'

I clawed up and slashed down, trying not to wince.

Kevin's eyes widened. 'Red, what …?'

'Magic blood!' I pushed my wrist towards his mouth. 'You'll heal before any wolfy-infections set in, right? And it's gotta be better than pig juice, go on.'

'No!' Kevin backed away, his hand over his mouth and nose. 'I could hurt you.'

'You won't.' I scratched deeper as my arm healed up. 'I – ow – I trust you.'

'You shouldn't!' His eyes were glued to the thick red trails on my wrist.

He reached down, feeling the sink until he found the tap, then twisted the knob and yanked my arm under the water, chewing his lip anxiously as the blood washed away.

Then he let go and pushed past me, grabbing his hot chocolate from the ledge and downing the whole thing, before blurring into the bedroom and chugging my drink too.

He was shaking.

'OK,' I said. 'This was a terrible idea.'

I started towards him, but he darted into the hallway. I ran after him.

'Stay back!' he snapped.

'No!' I grabbed his hand. 'Kevin, I'm sorry. I … I … That was stupid of me.'

'It's not your fault!' he said. 'It's mine. I let you think I was – what? Nice? Or safe? Or – I dunno! I don't know what I thought we were doing, but I was wrong.'

He tried to let go of my hand. I held tight.

'Evie, please. Just let me go.'

'No! *I* messed up, OK? I saw how you were in the crypt. I should've thought, but I didn't. I never do.' I stepped closer. 'I know you've been through some stuff.'

'You have no idea what I've been through, or done.' He laughed humourlessly. 'You wouldn't trust me like that if you did.'

He turned away, so I moved around to look at him again.

'I know you lost yourself at first,' I said. 'I'm sure you made mistakes. But it's OK. I'm not judging, I promise.'

'You should judge!' Kevin yanked his arm away and stepped back. 'I'm not what you think. It wasn't this sad, tortured TV monster thing. It was – worse. I'm worse.'

He started toward his room. Like he was getting away that easily?

'I don't believe that. You *saved* Kate.'

'Oh my GOD, Evie! Don't be one of those.' He wheeled back around, his eyes blazing so bright I jumped away without meaning to.

'One of what?'

'Those girls!' he said. 'The stupid ones, in the books, who don't care what the monster's done. I've killed people, Evie. Not just at first, not just by mistake. Not 'cos my soul was cursed, or I didn't know what I was doing, or whatever. I knew. And I did it for years, and I liked it. OK? So, please, care. Judge! Because that's me.' He wiped his eyes angrily.

'I'm not good, like you, Red. I try, but it doesn't matter what I want to be. You don't do stuff like that and get to come back from it.'

My heart stabbed again. I knew what he'd just said, but he couldn't be bad. Not after everything I'd seen. Still, he didn't think he deserved sympathy, so fine.

'You done?'

Kevin blinked in surprise. 'What?'

'That whole angsty monster rant? Is it done? Can I talk now?'

'I ... I, um ...'

OK, dumbstruck. Perfect! 'First of all: don't yell at me. Ever. You wanna spiral into some self-loathing crapstorm? Fine. But don't take it out on me.'

'I wasn't –'

'Second,' I said, 'don't call me stupid. It's not stupid to give the guy who just saved my sister's life the benefit of the doubt. Or to not know things you haven't told me. I'm not a freaking mind-reader, Kevin. I'm your friend.'

He looked like he was about to object again, so I held my hand up.

'And you saved my life too. You stopped me running away, into Ashton's guys. And then you taught me not to be scared of myself. You've helped me in ways no-one else could, so don't act like it's my fault for seeing the best in you. You've shown me so much of it.'

I didn't glare as I finished – that might have been overkill. Instead, I took his hand. Kevin looked down, surprised, gave a sad squeeze and tried to loosen his grip. Nope.

'And you can't push me away for my own protection,' I

said. 'I need you! My mom's missing, my sister's a vampire, I have an evil wolf-stalker and now, apparently, there's a town of psycho-vampires after me.'

'Wait, after you?' Kevin's eyes burned bright again. 'Specifically? Are you sure?'

He looked ready to punch someone.

I nodded. 'That's what Felix said. He told Kate they didn't want to hurt me, but that doesn't sound true. Right?'

'Right,' agreed Kevin.

He grabbed my other hand with urgency-bordering-on-panic. 'Red, you can't stay here if Ashton's after you. He'll find a way. I'll call Jim, he'll have somewhere.'

'I can't go!' I said. 'Kate needs you as her vampire Obi Wan. And I need her. I can't do this alone. Unless –' I paused. 'You came with us? Just for a bit.'

Kevin's gaze fell from mine. 'I'd love that. But if I leave Brightside, Ashton's gonna destroy the whole town.'

'What?'

'He wants me to come back to him. He said he'll wait as long as it takes, but if we run he'll kill everyone in Brightside – and all the towns around us.'

Wait! *Back to him?* 'Dude, were you part of the psycho-brigade?'

Kevin shook his head. 'Not exactly.' Then, just as I was about to breathe a sigh of relief, he added, 'I was more like his proto-psycho.'

His eyes met mine again. His hold on my hand loosened like he was waiting for me to run. I held his gaze, and hand, as I tried (and failed) to fake calm.

'Proto-psycho? What does that mean?'

Kevin gulped. Somehow, he looked more scared than me.

'I've only talked about this once in twenty-three years,' he said. 'But Ashton ruined my life, and now he wants to ruin yours. So – how about a hot chocolate and a chat?' He smiled, half-heartedly. 'Then you can decide if you want to keep holding my hand.'

24. Evie (and Kevin-ish)

Obviously, Ashton had a tragic backstory. You know, the sort you could use to justify decades of mass murder? Or the sort he could, anyway. He'd been married, with a son a bit older than us and a daughter a bit younger. They'd led this idyllic country life, until the day he came back from hunting to find his son sobbing over the torn-up bodies of the 'womenfolk'.

Poor boy was still holding the axe he'd used to fight off the werewolves, and nursing a bloody bitemark. Ashton knew what that meant, so he hugged his son, then used the axe one more time – before burying his whole family behind their cabin.

Next came the predictable seeking-vengeance bit. Ashton started following strange killings across different towns, looking for wolves. Just like my mom did. And, like Mom, his wolf-hunt also brought him straight to a hot vampire.

His was called Ava. Ava was super-into Ashton's whole brooding-widower vibe and turned him so they could be together for ever. At which point, Ashton dumped her and took off, using his new vampy-super-powers to become the

Ultimate Lone Wolf-Hunter. And he stayed alone, for years, until ...

'He got bored, I guess?' Kevin said. 'And we got unlucky.'

'We?'

'Chris and I.'

Oh yeah, Chris. Who, it turned out, was Kevin's little sister. They'd been coming back from the movies when eight-year-old Chris spotted a raccoon, and chased it down an alleyway to share her leftover popcorn. Kevin followed her, of course, in a slow grumpy-big-brother way – until Chris screamed. Then adrenaline flung Kevin around the corner, ready to save Chris from the cute-but-vicious furball.

Instead, he found Ashton, fang-deep in Chris's neck.

'So I ran at them,' said Kevin. 'Like I could really save her.'

He did save her, though. Sure, Ashton could've killed Kevin. Or taken them both, or killed them both or – whatever he liked, really.

But what he did was laugh as Kevin shoved him aside.

'I told Chris to run,' said Kevin. 'She thought I'd be right behind her, but then Ashton grabbed me and blurred off.'

Kevin was terrified, naturally. He knew he was going to die. He just had no idea how much worse things would get after that. Because brave, loyal Kevin was everything messed up Vampire Dad Ashton wanted in a 'son'.

So, after explaining how easily he could find Chris if Kevin didn't 'work out', Ashton murdered him – and remade him as his own blood-junkie progeny.

'It didn't take long,' said Kevin. 'I woke up, starving, with no impulse control. And Ashton had brought home some guy. He ripped his throat open, and threw him to me. I … I couldn't stop myself.'

Afterwards, Kevin sobbed and puked, and tried to kill Ashton.

'I didn't even mean to, but I couldn't control that either. So Ashton beat the crap out of me, then locked me in the basement with that body until my impulses settled.'

Eventually, Ashton brought Kevin a mug of fresh blood, and they had a 'chat' about how things were going to be.

'He said he knew this was hard,' said Kevin. 'But we had a calling: our powers and appetites meant we could clean up the streets, like super-heroes.'

As he spoke, Ashton had played with a scrunchie he'd stolen from Chris's hair – to remind Kevin of their 'deal'. So, when he said they were going hunting, Kevin didn't argue. But when Ashton cornered some sketchy guy in an alleyway and told Kevin to kill him, Kevin couldn't do it.

Ashton could, though. He tore the guy's jugular, then forced Kevin to drain him. They tried again the next night, and the next, almost like Ashton was being patient.

But when Kevin refused for the fourth night, Ashton lost it.

'He dragged me home, flung me in that basement and left me there. It took a few days to really get hungry. Then I felt horrendous. My body swung between burning and freezing. My stomach kept retching even after it was empty. I couldn't stop shivering.'

'Like withdrawal?'

'That's exactly what it was.' Kevin looked ill just remembering. 'By the time Ashton opened that door, I couldn't even think straight. I just burst onto the street and grabbed the nearest person. If Ashton hadn't gotten there –' He gulped. 'She was only about ten, Red. I didn't kill her, but I know I hurt her. She was already bleeding when Ashton pulled her free and yelled at her to run. Like he was her hero.'

Ashton hadn't cared about the girl. Kevin knew that now. He'd probably smelt her coming, and released Kevin knowing what would happen. Knowing hurting a kid who could be Chris would scare him into co-operating. And it did. They found some poor guy down the darkest alley and this time Kevin didn't hesitate.

'Afterwards, I felt warm and buzzy. And strong.' Kevin's jaw flexed, furiously. 'When Ashton asked if I wanted to do it again, I said yes.'

I must have looked horrified, because he looked even more ashamed.

'I told you, I'm not good.'

'No! He – he didn't give you any choice.'

'He didn't make me *like it*, though.'

Didn't he? When the alternative was torture, or hurting kids, or Chris getting turned too? Ashton swore he knew who the bad guys were, that he just 'had a sense for it', so why wouldn't Kevin convince himself it was fun?

There was no escape either way.

'And he was so proud of me when I co-operated,' said Kevin. 'He'd even hug me. My own dad never did that. It felt better than being scared. I started wanting to make him proud. Once Ashton saw that, he said I was ready for the real hero stuff.'

As in: wolf-hunting. Ashton taught him to fight, use weapons, tear heads – all the skills he couldn't teach while Kevin might've used them against him.

'But I was past wanting to leave,' said Kevin. 'I had nowhere to go, and I liked fighting. It let me pretend I was in control, not just the strung-out, mass-murdering sidekick to Captain Psychotic.'

So that was Kevin, for years. One half of the demonic duo – feeding on 'bad guys' to defeat the monsters. Until Chris tracked him down.

'Wait, Chris?' I said

'Yep.' Kevin smiled. 'Chris!'

Chris, the badass – who knew a vampire had taken Kevin, no matter what the adults said. And never gave up on finding him, even when everyone else did. She was out on her bike postering, every week, for years. She even saved her pocket money as a reward. But no-one called.

So when she turned eighteen she bought a camper van, hooked a motorbike on the back and spent two years following creepy-death trails, just like Ashton and Kevin, and Mom and – oh, probably everyone? Who knew *that* was a thing?

And, twelve years after she lost Kevin, she found him again.

He and Ashton had just taken out a wolfpack, and gone their separate ways to 'refuel', when Kevin spotted Chris's posters.

'I felt ill,' he said. 'Someone was still looking for that dork in the photo, and I wasn't him any more.'

Still, he'd ripped a poster down, blurred to a phone box and dialled.

'I swear,' he said. 'I've never been more scared of anything than I was listening to that dial-tone. I nearly hung up. But then Chris answered, and I – I thought I'd dialled the wrong number. I mean, she was a *woman*, but Chris was a kid. Right?'

Chris had known Kevin's voice, though. It took everything he had not to slam the phone down when she said his name. But he didn't, and they arranged to meet at the diner downtown.

'And there she was,' said Kevin. 'All grown up in biker leathers. Honestly, my first instinct was to lecture her on how dangerous motorbikes are. Then I remembered how dangerous *I* was and – and what the hell was I thinking, meeting her? That wasn't safe for either of us.'

But then Chris threw her arms around him and he burst into tears. And they stayed hugging and sobbing, until a waitress suggested they get a booth. And some food.

Then they talked for hours.

Chris knew what he was, of course. It wasn't the best-case scenario (that would be amnesiac-university-graduate-turned-fantasy-novelist) but that was OK.

She'd planned for this, she said. They could deal with anything, together.

'But I couldn't go with her,' said Kevin. 'Ashton needed me. Besides, what kind of a life would that be for her? Taking care of a blood-crazed monster for ever?'

He stopped, realising what he'd said. Or at least what I might have heard – given my family history and Kate's situation. But I was busy remembering how Chris's eyes lit up talking about him.

'Pretty sure she thinks you're worth it.'

'Yeah, she's said that,' said Kevin.

But Past Kevin hadn't believed her. He'd stuck to his 'no' and, eventually, seen Chris back to the campsite – where Ashton was waiting.

'He'd been worried, he said. Like maybe we'd missed a stray and I was in trouble.'

So he'd followed Kevin's scent, then caught Chris's. And he was furious.

'I tried to explain,' said Kevin. 'I mean, I wasn't leaving. And Ashton understood family, right? But the way he looked at Chris terrified me. I said we could go, right then. Just him and me, and I'd never see her again. I swore it.'

But Ashton couldn't just leave Chris. She'd tried to steal his Kev; he needed her gone. And he needed Kevin to do it.

'And when I said "no", God, he moved so fast! Grabbing Chris by the hair and shoving her under my nose, taunting me about all the things I'd done, so she'd hear exactly what kind of a monster her big brother was. He made this cut on her neck, just there.' He indicated the side of his throat. 'And I was still so hungry. My fangs were out before I knew what I was doing – but then Chris screamed.

Suddenly I had Ashton on the ground – and Chris was halfway across the campsite. The force had knocked her clear. So I yelled at her to get to her van. Ashton's always been stronger than me, but I figured if I could hold him down until she locked herself inside, she'd be safe, 'cos he couldn't go where he wasn't invited.'

But Chris wasn't eight any more. Sure, she ran, but only to grab the stakes she apparently travelled with now.

'And when I saw that,' said Kevin, 'I dunno, it's like it gave me strength. I managed to smash Ashton's head against the ground and pull free. Then I grabbed Chris and got us the hell into her van.'

Cool, eh? And it got cooler.

Chris got cooler. 'Cos as Ashton screamed furiously and Kevin freaked out, Chris climbed in the front of the van, told Kevin not to look, and dumped a bag of poppyseeds out the window.

'Poppyseeds?' I said.

Kevin nodded proudly. See, his sister was super-resourceful, and far better at research than Kate's sister, because apparently Vampire Compulsive Counting Disorder is a thing – they can't pass spilled seeds until they've counted every single one. So all those teeny dots in the dark bought the head-start they needed to lose Ashton.

Once they were in the clear, Kevin realised he had no idea what to do next.

Chris did, though. Because Chris is awesome.

She'd made friends in slaughter-houses all over the country – plus, her new sketchy-but-sweet friend Jim had built a 'monster rehab' bunker where Kevin could quit human blood and adjust to the animal type, in the comfort of rein-forced concrete and steel (with Hollywood's finest sci-fi and fantasy movies to distract him).

'I didn't think I could do it,' said Kevin, 'but I wasn't going back to Ashton. He'd tried to make me kill Chris – and I'd almost done it. Hard to keep kidding yourself you're the good guy after that.'

So, he did quit. But not for ever. At least, not all at once.

'Chris said, just do one day,' said Kevin. 'And when I got through that, then I gave up for the next day. Then the day after and – and that's what I do. One day at a time, for the past twenty-three years.'

'Until today,' I said, realising.

Twenty-three years, and I'd made him break his sobriety.

'Oh, don't worry,' said Kevin. 'Turns out trying not to kill someone *too much* is a huge buzzkill.' He laughed, until he realised I wasn't laughing too. 'Sorry, that's not funny, is it? I told you, I'm a terrible person.'

'You keep saying that,' I said. 'But Ashton tortured you. He threatened you. You were just trying to survive, and protect Chris, and you've been clean eight years longer than I've been alive. Ashton messed you up, but you're not what he tried to make you.'

Kevin's head drooped guiltily. 'That's exactly what I am, Red.'

'Nuh-uh. Chris said –'

'Chris can't see inside my head.' Kevin lowered his voice to hiss that. 'She knows I still hunt the odd wolf, but she doesn't know how much I enjoy it. And she doesn't know the reason Ashton's still here is because three weeks ago we took out a wolfpack together. And it was amazing.'

My stomach formed a sick knot. 'What?'

'You heard me.' Kevin leaned forward. 'Ashton's not here clinging sadly to some past glory. He's here because he knows how close I am to going back.'

25. Still Evie

Back?

My head thumped. My muscles twitched.

Ashton had kidnapped Kevin. He'd tormented him; he'd broken Chris's sweet bookworm of a big brother and remade him as a blood-addicted mass-murderer.

'Dude, how could you go back? He ruined your life.'

'And murdered my parents,' said Kevin. 'While Chris was getting me clean, he went to my hometown and massacred every Harris in the phonebook, just to be sure. They never even knew she'd found me.'

Oh my God. 'So he's *evil* evil.'

'He's … complicated.'

'Dude!'

'I'm not defending him,' said Kevin. 'I want to tear that smug grin off his face and rip his heart out. But –'

'But *what*?' How could there be a 'but'?

'He was my friend. I barely spoke to anyone else for twelve years. He scared me, and hurt me, and – and made me feel special, and loved.' He pulled his glasses off and rubbed his eyes furiously. 'I think he really broke me, Red. And I'm not sure I've come back together properly.'

He did look broken. His eyes were all pink-rimmed and he was squeezing my hand like he was scared I might let go.

Still, I had to say it. 'So you snuck out to team up with him behind Chris's back?'

'No!' Kevin looked like I'd slapped him, but also like he'd deserved it. 'I – it wasn't like that. Look, there were wolves in Brightside, about a month ago. Just a few strays, I took 'em out no probs. But then more showed up, and these were way more co-ordinated than I'm used to. Caught me totally off guard. I'd have been done for – if Ashton hadn't been tracking them too and swooped in to save me, just in time.'

Swooped in? 'Ooh, heroic. Did he hum his own theme music too?'

'No.' Kevin half-laughed. 'But he did order his army to stay back, so we could finish off the pack together. And, I know it's horrible, but it felt *right* and fun – and Ashton saw that. When we were done, he made this big proclamation to his men, about how fate had brought us back together, and I'd be helping lead them as we took out the wolf camp.'

'There's a *wolf camp*?'

Kevin nodded. 'In the Rockies, somewhere. We never looked for it. Even if we could've gotten in uninvited, two vampires against an entire camp wouldn't stand a chance. But a whole army –' He paused. Guiltily. 'I was actually tempted, for a sec. Then I snapped out of it and tried to kill him, so he beat me nearly unconscious, followed my scent here and dumped me on the porch. And he's been here ever since – hunting down locals, building his ranks – and waiting for me to crack and "accept my destiny".'

'Why didn't he just take you, if he wants you back that bad?' I asked. 'Doesn't sound like you could've stopped him.'

'I couldn't,' said Kevin. 'That's the point. He needs me to choose, so his guys can see that I really never stopped being his. And maybe he's right, eh?'

He looked at me, all stereotypically hot, self-loathey bad boy. But so scared too.

I squeezed his hand tighter. 'He's not.'

'Really?' said Kevin. 'Because I *liked* scaring you, Red. I wanted an excuse to –'

His eyes flashed, finishing the sentence for him. I tried not to flinch.

'And I lied,' he said. 'Kate's blood did give me a buzz. So I'm not even clean any more. I'm just the asshole letting an entire town die for me. I've been justifying it, like, they'd be killing people anyway – but a whole town? What's that doing to the people left behind? Plus, Chris gave up her life trying to fix me, and I'm too broken for that. But if I left –'

'She'd come after you again,' I said. 'And Ashton would kill her. Don't pretend you don't know that!'

Kevin chewed his lip, and glanced towards the closed door – like he was looking straight through and across the hall at his sister. Then he gave this pissed-off half-laugh, ripped his glasses off and slammed his face into his hands.

'You're right,' he groaned. 'If I leave, I'll get her killed. If I stay, I'll get everyone else killed. Including you. So –'

'Don't worry about me.'

'Of course I'll worry about you, you're my ...' He looked up. The intensity as our eyes met made my stomach flip – and his cheeks flush – even though he only finished with 'friend'.

Coming from him, that didn't sound like a small thing. My heart didn't think so either, the way it sped up. Which he could hear, obviously.

His cheeks got a little pinker, but his eyes were still scared and angry. So I leaned forward. 'I am your friend. And whatever you do about this, I'm doing it with you. Besides –' I grinned. 'I've always wanted to storm an evil lair.'

'What? No!' Kevin looked horrified. 'Red we're not – even if I wanted to, Ashton's base will reek of human blood. I can't trust myself around that, especially after tonight. And they'll kill you.'

His hand gripped mine like he was scared to let go.

'So we're just gonna sit here, then?' I said. 'Wait for Ashton to get bored and come after you anyway? 'Cos you know it'll happen.'

'I do.' He sighed. 'But I didn't tell you this so we could fix it. I just thought you should know. My crappy past has ruined your life. And I'm sorry.'

He glanced down at my hand, and it felt very 'in his' as he chewed his lip nervously, before looking up. He was trying to meet my gaze, but my eyes were still drawn to his lips.

'Kevin.'

He shook his head. 'We're not storming the base, Red. But Ashton *is* after you – you still need to be prepared. So –'

He blurred, and suddenly I'd been yanked upward and flung towards the stove.

'Hey!' I caught myself on the saucepan rack, spinning to face him as I landed. 'Stop changing the subject!'

Kevin glowed his eyes and quirked a bad-boy smile. 'Make me.'

Ooh, my tummy-butterflies had no sense of timing.

Neither did I apparently. I'd barely moved when Kevin sprang forward, catching me mid-air and barrelling me into the floor.

My skull didn't crack on the tiles – Kate had taught me to tuck my chin in – but pain jolted across my shoulders. I grabbed Kevin's wrist, flicked my leg around his and flipped him over so I was on top.

'All right –' I started, but then he wrenched his hands free and sent me flying back, towards the wall.

He caught me before I hit, but the brush of his fangs on my neck reminded me I would've been in trouble if this was real. I grabbed his hair, yanking back, and was about to fake-rip – but he caught my wrists and pushed me into the wall, chuckling triumphantly as he eyed my neck again.

Without thinking, I leaned forward and planted my lips on his.

He froze, surprised, so I pulled my arms free and sent him hurtling onto the countertop, before springing over to imaginary-stake him.

'See? I can handle myself.'

Kevin pushed himself up on his elbows, still flustered. 'That wasn't fair.'

'Does Ashton always fight fair?'

'Well, he's never done that.' Kevin moved a little closer, and my belly-butterflies fluttered into overdrive.

My lips tingled, and his eyes flitted back to my mouth.

'You want a rematch?' I asked.

'Which bit?' Kevin's lips were so close to mine, and I already knew they tasted of chocolate. I also knew we should be talking about Ashton, but ...

'Oops, sorry, guys!'

'Chris!' Kevin jumped, knocking us both off the counter.

We landed in an awkward heap, untangled ourselves from each other at monster-speed and leapt to our feet as Chris sniggered.

'We ... we were training,' said Kevin, blushing.

'Uh-huh, yep.' Chris drained her wine glass, then nodded at the mess of knocked-down pots, broken mugs and spilled hot chocolate. 'How 'bout you two reckless teens keep "training" in your room, eh? I'll stay here and be the responsible adult.' She hung the pans back up and turned her attention to the hot-chocolate puddle. 'Now!'

I looked at Kevin, who shrugged like there was no point arguing and started towards the door, so I followed him.

26. Still still Evie

I'd never been in a boy's bedroom before. Or a vampire's, but that's probably less surprising.

Either way, it was tidier than mine. Like, I assume he had clothes, but they weren't layered three-deep on the floor like a normal person's. Every book in his giant wall-sized bookcase stood upright, in its own space, instead of slopping over half-open with another three books jammed on top. And there were no dirty socks between any of them. In fact, there were no dirty socks anywhere – I would've smelled them!

'Thought you said you weren't clean,' I quipped, and immediately regretted it. An addiction joke? Really, Evie-brain?

'Sorry,' I muttered.

Kevin chuckled. 'Nah, I'd prefer you to make a crappy joke than walk on eggshells around me, Red.'

Just as well, 'cos then he turned to face me, and suddenly I couldn't promise to take *any* sort of care with my words. My belly-butterflies reached my brain, and my 'storm the castle' arguments mushified as Kevin stepped towards me.

'Wait, Ashton –' I tried vaguely.

'It's Kevin,' said Kevin.

But he knew what I meant. He also knew what he was doing, distracting me by being all handsomely right there. He could hear my pulse as he brushed my hair out of my face and moved in closer, putting his arm around my waist and – shaking?

Aw, he was nervous too! And *so* dorky-cute and … Oh, screw it. Ashton would still be holding the town hostage in five minutes. I stretched up towards him.

'I can't believe you're real,' murmured Kevin.

I couldn't believe any of this was real. A hot vampire, saying things like that? Looking at me like this, giving me full-body butterflies? No wonder Mom was laughing with Invisible Batman, it was freaking surreal.

But, it was also Kevin. And he was more than some undead hunk or Reformed Evil Robin. Wait!

'Batman!' I gasped.

Kevin's eyes widened. 'What? Uh, I mean, it's Kevin.'

Nice try, but he knew exactly what I meant. Holy crap!

'You heard us, watching that video. You knew Mom was with one of Ashton's guys. Or maybe with Ashton? The head of an anti-werewolf army, grabbing drinks with a scientist who specialises in wolf-suppressants? You didn't think that was worth mentioning?'

Kevin shifted uncomfortably. 'Red –'

'SHUT UP!' I snapped. 'Mom's looking for my biological parents; Ashton's looking for the wolf camp. You don't think he lured her into his base, so he could force her to work for the psycho-squad?'

Kevin didn't speak, but his tortured jaw-flex said it all.

193

My head pin-prickled. 'Is Ashton Bruce Wayne?'

'I – I mean, there've been so many Batmen …'

'KEVIN!' My eyes burned. 'Did my mom leave that diner with *Ashton*?'

Kevin gulped, hard, then nodded. 'I think so, yeah, but –'

'But *what*?' A shot of white-hot pain hit my spine. Ashton had my mom, and Kevin had known it. My hands throbbed with the urge to claw something. 'Where are they?'

'Evie, calm down.'

'I AM CALM!'

Kevin moved away slightly. 'OK, you're calm. So then you know you can't rescue your mom if you're dead?'

My head was starting to splinter. My gums were tingling.

Kevin didn't want to help? Fine! 'I'll sniff them out myself.'

I started towards the door, but Kevin was already there, blocking the way.

'Move!' I snapped.

He shook his head. The urge to just rip through anyone who got between me and Mom pulsed hard. If I changed now, I would lose control.

'Kevin, I don't want to hurt you.'

'Then don't leave!'

My vision was blurring, but I could see the desperation in his face.

'I'll go,' he said. 'I'll make Ashton invite me in and –'

'And what?' I snarled. 'You already said you can't trust yourself up there. I'm not trusting you to get my mom. Now, MOVE!'

I grabbed the front of his shirt, ready to fling, but he ripped my hands loose and shoved me into his bookcase, yanking my head aside and – 'OW!'

There was no blood, he'd kept his fangs in, but my inner wolf still snarled as he stepped back. 'You bit me.'

'Barely,' he said. 'Look, I've never gone easy on you, but I haven't tried to hurt you. Ashton will, and he's faster and stronger than me. If I can do that, he'll do worse.'

His eyes were locked on mine and his face couldn't seem to decide between 'badass-hero' mode and its new 'terrified-friend' setting.

'Red, if you storm their base, the best-case scenario is you die,' he said. 'The worst case is they keep you and use you as leverage over your mom. Like he used Chris on me. Is that what you want? To hand Ashton the tools to torture your mom into becoming his evil-scientist sidekick?'

Another pain-wave hit. I curled my fingers into my palms and fought back. Kevin was right. I couldn't save Mom by hitting beast mode and racing out to 'search and destroy'. I needed a plan.

'All right,' I said.

Kevin tilted his head, uncertainly. 'All right … what?'

My head thumped. I took a deep breath, forcing my brain to work through the wolf-jolts and pain.

'Evie?'

'SHUT UP! I'm wolfing off.' I closed my eyes, then focused, like Kate had told me, on each part of my body in turn. My hands tingled, until I told them to relax. My stomach twisted, so I breathed into it until it unravelled.

Slowly, all the head-splitting body-twisting vanished, and I could think again.

'You OK?' asked Kevin when I opened my eyes.

'*I'm* OK. *We're* not. You lied to me.'

He nodded. 'Fair enough. Although, in my defence, I was just trying to protect you from racing out to do something reckless and impulsive.'

Reckless and impulsive, eh? I should've been touched he knew me so well, but –

'Yeah, I love when guys make my decisions for me,' I said. 'Way more romantic than letting my sister do it. Move!'

I started to push past him again. His eyes widened in panic.

'You're still going? But you wolfed off, you meditated. I thought you'd realised it was pointless to –'

'Storm the base?' I said. 'Right. I won't storm, I'll walk in, and offer my services as a Trojan wolf.'

'Trojan ... what?' Kevin's brow dipped. 'What do you mean?'

'Like, a double agent for the psycho-squad.' I might've been furious, but I was too proud of this plan not to brag. 'Betrayer of wolfkind. I'll tell Ashton, if he lets Mom go, I'll join the wolf camp. That's all they need, right? Someone to sneak out, invite Ashton's army in, and then – boom! Epic underworld battle.'

I couldn't quite read Kevin's expression. His mouth gaped slightly, and he seemed to be searching for words long before he found them.

'Red, that's brilliant!'

Duh!

'But it's not gonna work.'

'Oh, you think starting an inter-species battle royale and then hoping to sneak out un-mauled is a bad idea?' I laughed. 'But it's a good cover story, right? If he buys it, it should get me close enough to kill Ashton and free Mom.'

Kevin thought. This weird look crossed his face. Then he shrugged. 'I mean, he's cocky as hell; he'd *never* consider anyone could double-cross him. But collaborating with a wolf? Even one who could get him into the camp?' He chewed his lip, then looked at me. 'I should go too.'

He raised his eyebrows hopefully.

'No way!' I said. 'I don't need you and your precarious sobriety threatening to screw this up just 'cos you think I'm too helpless to –'

I stopped. Something had moved down the hall. I tried to listen, but Kevin leaned closer, his voice low and urgent: 'Red, you won't even get through the door without me. Kate'll crash early tomorrow – transition day's exhausting. We can prep together and go once she's out. Just don't do anything without me. Please?'

He looked so cute and worried – totally unfair given that I was still super-furious. I was about to tell him to piss off again when –

'*Evie? EVIE!*'

KATE! We jumped to our feet, panicking in sync as something metallic crunched in room 2.

'She broke the door handle,' muttered Kevin.

The door handle? Oh, crap.

My undead sister had just discovered her new super-powers.

27. Kate

Evie?

I was barely awake, but already bolt upright. Last time I'd seen Evie, she'd been tearing the head off that Donnie vamp and then … what? How did I wind up here?

Where *was* here? Wherever I was, it was dark.

And then, suddenly, it wasn't.

No, that's not quite right. The dark was still there, I could still see it, but I could see everything inside it too. And I could smell blood, and chocolate.

And – Evie? My stomach grumbled.

I looked around. I was back in the guesthouse. Which was good, except Evie wasn't here. *No Evie, just her scent?*

What had happened last night?

'Evie?'

I remembered getting a few hits in on that Frat Boy vampire. Then he'd overpowered me and smashed my head into something. I'd felt my skull crack.

Everything after that was blurry. I remembered pain, and blood. Fangs sinking through my skin. And Evie, screaming my name. Where *was* she?

'EVIE!'

I jumped out of bed. At least, that's what I meant to do: jump up, go open the door and find my sister. But I'd barely thought all that when I was there, at the door, holding the handle. The handle was not attached to the door.

There was a thump of footsteps outside, then the door burst open.

Literally. It splintered, as Evie and Kevin smashed through.

'EVIE!' She was OK.

I pulled her into a hug – and my canines jolted. There was a blur, a shot of pain through my arms, and a crack as something shoved me into the window.

No, not 'something' – Kevin.

'Red, run!'

He pinned me back, my arms yanked wide where he'd pulled Evie from my grip. She was still in the doorway, looking confused.

'Let. GO!' I snarled at him.

Something smelled delicious. It filled my lungs, tearing at my stomach. It was everywhere. Every*thing*. And Kevin was keeping me from it.

'Red!' he said again.

'Kevin, it's OK. It's Kate, she wouldn't –' She stepped forward.

My stomach lurched. I found myself snarling, pulling against Kevin's grip as he tightened his hold. Evie jumped back, and a furious beat pounded the air like a frightened pulse. It made the scent sweeter.

'Red, get to the kitchen!' yelled Kevin. 'Get a bottle from the fridge. GO!'

Evie ran, and the scent waned.

It was still there, still delicious – but the urgency in my fight slipped. Kevin loosened his grip but stayed blocking my way to the door.

'Move,' I said.

'No. You don't want to hurt Evie.'

'Of course I don't –' I stopped.

The hunger-rage was lifting, letting my brain pull the pieces together with sickening clarity. That smell, the one still making my teeth twinge. It was Evie!

My mind raced, replaying the tiny snatches I remember from last night: pain, blood, fangs. I touched my neck, where the bitemarks should still have been healing.

Nothing.

'I should be hurt,' I said. 'Felix cracked my tailbone. That freak fractured my skull. I got bitten. And now I'm fast and strong and … hungry for Evie?'

I could still smell her. My gums ached.

'Kate,' said Kevin.

'Shut up!' I yanked my hands free, touching the pulse-point under my jaw, before grabbing my wrist and pressing down lightly.

Sympathy flooded Kevin's face. 'You're checking for a heartbeat?'

'*SHUT. UP!*' My eyes stung.

I only thought about looking in the mirror, but suddenly I was there – wishing I wasn't, because my eyes were burning amber just like Felix's had.

And my cuts and bruises were gone, along with all my old scars.

'Shit!'

'Hey, it – it's OK,' said Kevin. 'You're OK. Everything's gonna be OK.'

No-one who said 'OK' that much could possibly mean it. And how could he? I checked my reflection again. It was creepy, airbrushed perfection. No dark circles, no blemishes, no signs I'd actually lived.

'But I *have* a reflection,' I muttered.

'Yeah,' said Kevin, sliding in beside me. 'I can see myself too.'

I stared at the empty space in the mirror, where Kevin should have been, then turned to face him. 'What the –?'

He flicked his fangs down, sheepishly. 'Surpri–'

Suddenly my fist was out, and he was crashing into the wall by the door. Oh my God! Did I just do that?

'Sorry!' Somehow, I was over beside him already, helping him up. 'I'm so sorry, I – I didn't mean to – are you OK?'

'Peachy.' Kevin smiled, wiping the blood from his mouth. 'And it's fine, just impulse stuff. Your brain needs a few hours to catch up with your body, that's all. Look, no harm done.'

He held up a gleaming fang I must have knocked out, then ran his tongue along the gap. A new one was already growing in. *Oh God, this was real.*

'You're a vampire, like them?' I gestured toward the window, to outside.

Kevin shook his head. 'We're not like them, Kate.'

For some reason, that 'we' hit hard. Like hearing it out loud wiped away the tiny shred of denial I hadn't realised I'd been clinging to.

201

'No,' I muttered. 'No, I can't be a vampire. I've got too much to do.'

Then another thought hit: a sudden, horrible realisation that ripped through my unbeating heart like a stake. I hadn't just tried to *bite* Evie ...

'I tried to *kill* her!' My knees buckled.

Kevin caught me and pulled me up. 'Hey, this isn't your fault, OK? These impulses are strong. But you're stronger, and once this bit's passed –'

'What? I'll never be hungry for her blood again?' I found that hard to believe, the way my mouth watered at the thought.

Then, with the worst possible timing, that stair in the hallway creaked, and Evie filled the air again. Kevin's eyes flashed with panic.

'I'll be right back,' he said. 'Try not to breathe.'

He vanished, pulling the splintered door as shut as it could get behind him.

I clenched my jaw and clamped my hand to my nose, but she'd already flooded my senses. My appetite burned. Tears pricked at my eyes, I couldn't do this.

I was supposed to keep Evie safe, not be the thing she needed saving from. The thing I'd stake to protect her. I'd only just glanced at the wooden chair by the desk when –

'Katie, stop!'

'RED, DON'T!'

Evie raced in just in time to wrench the smashed chair-leg from my grip, and flung it across the room. Her scent hit, my stomach lurched and my fangs came down – straight into Kevin's arm, as he shoved us apart.

'Ow!' He uncapped a plastic bottle and shoved it into my hands. 'Drink. Now! Red, I told you, stay outside.'

The blood in the bottle was cold. It smelt dead and gross, but it wasn't Evie's. I wondered if I should chug the lot, then found myself already glugging mouthfuls of pig-tasting gunk. I stopped, gagged and kept going.

'I wanted to make sure she was OK,' said Evie.

'Well, I'm not!' I gulped my last mouthful. 'I can't be near you, Evie.'

'It's just for a few hours,' Kevin said. 'Until her impulses settle.'

Evie's arms twitched. I could see her fighting the urge to hug me.

Instead, she said: 'Fine. But no more self-destruction attempts, we didn't bring you back so I could lose you three minutes after you woke up. Dork.'

She was trying to sound casually grumpy, but her voice was shaking. So was she.

'Deal,' I said.

'Now, go lock yourself in my room,' added Kevin. 'Read a book or something. If you're hungry, there's Oreos in my desk. Just don't leave, OK?'

'Yay, sugar!' Evie disappeared in a rush of fake excitement.

I burst into tears – huge, body-quaking floods – as I sank to the ground.

Kevin sat down beside me. For a moment I thought he might try to hug me, but he was smarter than that.

'It will pass,' he said. 'I promise.'

'And then I'll just be a regular blood-thirsty psycho-monster?'

Kevin straightened up slightly. 'Wow. Yeah, none taken.'

I gave a snotty snort-chuckle, so Kevin handed me a tissue, then shifted awkwardly and cleared his throat. 'Uh, there's something you need to know about last night.'

'There's probably a *lot* I need to know about last night,' I said. 'Last thing I remember is that freak infecting me, or turning me or – whatever vampires do.'

'Turn you.' Kevin cleared his throat again. 'But not with a bite, that's werewolves. Vampires have a – a whole process. It can't happen by accident, Kate.'

He paused, guilt written all over his face.

'Wait, you mean – did *you* turn me?' Something flared inside me.

'You were dying,' said Kevin. 'Evie was a mess. I couldn't let her lose you.'

'So you gave her a sister who can't stop trying to murder her? That's better?'

My fist flew by itself. Kevin caught it, expertly, along with the second one a moment later. He held on to both, as his eyes met mine.

'It *is* better,' he said. 'You're still her sister. And you're my – whatever you want to call it. Our blood is in each other's veins. That sort of thing mightn't mean much to the psycho-squad out there but it does to me. With you. I'm not going to let you hurt Evie or yourself. OK?'

He looked so genuine. I yanked my hands from his grip and sat on them, so I wouldn't try to punch him again. 'Didn't have you pegged for a sentimentalist, Kev.'

Kevin winced at the name, but didn't correct me.

'Oh, yeah. I'm a big schmaltzy fuzzball of emotions,' he said. 'Look, I know what I did to you. I know it sucks. Someone did it to me too, remember? But I'm not him, so you're not going to be me. You're better than that.'

I almost said I knew I was better than him, but then I remembered him holding me back from Evie, and wound up choking on a sob instead. Kevin moved to put his hand on my arm, then changed his mind and elbow-bopped me on the bicep instead.

'Listen to me,' he said. 'I saw Evie when she thought you were dead and – and she was not OK. She needs you. So if you ever feel like you can't keep going just – do it anyway. For her, all right?'

I was going to nod, then I caught sight of my makeshift stake again and wound up lunging for that. Kevin pulled me back and kicked the chair-wreckage out of sight in one movement. The tightness of his grip was weirdly comforting.

'Let's get you away from spiky wooden things for now, eh? You want pizza?'

'Pizza?' The unexpected randomness made me sob-snort. 'We're vampires!'

'True, better double stuff the crust,' Kevin said too cheerily. 'This metabolism is a lot, and pig's blood gives us what we need but it's not what we're craving. So, filling up on other things keeps your appetite from getting too – y'know ...'

'Murdery?'

'Right.' Kevin smiled. 'Now come on, you can help me make the base!'

And, with that, I let my nerdy vampire non-friend guide baby-vamp me to the kitchen for pizza, so I wouldn't accidentally murder my sister.

This would be a lot to explain to Mom.

28. Kate again

The kitchen was good.

The kitchen felt safe.

The kitchen reeked of disinfectant, blood and hot chocolate; all strong enough to overpower any leftover Evie scent. Plus, the lack of potential self-staking implements meant Kevin could let go of me once he felt my body relax.

'OK,' he said. 'Let's work on your impulse control.'

'What about pizza?'

'Pizza *and* impulse control.' Kevin quirked a grin. 'A little "wax on, wax off", if you know what I mean?'

'I don't.' My stomach grumbled, unhappily. 'But *you* can wax off if you're going to be weird while keeping me from food.'

Kevin laughed. 'We'll get to the pizza. First I need my measuring cups. They're in the middle drawer on the breakfast bar. Can you walk over and –?'

I was already there, holding the cups. Kevin sighed.

'Great. Now put them back, come here, and *walk* there. Slowly. Focus on lifting your feet, moving one in front of the other.'

'I know what walking is, thanks.' But my body kept racing ahead. I was back beside Kevin before I'd finished that sentence. 'Oh.'

'It's OK. Try again. You're stronger than your impulses. You can control them, it just takes practice. Now, you focus. I'll get the ingredients together.'

'Focus', he'd said. Like it was easy. Just die, wake up monstrous, nearly kill your sister – then really *focus* on moving your feet.

I gripped the counter to keep from zipping ahead and wound up snail-crawling towards the drawer. My body couldn't seem to figure out a mid-speed.

'Why am I even practising?' I asked. 'Won't I be fine, once I adjust?'

Kevin hesitated by the olive oil. 'I didn't say fine. I said this will pass, and it will. You'll have more control over your impulses once your body and brain sync up.'

'But I won't be fine?'

Kevin put the oil and baking powder on the counter, then sighed.

'You'll be better, but part of being a vampire is being a predator. You're faster than you're used to, and stronger. And you're gonna have violent urges. You need to be on top of them, especially around Evie.'

'You think I could still hurt her?' The countertop cracked under my grip.

Kevin spooned some sugar and salt into a bowl, avoiding my gaze.

'I think you *could*,' he said. 'I don't think you *will*. But you know how she smells. And that's with all her blood on the inside.'

'Well, that's where it's supposed to be,' I said.

'Mostly,' said Kevin. 'But if twenty-three years with Chris has taught me anything it's that, once a month, things get challenging.'

'Oh.' I hadn't even thought about that.

'Don't worry, you'll cope,' he said. 'You just need to be prepped. I stock up on extra blood, comfort eat, try not to breathe much around her. Also, tampons help.'

'Tampons?' My hand flew to my nose. 'Isn't that uncomfortable?'

'Not for *me*, for her,' said Kevin.

'Ah, yes. That makes more sense.'

I'd reached the drawer, so I found the cups and handed them to Kevin, who set about measuring and mixing ingredients. It was oddly comforting to watch. Something normal on a messed up night.

'What if I can't control it?' I asked.

'You can,' said Kevin. 'Evie's the biggest challenge. She smells better than anyone I've ever met. If you manage around her, you can do it around anyone.'

'But if I can't?' I said. 'And if you think I might hurt Evie, or anyone else …'

'Kill you?' Kevin tipped the dough onto the counter and started kneading. 'Fine, I'll add you to my list. But it won't come to that. Hey, grab the rolling pin?'

He nodded to the utensil holder by the cooker, back the way I came. I groaned, then started the snail-crawl towards it.

This time, Kevin joined me. 'If it helps, I spent twelve years as a desperate blood junkie before Chris found me and – well, now look!' He straightened his glasses. 'World's dullest monster, but I'm sober.' He veered off to the fridge. 'OK, what are we thinking for toppings? Mozzarella, obviously. And – pineapple? Yes? No?'

My stomach twisted, and not just at the thought of pineapple pizza.

Twelve years, he'd said.

You could kill a lot of people in twelve years. People who didn't stop being dead just because you've retired from serial killing. And now here he was, chatting away and cooking for me, like Hannibal Lecter.

'Kate?' said Kevin. 'You've gone pale. You hungry again? Here –'

He pulled another bottle of blood from the fridge. I fully intended to knock it out of his hands, but somehow I wound up chugging the lot. It was only when the bottle was empty that I crushed it up and hurled it to the floor.

The impact was kind of lost by then.

'This actually goes in recycling,' said Kevin, picking it up. 'Are you all right?'

'You've killed people,' I muttered. 'You're a ... a bad guy?'

Kevin's jaw flexed. 'I keep telling you, I'm not a hero.'

He did, he'd said that. I'd assumed it was self-deprecating brooding, but –

'Kevin, I've got to ask,' I said. 'Everything going on here, the vampires and the missing giants, that's ... nothing to do with you, right?'

Kevin's grip on the crumpled plastic tightened, his knuckles whitening with the strain before he answered. 'It's everything to do with me.'

My blood froze. 'You're gonna need to explain that.'

Kevin laughed humourlessly. 'Course I will.' He handed me the rolling pin, then sighed. 'You roll, I'll talk. Just try not to whack me *too* much with that thing. Impulse control and all.'

'I can't make any promises,' I said. 'Now, backstory!'

*　　*　　*

My brain must have finally synced up with my body because, yes, I'd smashed the rolling pin, a few mugs and part of the countertop. And, sure, I'd cracked a couple of Kevin's ribs in an unexpected hug. *But* I waited until he was finished talking before zipping towards the back door.

'I'm gonna kill him.'

'Stop!' Kevin appeared between me and the door. 'You can't.'

'Oh, I shouldn't kill the psycho who's after you and my sister? And destroying this town?'

'I said "can't", not "shouldn't",' said Kevin. 'You need to be invited in, Otherwise –' he winced '– it's like your brain's being ripped apart whilst *on fire*. You couldn't think, never mind take out an army and kill Ashton.'

'Then I'll get myself invited,' I said. 'I'm charming.'

'You're a hot girl,' said Kevin. 'Ashton won't want you distracting his guys. He only took your mom because –'

'Mom?'

Kevin's eyes widened. His mouth formed a perfect 'O'.

My whole body went cold. 'Kevin, my *mom*?'

That 'O' gaped uselessly, so I shoved him back, into the door.

'I am *really* struggling to control my impulse to rip your arms off,' I said. 'But if that sicko has my mom, and you're hiding it from me –'

'I'm not!' Kevin wriggled free. 'I was just waiting until you were synced, so you wouldn't go racing out like Evie wanted.'

'Evie knows?' There was a crack. I pulled my fist from the wall beside the door and shook the plaster off. 'You told her, then left her alone for … what? An hour and a half?'

'But I've stalled her,' said Kevin. 'I said we'd go together. I wanted to buy *us* time to work out a way to stop her and –'

'And she agreed?'

Kevin hesitated. 'I mean, it's an agreement-in-progress, but –'

'So "no" then?' I shoved past him and raced up the stairs. 'Evie! *EVIE!*'

The door at the end of the hall was open. A half-second glance inside told me that (a) this was Kevin's room, and (b) it had been a lot neater before someone had quietly gnawed his desk and chair, then claw-shaved the legs into vampire stakes.

'She promised she'd stay in the room,' said Kevin, sounding hurt.

'No, she said, "Yay, sugar"!' I snapped. 'That's *not* a promise. Idiot.'

I wheeled around and raced to our room. Another mess.

'Well, we didn't hear her come downstairs,' I said. 'So she's here some… what?'

'Um.' Kevin yanked the curtains apart, revealing a huge hole in the window-pane. 'That's how she left last time.'

'Oh, you're kidding me.'

There was a smash from down the hall, then a *THUMP!* outside.

We both knew what we'd see before we looked, but the sight of Evie's body flat-out in the snow still sent me over the edge.

Literally.

29. Kate again

Broken glass ripped my shins, as I hurtled toward the ground.

I twisted my body, landing squat on my feet, before jumping upright and racing over to where my bloodied baby sister was pushing herself up.

'Evie!'

She shoved me back and scrambled to her feet. My heart stabbed: she was scared of me. 'Evie, it's OK. I'm all right.'

Evie stepped forward. 'You're you?'

'Just a little deader.' I held my arms out, ready for my hug.

Instead, she pushed me away and yelled: 'Good, then STAY. HERE!' before snatching her backpack and racing off – right into the tattooed giant who'd appeared out of nowhere.

'Well, don't you smell delicious?' He grabbed her.

My fangs snapped down. I rushed forward, then jolted back.

'Nuh-uh, gorgeous.' The monster gripping my arms reeked of blood. 'Not if you want her to live – right, guys?'

There was a murmur of agreement, as five more amber-eyed monsters closed in.

'Leave her alone!' yelled Evie. 'I'm the one Ashton wants. I'll come with you – no tricks. Just let her go.'

'No tricks? Really?' A preppy-looking blond guy ripped her bag open, unleashing a cascade of home-made stakes. He picked one up and turned to me.

Evie growled.

Preppy smirked. 'Hey, y'all haven't seen our buddy Donnie and his crew, have ya? They went out for you, and never came back. Almost like …' He tapped the point of the stake over my heart. '*BOOM!* But you wouldn't do something like that, right?'

Evie's growl reached danger levels.

The tattooed giant tightened his grip. 'Ooh, puppy likes the dyke! Maybe we'll keep her, eh? A little insurance –'

He exploded.

The surprise made Preppy let his guard down, and the blood-breath monster behind me loosen his grip. I slammed my elbow into his solar plexus, then drove my fist into Preppy's chest. Blood Breath snarled, so I spun out of the way, back-kicked him into his friend – then watched him burst into gore.

Preppy barely flinched as the friend he'd accidentally staked rained onto him. Instead, he glowered at me. 'Or maybe we won't keep ya, huh?'

Over his shoulder, I saw Evie rip the head off a vampire in a fedora, before spinning to help Kevin with the last two. They made it look easy.

Preppy charged.

I slammed my arm down, catching the stake as he tried to drive it through my heart, and yanked hard. He kept his grip, until I smashed my left palm into his nose, sweeping his legs from under him so he crashed to the ground.

I dropped down, stake raised – and his eyes widened. Cass's huge, unblinking eyes flashed through my mind, along with the terrified face of the vampire I'd killed.

My stomach twisted. Preppy was huge, but only about eighteen. Maybe Ashton had tortured him too. Maybe he was just broken, like Kevin.

I lowered the stake.

Preppy smiled, then grabbed it and flipped me onto the ground. My head smashed against the path and, for a moment, there were three of him.

Then there was none.

His gore turned to dust, covering my favourite hoodie in vampowder and bad memories. Kevin kept his stake up and raced off as Evie helped me to my feet.

I needed help; I was shaking.

'You OK?' she asked. 'I thought you had that – what happened?'

Kevin returned before I could answer. 'He got away.'

'Who?' I said.

'Some biker-looking freak,' said Evie.

'Who's gonna report everything back to Ashton,' said Kevin. 'So if he didn't know there were two of you, he does now. Plus, he'll figure out I turned you, Kate – so he'll know I've tasted blood. And I just left the house to help here, so obviously Chris isn't my only weakness any more. All in all, yeah. Productive few minutes.'

He scowled at Evie.

She folded her arms and glared back. 'Well, if you two hadn't tried to stop me –'

'You'd be dead? We know.' Kevin gathered up the rest of the stakes, wrapped them in the ripped backpack and started towards the house. 'Let's get back inside before anyone else swings by. Oh, and Evie?'

'What?'

'You owe me a new backpack.'

*   *   *

'I didn't *lie*.' Evie was still grumpy as Kevin sliced the slightly charred pizza and set it on the breakfast bar with mugs of blood. 'I just felt useless, reading *Good Omens* while you looked after Kate. So I thought –'

'No, you didn't,' I said.

'What?'

'You didn't think, Evie! You ate the furniture, then smashed a window to go storm a vampire nest – forcing your possibly still blood-crazed sister to jump after you while you're all cut up and delicious smelling! That's the opposite of thinking.'

'You weren't supposed to follow me; you weren't supposed to know I was gone. I would've used the broken window, but –'

'You heard us and jumped through the nearest one instead?' I said. 'We know. That's *not* thinking.'

'Neither's freezing up mid-battle and almost getting yourself re-killed,' said Evie. 'Or are we not gonna talk about that?'

She was being bitchy-defensive now. Mom would've been all over that, but the best I could do was chew my burned pizza and try not to think about the gleeful hate in Preppy's face as he almost murdered me.

'Evie, that's not fair,' said Kevin.

'Neither's me having to watch her die in the first place!' snapped Evie. 'Or Mom being held hostage by wolf-hating psychos, or *you* having your life wrecked 'cos that asshole missed his son. It all sucks. This whole stupid monster world! And if Kate's too nice to even protect herself –'

Her lip wobbled, and suddenly I was on the other side of the table, hugging her.

'I don't want you to die, Katie,' she said. 'I'm sorry if I was stupid, but we need Mom. You need her! All this taking care of me, dealing with vampires and werewolf stalkers, being *undead*, and – and missing Zoe ... I just wanted Mom back. For you.'

Pain stabbed through my pointless heart.

'Oh, Evie.' I pulled her as close as I dared without cracking anything. 'There's nothing I'm OK with risking you for. Not even Mom. We'll figure out a way to get her back, but not one that'll get the whole family killed, OK?'

'Fine,' said Evie.

It wasn't, clearly, but her plan A had just gone out the window, been attacked by vampires and forced to retreat, so, reluctantly, she agreed to my lie.

And, after showers for everyone and some power-honing training for me, we all agreed when Kevin suggested staying on a fold-out bed in our room for tonight, to make sure none of us did anything else stupid.

I wasn't delighted about being babysat, but I really was starting to flag. It would be useful to have a less-exhausted pair of ears listening out for Evie.

Which is why his voice was the first thing I heard, six hours later, when –

'Evie, don't!'

I was on my feet just in time to catch Kevin before he hit the wall. He shook me off, and snapped his attention towards the empty doorway. 'She's gonna kill him!'

'What? Who –?' I stopped, as my ears caught a whimper from downstairs.

'I'm sorry!' *Felix!*

I started for the door, but Kevin pulled me back.

'It's morning. If we're going out there, we need to cover up.' He grabbed my hoodie from the floor. 'You got another one?'

'Evie does,' I said. 'Go, I'll find it. And here –' I tossed him the tranq gun from under my pillow. 'Just in case.'

Kevin pulled the sweater on, yanked the hood up and raced downstairs. My eyes stung as I emptied Evie's bag onto the bed. *She wouldn't.* I really wanted to believe that. But I'd seen her rip a lot of heads off recently. She found this easy.

And Felix had gotten me killed.

He was definitely about to die.

30. Evie

I woke up furious. My claws were out, but I wasn't sure why until my ears focused, and I heard the voices downstairs.

'Please, I need to talk to her.' It was Felix.

A growl started in my throat. I forced it back.

No need to wake the others. I could deal with this.

'I said she's not here.' That was Chris.

'Then I'll wait until she comes back,' said Felix.

I slipped out of bed and tiptoed towards the door as Chris said: 'GET OUT!'

Nah, stay, Felix. Just a moment longer.

I slid between Kate's bed and Kevin's fold-out, quietly. Just a few more steps.

'Evie?'

I glanced down. Big mistake. My eyes were angry-burning. Kevin was up in a flash. 'What's –?'

'Not until I see her,' said Felix.

Kevin's eyes widened. 'Oh, no. Evie, don't.'

I didn't have time for this. I shoved him back, harder than I should have, then turned and raced down the stairs.

* * *

220

I don't know if Felix saw me before I grabbed him by the throat, but he sure as heck saw my eyes as they darkened and burned yellow.

'I'm sorry,' he whimpered.

'Sorry?' My fingers tingled, growing wet with his blood. I'd *make* him sorry.

He sniffled and ... oh my God, was he crying?

'Give me one reason I shouldn't rip your head off right here, asshole.'

Felix shook his head, wincing as my claws dug deeper into his skin. 'I can't.'

'Evie –' started Chris.

'It's OK.' Felix winced again.

He deserved pain. But then his eyes met mine, and all I could think was how red and puffy they were. He looked exhausted.

'Just give me five minutes,' he said. 'Please. You can do whatever you want after, but let me talk, OK?'

My claws drew back by themselves. He was trying to make me feel bad for him. But I wasn't Kate, so I shoved my face up to his and snarled. 'Oh, you wanna talk? Like those freaks wanted, when they killed my sister? When you *got her* killed?'

My fingers tingled again, and he gasped as my claws dug back into his skin. I was vaguely aware of the sound of curtains being pulled over, but I was too focused on this wimp to pay attention.

'I did, I know.' He was full-on sobbing now. 'I'm sorry. It keeps playing in my head on a loop. I can't stop it, and I can't take it back.' He sniffled pathetically. 'They said you'd arrived in Brightside first, that you'd hurt people first. And I know

221

that's not true, but I was bleeding out and I ... I should've just died. I'm sorry, Evie.'

Images of Felix, half-dead and terrified, surrounded by Donnie's sneering goons, flashed through my head, making my heart ache. *Stop it!*

'Hope you're not waiting for me to disagree,' I growled. *That's better.*

'No, kill me,' he said. 'I don't care. There's just something you need to hear first.'

His heart was pounding and – wait, his heart was pounding? My claws drew back.

Felix dropped to the ground. He slapped his hand to his neck, but his eyes stayed on me as he sat sobbing and bleeding and – oh, he'd peed himself.

He was sitting in pee.

'I'm gonna have to clean that up, aren't I?' Kevin's voice made me jump.

I spun around. He was sitting on the stairs, holding the tranq gun and smiling slightly. 'I honestly thought you'd kill him, Red.'

'I can wait five minutes while he explains that pulse.'

'Yeah, I noticed that too.' Kevin blurred beside me. 'All right, freak. Who *are* you, really?'

'What?' Felix cowered into the wall, away from Kevin. 'I ... I'm me. Felix.'

'And you're human again?' Kevin laughed nastily. 'Yeah, not how this works.'

He yanked Felix to his feet, swiped his fingers across the blood on Felix's neck and sniffed before, very gingerly, sticking the bloodied finger in his mouth to taste it.

'KEVIN!' Chris looked horrified.

Kevin just looked confused. 'There's dust in his blood, Chrissy. The same dust I tasted in the air last night. It's like someone turned him, but – but then –'

'Exploded.' Felix nodded frantically. 'When Evie ripped his head off. Right!'

'So now he's *human*?' asked Chris. 'You said that couldn't happen.'

Kevin's eyes raced, side to side, as his brain clicked the pieces into place. 'That's what Ashton said. But then, he wouldn't want me to know the one thing that –'

Suddenly, his eyes blazed.

Felix whimpered, but Kevin's anger wasn't aimed at him any more than his fist was, when he smashed it through the window.

'Kevin, STOP!' Chris raced over, wrapping Kevin's still-bleeding hand in hers. 'Whatever you're thinking, don't! OK? Ashton's stronger than you, and we're fine as we are. We'll be fine.'

'Fine?' Felix laughed, until I glared at him.

'Just promise you won't do anything stupid?' said Chris.

Kevin hesitated, then hugged Chris. 'I won't. I love you.'

'I know,' said Chris. 'OK, I'll get paper towels and clean up here. You find Felix some new pants. And *behave*.'

She left for the kitchen. I waited until the door shut, then turned to Kevin with a whisper: 'Was that "I won't do anything stupid" or "I won't promise not to"?'

Kevin shrugged. 'Let's see how the night goes, eh?' He turned to Felix. 'In the meantime, I think we should take this upstairs.'

To Kate? 'Sounds fun!' I grabbed Felix and shoved him forward. 'Let's go.'

* * *

'Oh, hey, pal!' Katie was on the bed, wearing my hoodie.

She waved, as I pushed Felix in. He shrieked and stumbled backwards, almost smacking his head against the drawers before Kate blurred and caught him.

'Careful! Wouldn't want anyone getting hurt, eh?'

She lifted him to his feet, then off them. I would've thrown him against the wall but she placed him down, dusted him off – then stepped forward until he backed into the wall by himself.

'K-Kate,' he stammered, 'you're alive?'

'Good question.' Kate flicked her fangs down. Felix whimpered. '*Alive* implies a life, and I don't get one of those, do I? I won't grow old, or up. No university, no PhD, no research position at the kids' hospital – heck, no kids. No settling down with someone nice and living happily ever after.' Her eyes flamed as she cornered him. 'I've an eternity ahead of me. And no life at all. Thanks, dude.'

She raised her fist.

Felix flinched, but Katie just laughed – a little nastier than I was used to – before taking his hand, folding his fingers down and fist bumping, lightly.

'K-Kate,' said Felix. 'I'm sorry, what I did –'

'Sucked? Yeah. But you can't undo it by sobbing so –' She paused, then retched. 'Why do you smell like a port-a-potty? Can we hose him down or something?'

Kevin sighed. He had to be itching to hear more about the re-human-ing, but Felix really did reek of pee, especially to our monster-noses.

'Yeah, I won't be able to focus on anything if I'm trying not to puke,' I said.

'Fine,' said Kevin.

He vanished into the bathroom with Felix. There was a thump, an 'ow!', and the slosh of running water. Kate winced uncomfortably.

'Clean yourself up,' Kevin said. 'I'll get you some clothes.'

He blurred off, leaving us to supervise the skinny goth sobbing in the shower.

Old Evie, the one who hadn't just sat holding her sister's lifeless body, might have felt bad for him. New Evie just felt a rush of – what's that German word – *Schadenfreude*? Meaning happiness at the misfortune of others? Yeah, I was feeling that in buckets.

'Hey, bring him a sandwich too,' Kate called after him. 'He's probably starving.'

'A sandwich?' I said. 'Kate, he threw you to the vampires!'

'I know. I was there.'

'And I was there afterwards!' My head prickled at the memory. I squeezed my nails into my palms, letting them claw up slightly, but images of pale, vacant-eyed Kate flashed through my mind anyway. For about the zillionth time since last night, the pain of almost losing her hit my gut.

'You're bleeding!' Kate clamped her hand over her mouth, but her stomach rumbled anyway. *Crap!*

I raced into the bathroom. Felix's pulse went insane behind the shower curtain.

'Relax,' I said. 'I'm just washing blood off my hands so my sister doesn't try to bite me. Again. Because that's a thing I have to worry about now. Thanks.'

'Evie –' he started.

But I didn't care, so I left. Kate was nibbling on Cass's chocolate-coated seeds when I came back in. She swallowed, guiltily, and edged away.

'Kate, it's OK,' I said. 'You can't control your belly-grumbles. And look –' I held my hands out to show her. 'All better.'

Kate's eyes flicked from my palms to the meds bag, suspiciously.

'You're suddenly healing a lot faster,' she said.

'I've got super-senses now too.' I said. 'And powers, obviously. Which I can control as long as I can control my temper.'

Sure, when I got angry I was in danger of accidentally murdering someone, like I almost did with Felix. But I wasn't about to go into that. Kate's jaw was already flexing unhappily. She looked … 'pissed off' was the wrong phrase, but 'worried' wasn't quite right either. Like, grumpy-concerned? Is there a German word for that?

'So, you're off your meds?' she asked.

'I don't need them, you said so yourself last night. There's no inner monster, there's just me. And I can control this. Plus, this way we limit my silver exposure so –'

'It's not about you!' snapped Kate.

Her expression softened the moment the words were out of her mouth, but it was too late. I was already thinking about the other thing she'd said in the bathtub last night. About not knowing who she'd be if I was all me.

'So, it's about you then?' I said. 'Being scared I won't need my big sister any more if I don't need protecting? 'Cos that's bull-crap, I'll always need you.'

That had started off angry, but somehow ended with me fighting back tears. I'd just doomed Kate to immortality rather than lose her. Maybe I wasn't in the greatest position to get all self-righteous about *her* co-dependent insecurities.

Kate's face tried on about fifty emotions, before settling on sad exhaustion.

'I know,' she said, 'and I'm sorry I snapped. I just … This isn't about our messed up family dynamic. It's about your stalker.'

'Rom?' What did he have to do with my meds, and why was I only hearing about it now? 'Another secret! Cool. Love those.'

'Says the girl who dropped her meds without discussing it?' Kate *touché*-d, Momly. 'This wasn't a secret, Evie. I just didn't want to add one extra stress on top of all – *this*!'

She gestured around, like Ashton's monster mob and the absence of Mom were somehow all right here in the room with us. My head prickled.

'Well, consider me stressed, now go on.'

So, on she went, telling me about my parents and their buzzy little in-built tracking instincts that sounded a lot like my angry-bee headaches. How she was worried that, without my meds, Not-Evie would be broadcasting my signal all over the place for any wolf to pick up. Just like Rom said he had, in Toronto.

'I can't go back on my meds,' I said. 'They make me weak, and they barely work. And we're surrounded by psycho-vamps who keep trying to kill us, plus you need my silver resistance down in case you have to stop me.'

Kate groaned, because I was right. 'So you just want to keep broadcasting to the world, and if he shows up he shows up? Is that what we're going with?'

I shrugged. 'I mean, Human Kate's already kicked his ass once. Also, you know, a town full of wolf-hating vampires? Might be problem solved, eh?'

'That's a ... horribly valid point.' Kate shuddered. 'God, we're going to need some serious therapy after all this.'

'We'd get, like, two sentences in before being committed,' I said. 'But hey, padded cell. Quiet. Sleep.'

'I wish.' Kate chuckled, tiredly, then pulled me in for a hug. 'OK, we'll just meditate more, then. And keep power-training. I'll get used to drinking blood, we'll find Mom and – and we'll be all right.'

'Of course we will,' I said. 'We're us! Now with extra magic.'

'Magic.' Kate smiled. 'I like that.'

She passed me the seeds, and we sat on the bed – a were-wolf and a vampire sharing treats made by a dead girl, while her traitor ex-vampire boyfriend sniffled and sobbed in the shower. Just one of those days, eh?

31. Kate

'Why are you being so nice to me?' asked Felix, as we settled into room 4.

'She's making us,' said Evie.

'We're not,' I said, because we weren't, really.

Kevin had fed him; I'd insisted we move room when I noticed him shivering by our broken window; and Evie just hadn't murdered him.

'Did you expect us to torture you?' I said. 'We're not monsters.'

Kevin pulled a face. 'I mean ...'

'OK, fine, we're monsters,' I said. 'But we're not the bad guys.'

'*They're* not.' Kevin spun a chair backwards and straddled it in front of Felix, like a parody of someone trying to play bad cop. 'I'm full-on nightmare fodder. So how about you tell us why you're here? Because don't let that grilled cheese fool you: I'm still on the fence about killing ya – and I'd enjoy it.'

He was so melodramatic, I nearly laughed, but Felix winced under his glare.

'O-OK,' he stammered. 'So, Donnie and his guys caught the wolf-scent off Cass, from when she hugged Evie, I guess, and – well – you know what they did to her. Then they dragged me back to Ashton and … and hurt me, until I told them about you, Kate.'

'Me?'

He looked so ashamed. 'I thought, if one of you *was* a werewolf … I mean, you're so badass. And Evie's so cute.' Evie snarled. Felix gulped down a whimper, then continued: 'Anyway, Ashton flipped out. He said Kevin had really lost his way if he had a wolf here. So they needed to bring you both in now. It was Donnie's idea to kidnap you, as bait. But there were other ideas too. That's why I'm here.'

He paused, trembling, and forced himself to make eye contact with Kevin – who raised his eyebrows and tilted his head. 'Because –?'

Felix gulped. 'Because Ashton's next favourite idea was to burn this house down and grab you all on your way out. Including your – sister?'

'Chris!' Kevin's eyes flamed. 'OK, new plan – I'm going to kill him.'

He tried to zip to the door, but Evie caught him and pushed him back onto the bed.

'Dude, it's barely noon, you'll flame-grill yourself,' she said. 'Besides, you're not storming Ashton's lair alone, right, Kate?'

'What? No!'

'See?' She grinned, misunderstanding me completely, and took a notepad from the nightstand. 'Now – we need a plan. Kate, what's our stake count?'

She flipped the pad open and looked at me expectantly.

I shook my head. 'That's not what I meant. Ashton's got an army. Kevin and I can't even get in without an invitation, despite his impulsive freak-out there. *We* can't –'

'Fine, stay!' Evie slapped the pad shut, grouchy suddenly. '*I'll* stop Ashton and get Mom back.'

She tried to glare at me, but I could see the fear in her gold-shimmering eyes. Kevin was already between her and the door.

'Red, Kate's right. I did freak out, obviously. If you hadn't stopped me I would literally be barbecued geek right now.' He laughed, trying to placate her I think. She just kept glaring. 'And I get it. Your rage-impulses run deep too, but Kate and I can't go in uninvited. And you going alone would be –'

'Suicide?' she said. 'Yeah, maybe. But what's the alternative? You can't run or Ashton will destroy Brightside. And you can't stay without him torching the house. So it's a choice between me, or me plus you guys plus anyone who comes to put out the burning building and walks straight into a gang of killer jock-monsters.'

I felt a sick jolt.

She was right. The first responders would be like moths to an actual monster-filled flame. We couldn't let that happen. But I couldn't let her go either.

'We'll think of something,' I said.

Or lied. Again. Evie's eyes blackened around the edges. 'Really? Because you said that last time, now you're telling me you two can't even get in. And we are *not* doing nothing! Mom's up there, so –'

231

'What, um, what if I got Kate and Kevin in?'

The room went quiet.

We all turned to look at Felix – sitting there all tiny and terrified, chewing anxiously at his thumbnail.

Kevin stepped forward, towering over him. 'What?'

Felix gulped. 'I … I joined the horde, right? I know they were planning on killing me. And now I'm human again – but they never disowned me. Their base is still technically my home. So I could invite guests, couldn't I?'

'Sure,' sneered Kevin. 'Or set us up again. Girls, I've decided, let's kill him.'

He was joking. Revelling in his bad-cop role, because I couldn't seem to help playing good cop. I think. I hoped.

But Felix was nodding. 'Fine! But do it in style, eh? Ashton's got guards all around the front of the house. If you're really doing this, you need someone to go in first and draw them off.' He held his hand up, then pointed to himself.

Evie laughed. 'You? Dude, no offence – or loads of offence, whatever – but you're not exactly slayer material. You wouldn't last five minutes.'

'So?' said Felix. 'All I have to do is distract them long enough to get you in, give you a shot at Ashton. He's turned every vampire in town, except Kate. And Kevin turned her. So, take Ashton out and – BOOM! Everyone's human again.'

He grinned, and my stomach gave a weird twist – half-ill, half-excited.

Felix was right. If we could get to Ashton, we didn't have to worry about destroying the horde. They'd all just be people again. So would I.

'But you'll be dead,' I said.

'I already should be,' he said. 'Look, you're not the only one Evie saved last night. My heart started beating the moment she took out Donnie. Now I'm all de-vamped, with this bonus life I don't deserve and don't particularly want. So let's trade it in for a dead Ashton, restore balance to the force, or whatever. It'll be fun.' He laughed,

No-one else did, unless you counted Kevin's derisive snort.

'So, you're what? Volunteering as tribute?' he said. 'Sacrificing yourself for us, to atone for your lousy misdeeds? We're supposed to buy that?'

Felix hesitated, then shook his head.

'No,' he said. 'I wish this *was* just about you, Kate. But they killed Cass. They've ripped my town apart. They *tortured* me! I'm not strong enough to dust Ashton myself, but the three of you together really could.'

His chin quivered, like he might burst into tears again. I was half-tempted to give his arm a reassuring squeeze. Instead, Kevin leaned over – and yanked him off his feet, shoving him against the wall so hard I heard his head go clunk.

'Kevin!' I yelped.

He didn't even glance at me, just snarled straight into Felix's face: 'I'm going to say this once, creep. I've had two real friends my entire life, and you got one killed and made the other one watch. So let me be really clear: if I even suspect you're putting anyone in this house in danger, you'll see exactly why Ashton wants me leading his psycho-army. Got it?'

Felix nodded, and Kevin dropped him to the ground.

'Cool.' He took the notebook from Evie and flipped it open, smiling. 'Then how about we start plotting your imminent demise, eh?'

* * *

'OK, one more time,' said Evie. 'We swoop in, find Ashton in the "throne room". BOOM! Dust. BAM! Human –' She pointed to me and Kevin. 'Town? SAVED! We find Mom, we hug, we kiss. Everyone's a hero, credits roll! Did I miss anything?'

'Yeah, the bit where you're not coming,' I said.

'Nah, that didn't test well in the previews. Sorry, Kate.' Evie smiled, too brightly, then turned back to the map Felix had drawn of Ashton's 'evil lair'.

It wasn't the graveyard – Ashton was too self-aware for that. Instead, they'd taken over a huge farmhouse a few miles past the crypts, where he mostly hung out in the huge base-ment bar he called his throne room.

'Ooh, do they have bottles of spirits?' asked Evie. 'We could make Molotov coc– wait, no. We're flammable too, I forgot. Never mind.'

'Evie, this isn't a game!' I said.

'No, really? I watched you die. I know what the stakes are. Heh! Stakes.' She paused, waiting for me to laugh. When I didn't, she continued: 'Speaking of which, what *does* happen once Ashton's dead? And it's just you and Kevin in a house of giant mass-murdering humans?'

'Well –' I started, then stopped.

I knew what she was getting at, and she was right. Felix had seen Brightside's missing giants gleefully comparing kill-counts and laughing at their victims' pleas. Ashton hadn't had time to break them like he had Kevin; he'd just cherry-picked the worst he could find and weaponised them.

Guys like that would hardly *love* us de-vamping them – and my fourteen years of judo could only do so much against an angry mob. Plus, everything Kevin knew about fighting he'd learned while basically invulnerable.

'We'll figure it out,' I said.

Evie laughed, like she'd won. 'This *is* us figuring it out – and I have. You need a monster body guard – case closed.'

'No!' There was another way, there had to be. And then it hit me. 'The tranqs!'

Evie raised an eyebrow. 'The tranqs that knocked that one guy out for three seconds and need to be reloaded constantly? What about them?'

She was still smiling triumphantly, but I was ahead of her now.

'We can modify them,' I said. 'Add something vampire-specific like –'

'Holy water!' interrupted Kevin. 'That's basically liquid sunshine, a dartful burning through your veins would be ...' He shuddered, gleefully. 'Let's do it.'

He was way too excited by this. Still, I wasn't objecting. We had the perfect alternative to throwing Evie into a house packed with monsters. I was happy too.

'OK,' I said, 'holy-water-and-sedative darts. Nice non-lethal cocktail to disable them before we kill Ashton and knock them out afterwards. No Evie required.'

There was an awkward silence. Or at least, Kevin seemed awkward.

Evie looked smug. 'You mean, the elephant tranquilliser? Is that not a teensy bit lethal to humans?'

I pulled my phone out and Googled quickly.

'I'm sure there's a safe minimum,' said Felix confidently, before I groaned. 'Or ... not?'

I showed them my screen: *Not for human use. Sudden death may occur even in cases of accidental contact or inhalation.*

'YES!' Evie didn't quite happy-dance at the validation, but she was close. 'I'm totally coming, and if any one of you tries to tranq me, I'll just follow you when I wake up. Alone. In the dark. Is that safer?'

She fixed me with a glare of badass determination.

I sighed. 'Fine. But stay with me and Kevin,' I said. 'I don't want you alone when the horde catches your scent.'

Evie gave a little victory-squeal. Kevin nudged me and leaned in.

'Are you sure we're not OK with a little smidge of murder?' he asked, like he'd just suggested a second helping of ice-cream.

I responded with my best Mom-look-and-slow-head-shake combo. 'No killing, unless we have to.'

Kevin pouted. 'Spoilsport.'

'Hey, at least burning-torture darts still sound like fun?' said Evie, trying to cheer him up. 'Might even give Felix a shot at surviving, eh?'

She tried to make it sound offhand, but it wasn't. Felix's mouth pursed awkwardly as he shook his head. 'I appreciate the thought, Madam Secretary. But I'd never reload fast enough to escape.'

'Oh. Right.' Evie's face fell. 'Wow, you really are useless. We don't need that kind of liability. Maybe –'

'You need me,' said Felix quietly. 'And it's fine. Stop worrying about me.'

'I'm not,' lied Evie. 'I don't care. I just –'

She paused, mid-thought, as her eyes lit up and she jumped to her feet, shoving her hand into her sweater pocket to yank out what was left of Cass's chocolate seeds.

'Hey! Wanna see a magic trick?' She dumped the seeds onto the coffee table and yelled: 'SHAZAM!'

My body twitched. *So many seeds. But how many? Forty, fifty, a hundred?*

Without warning, I was down on my knees beside Kevin, both of us scooping up seeds one at a time, dropping them into our hands and – *onetwothreefourfive* ... My head buzzed. I felt itchy. Nothing else mattered.

But still, somewhere outside the counting, I heard Evie trying to suppress her relief.

'Looks like Cass just bought you some reload time, dude.'

32. Evie

Kevin hadn't been wrong about Katie's transition-day crash. By dinnertime, I had to keep nudging her awake so she could finish her blood.

'Just a few more gulps,' said Chris. 'You don't want to go to bed hungry.'

Katie drained her mug, then slumped onto the table and snored.

Felix wasn't far behind. He struggled to stay conscious as we convinced Chris he should stay a few days to 'process his trauma', then zonked on the sofa the moment she agreed.

'Like a tiny, treacherous goth cherub,' mused Kevin, as he carried him to the fold-out by Katie's bed. 'I still can't believe we're trusting him.'

'Well,' I said. 'If he gets us all killed, at least you can say "I told you so"?'

Kevin grinned humourlessly. 'Yeah. Silver linings, eh?'

We tucked them in, then sat out in the hallway. The air was thick with nervous tension.

'Are you scared?' I asked.

'Of course I am,' said Kevin.

'Of dying?'

He hesitated, then shook his head. 'If we don't beat Ashton, dying's the best-case scenario. I'm more scared what he'd do if he decides to keep us alive.'

'Or what you'd do, in the blood-smelling den?'

Kevin nodded. I took his hand. 'You'll have us, remember? We like you too much to lose you to the dark side.'

'Oh, so you *do* still like me?' Kevin smiled, and my tummy flipped.

But I managed a casual shrug. 'Well, I'm not actively killing you, am I?'

Our gazes locked.

Suddenly my heart seemed super-loud. We were sitting really close together. Had we always been this close? Had I moved? Or had he?

Kevin chewed his lip nervously and – wait, crap, I was staring at his mouth. Eyes back up, Evie. Eyes back up! I looked up, at exactly the same time Kevin did. I swear we'd moved closer again.

He leaned in slightly, and then a bit more and – 'OUCH!'

Kevin jumped back, flustered, as I rubbed my gums. OK, not quite what I'd expected, given our last almost-kiss. But whatever.

'S-sorry!' He stammered. 'I didn't mean to ...'

'That's all right. It was both of us.'

I mean, mostly him, teeth-punching me in the mouth. But it didn't matter. The pain was starting to fade. And Kevin's split lip was already healed.

'Can I try again?' he asked.

'I'd like that,' I said.

And then his lips were on mine and it was ... Well, there was no teeth-clashing this time, at least. But there *was* an awkward mashing motion.

I tried kissing him back, but his mouth was so tense. And he was holding me so tight, I swear he was worried I might run off. I pushed away, gasping for breath.

Kevin gave a hopeful smile. 'Better?'

'Seriously?' *Crap!* I'd said that out loud.

Kevin groaned. 'Oh God! I'm a terrible kisser.'

'What? No, Kevin!' I reached for his hand again, but he was already on his feet, pacing embarrassedly.

'I'm sorry, Red. I just – I think I've spent so long reading about this stuff, imagining it and figuring I'd never get to do it. And then I met you and ...'

He stopped, tried to look at me and couldn't even do that. 'You're so beautiful. And fun and terrifying. And then I hear your heart when you look at me, and this shouldn't be real! You know? *You* shouldn't be real. You're too ...'

He stopped. He didn't have much choice, because I'd jumped to my feet and pressed my lips to his, mid-sentence. His entire body froze.

I pulled back. 'Dude, stop thinking.'

'I have stopped talking.'

'I said "thinking". I'll never measure up to thirty-five years in your sixteen-year-old brain. So shut it off and kiss me.'

His heart couldn't pound, but mine was loud enough for both of us as I stretched up to brush my lips against his. A tiny, light touch. But it made him smile, so I did it again, a little longer this time. And then longer again, and –

His lips moved on mine, softly, sending tiny tingles shooting through my body. He wrapped his arms around me, lifting me off my feet, and those tingles became one big rush as the kiss deepened. We toppled back against the wall. Our teeth clanked, but we just giggled.

'Sorry,' I said. 'That was my –'

'Ssssh,' said Kevin. 'No thinking, just kissing, remember?'

So I shut my brain off too, and lost myself in the softness of Kevin's lips and our … fourth? fifth kiss, I guess? Whatever. It was the perfect first kiss.

*   *   *

'Can I at least pretend I'm helping?' whispered Felix.

'Fine.' I let him grab the other end of the seed-sack and fake-help me lug it from The Health Story to Katie's car. 'Freakin' male ego.'

We were shopping together by default – I couldn't drive, Kevin and Kate would actually spontaneously combust, and apparently I'd draw too much attention just zipping back and forth with supplies by myself. So Felix it was.

My diminutive chauffeur was wrapped up like a bad Winter Soldier cos-play: scarf over his nose, hood yanked down almost to his eyes, shaggy dark hair covering the rest of his face. Luckily, the temperature was below zero so everyone else was similarly bundled up. But he still looked like an idiot.

'OK, poppyseeds – check!' He closed the trunk, then leaned against it to cross 'seeds' off the list. We'd gotten most of it: running shoes, holy water and stake-making materials.

The only thing left was – 'Pockets? Just … pockets?'

'Preferably with clothes attached,' said Felix. 'But yes. Let's go.'

We'd just left Ray's parking lot when –

'Say that again!'

Felix ducked back behind Ray's side wall, peering out in time to catch the shouter – a thirty-something-year-old woman with masses of dark curls and a huge bump under her bright-green maternity coat – yanking her scarf down and yelling: 'To my face this time, you self-righteous bitch!'

'Ooh, I like her,' I said.

'That's Heather,' whispered Felix. 'My stepmom.'

The Elsa-looking blonde in front of Heather smirked. 'Oh, sweetie. Calm down. That kind of stress is bad for the babies, and Lord knows they've enough going against them, between Addams Family reject parents and a serial-killing big bro– *OW!*'

The crowd that had gathered gasped. Heather scowled, rubbing her fist where she'd made contact with Ice Queen's nose. Her fleecy gloves had minimised the damage, but the rage was real.

'Shut up!' snapped Heather. 'You do *not* talk about Felix like that. Any of you.'

'Or what?' said Ice Queen. 'You'll rip us apart too? No, wait. If we say his name in front of a mirror three times, will he show up and stab us with a sharpened dice?'

A couple of the crowd sniggered. Heather glared at them.

'My son is missing,' she said. 'Sage Williams and Cass McCormack are dead. But sure, a grown woman made a second-rate Candyman joke, so laugh it up, assholes! Felix

242

is worth more than anyone here. And *you*, Summer Wilson. You can –'

The next words out of her mouth were not ones she'd be using around her babies, I'm pretty sure. But it must've felt good. She stormed off, leaving Summer and the rest of the town in scandalised silence.

'Well,' said Summer finally. 'Someone needs to take a prenatal chill-pill, eh?'

A few more of the crowd laughed, still buzzing from the drama. The rest dissipated off on their own errands. Beside me, Felix's breath sounded shaky.

My heart yanked so hard I'd swear there was a tiny inner Kate tugging its strings. I had a sudden urge to hug him, and I hated it. 'Felix –'

'It's fine,' he said. 'Let's go.'

It wasn't fine. I didn't feel fine. I felt ill.

Felix was sneaking around a town that hated him, buying supplies so he could risk his life saving them, while they mocked him to his stepmom's face.

'You know you don't have to do this, right?' I said. 'Any of it. You could just go home now. To your folks and your little nearly-siblings, we won't blame you.'

'I'd blame me,' said Felix. 'Look, I know what my chances are, even with the seeds, but – you've seen what I still have to lose. And the plan doesn't work without me. So I *do* have to do it. But it's OK, Evie. I'm OK with this.'

I felt a strange wobble. Inner Kate was having a meltdown in my chest. Felix must have read that in my face, because he pulled his scarf down to smile, before taking out his wallet and handing me twenty bucks.

'Here,' he said. 'I never did buy you that milkshake, Madam Secretary. So how about you grab us two to go? We can sit in the car, enjoy the healing power of ice-cream – and then go buy pockets, eh?'

I wanted to say I should treat him. He was about to die, so the least I could do was buy him a shake. But then he'd just point out twenty bucks is useless to a dead dude, and I didn't want to hear that out loud. So I said, 'Ooh, yeah! Chocolate brownie swirl, here I come,' and hoped he'd know what I meant.

I feel like he did.

33. Kate

Evie was still out with Felix.

Which was fine. I trusted Felix.

Sure, last time I'd been out with him he'd gotten me murdered, but that was two days ago. This was fine. Totally fine.

'Ow, Kate!'

'Sorry.' I pulled my hand from around Kevin's neck. 'You all right?'

'Peachy! Just focus, OK? Chris'll be pissed if you decapitate me.' He massaged his throat. 'Actually, let's leave the fighting. Show me a back-flip over the sofa.'

'From here?' We were half a room away.

'You're right, we're too close. Try it from the piano.'

It was weird, adjusting to these new 'super-powers'. I'd always been sporty, obviously (it was that or get eaten), and my judo 'mini-heroes' had been fan-childing over my 'Spider-man skills' for years: back-flips, front-flips, side-flips, all the flips. But that was in a human way. And I was not human any more.

245

I'd just front-flipped across the room, rebounded off the wall and done a triple-somersault to land Thor-style on the sofa when my phone buzzed with a text.

Kevin picked it up, in case it was Evie.

'It's Zoe, again,' he said. 'Are you sure you don't want to answer? That's her fifth text this afternoon.'

And possibly zillionth since we'd left Brightside.

I had replied at first, vaguely, trying to turn the subject around to school or movies or our mutual Hemsworth crushes. But Zoe always wanted to get back to me: Where was I? What was I up to? When could she see me again? *Where was I?*

Any other time, I would have been downright giddy over all the attention. Now, it felt like taking a salt-bath with my skin peeled off. I'd have preferred that, actually. Physical pain I could manage.

'I'll reply tomorrow,' I told Kevin. 'Assuming I'm human, and alive.'

Right now she was just one more reminder that my life sucked.

Kevin didn't quite manage to hide the disapproval in his face.

'What?' I said.

'Nothing.'

'It's obviously not nothing!'

'It's just …' said Kevin. *Yep, here we go.* 'I get you wanting to ignore her right now. I do. But … from *her* point of view, you're this smart beautiful badass she finally worked up the courage to ask out. And you immediately slammed the door, skipped town and started ghosting her.'

I should never even have told him about Zoe, but he'd seen my face when her first text arrived today. And he was a surprisingly good listener. He was just so invested now – shipping us, like we were some star-crossed couple in one of his books.

'I'm not ghosting her,' I said. 'I just haven't texted back for a couple of days.'

'Well, either way, she's freaking out. Look!'

He held my phone out, so I could read the last few texts.

My stomach dropped. He was right. In the two days since I'd stopped replying, Zoe's messages had gone from chatty and curious to downright desperate. The four I'd missed this afternoon were:

Why aren't you talking to me?

Did I do something wrong?

KATE! WHERE DID YOU GO? ARE YOU OK?

Whatever I did, I'm sorry. Please text back.

And her latest one was just a full line of crying emojis.

My heart stabbed. 'She can't possibly miss me this much!'

'As much as you miss her, you mean?' Kevin smiled, weirdly non-sarcastic, and an annoying flush of affection warmed my chest.

I was not comfortable with this level of sincerity between us. 'All right, fine! I'll text back, and then we're never talking about my feelings again, got it?'

'Deal!' Kevin pushed the phone into my hand.

I wrote something vague about 'family stuff' and hit 'send'. Then, as an afterthought, I added that photo of me, Cass and Felix outside 'Ray's Diner, Brightside, est. 1980 with a joke about my chatterbox cousins and bad take-out.

'All right, done! Now, can you please stop fanboying over my life, and –'

My phone buzzed. Zoe had replied already. My heart prepared to flip, but all she said was:

Exactly what I needed. Thanks.

'Everything OK?' asked Kevin. 'What did she say?'

'Um, nothing,' I said. 'It's fine. She just seems a bit …'

A bit what, I wasn't sure, so I pulled a face and hoped that said enough.

'Maybe she's kinda mad?' said Kevin. 'After two days of silence?'

'Yeah, maybe.'

Mad was all right. I'd take mad. Mad meant she cared.

I just couldn't shake the feeling it might be something worse.

*   *   *

Evie and Felix returned, and we smuggled supplies past Chris, up to our room to prep. But after the third time spilling poppy-seeds everywhere (because some of us kept trying to count them as others measured them into smaller bags), Kevin and I had to retreat to room 3, leaving Evie and Felix alone.

Which was fine. Obviously. Still.

Evie's giggle carried through the wall, and it took all my impulse control not to jab myself with a freshly filled dart as I spiked the lid back on.

'You OK?' asked Kevin. 'I thought you trusted him.'

'I do. I think.' Did I?

Maybe it was residual ill-ease from Zoe's odd texts or maybe it was Felix, but ... 'Something just feels off,' I said.

'I get that,' said Kevin. 'Like, he's funny now? Didn't he just betray us? Ow!'

He dropped his knife, along with the stake he'd been whittling, then sucked the blood off his thumb and glared towards their room, eyes smouldering like he might psychically burn a hole through the wall. He looked ... Not angry – jealous? Oh dear.

'Kevin, we need to talk.'

'Uh-huh.' He wasn't listening. He was too busy glaring.

'Look,' I said anyway. 'I get that we're stuck, biologically. Our frontal cortices are basically frozen in time. You are absolutely sixteen, but you've done a lot and –'

'They've stopped laughing!' Kevin half-smiled, still ignoring me.

'Kevin, I'm trying to –'

'Dude, you OK?' Evie's voice drifted out of room 4 as the door opened.

'Yeah, I just need a sec.' Felix sniffled.

The door clicked shut, and his footsteps passed our room, then stopped. I heard a faint dial-tone, before a hushed: 'Um, hey. How's it going up there?'

Kevin and I were up and by the door before Felix started his next sentence:

'So, we're doing it. Tonight. I've got this kickass utility vest with, like, thirty pockets. And holy water darts, and – poppyseeds? Apparently that's a thing?'

Felix's voice was shaking. I think he was crying. But he was also revealing our plan. My eyes stung as I edged the door open.

Felix continued: 'It's nearly dark. We'll leave soon. Please be waiting for me –'

'Oops!' Kevin grabbed the phone and tossed it down the hall.

I shoved Felix against the wall. 'Who was that?'

'What? I ... no-one!' Felix stammered, sniffling again.

Up close, he was a treacherous mess of red puffy eyes and runny nose – and my new vampire impulses were pounding down hard on the side of violence.

'Katie, stop!' Evie raced up, Felix's phone in her hand. 'Put him down!'

'What, like, over the balcony?' I looked at Kevin. 'Whaddya think?'

'I think it's a long drop for a snivelling wimp,' said Kevin. 'Do it!'

'STOP!' Evie yanked Felix free, then pushed him behind her. 'I know you're bluffing, but Felix didn't do anything. Look!' She held his phone out. The call was still going, the timer ticking away – under Cass's name.

'That could be anyone's number with her name,' said Kevin.

'All right. Let's check.' Evie hung up and called back. It went straight through to voicemail. 'Hey, you've reached Cass. Or, I guess, you haven't! Leave a message at the beep. Or text like a normal person, Dad. I love ya, bye!'

My stomach knotted so hard I wanted to vomit.

He'd just wanted to hear her voice. Talk to her again, like Mom did with recordings of Dad. Like I did sometimes.

'Felix –' I started

'It's OK,' he said.

'No, it's not. I'm sorry. I ...'

'Don't apologise,' he said. 'I get it.'

Evie glared past me to Kevin.

'What?' he said. 'You heard him, no apology!'

'You were gonna throw him down the stairs!' cried Evie.

'We were messing.' Kevin laughed. 'You know Kate wouldn't – wait, you wouldn't have. Right?'

'Right.' *I think.*

'See? All good.' Kevin flashed a cheeky grin. Evie's scowl didn't budge.

'Evie, it's OK,' said Felix. 'I haven't earned anyone's trust here, and Kevin's just looking out for his friends. It's a good thing.'

Poor Felix. He hadn't done anything wrong this time, but he still looked guilty as he took his phone and headed to his room.

He turned back when he reached the door. 'For what it's worth, though, I'm your friend too. You don't have to be mine, that's fine. But I'm all in. I promise.'

Evie glared at me and Kevin for a moment, then turned to chase after Felix.

'Are we terrible people?' I asked.

'Well, you're not,' said Kevin. 'He's right, we had no reason to trust him. And the way he was talking? What were we supposed to think?'

'I don't know! But maybe checking caller ID should have been our first move? Before death threats?'

Felix's muffled sobs drifted through the door. I don't care what Kevin said: I was the worst person ever.

'I'm gonna have to be nice to him now, aren't I?' sighed Kevin.

'I mean, he's probably going to die tonight,' I said. 'So ...'

'So, not for long?'

'I was going to say, "So, yes".'

'Oh.' Kevin winced. 'Yeah, makes more sense. OK, I can fake nice.'

*   *   *

He could, actually. Disconcertingly well.

He apologised nicely. He brought everyone cookies and hot chocolate nicely. He even suggested a quick self-defence lesson for Felix, while he whipped up another pizza from scratch (making a big deal of 'doing it properly' this time, because apparently Felix deserved better than the yeast-free, 'no rise' crust we'd made during impulse training).

I'd have sworn he actually liked him, if I didn't know better.

None of us were especially hungry, come dinnertime, but we sat together anyway like a big, weird family – waiting for the sleeping pills Kevin had slipped into Chris's Coke to take effect. (He'd gotten them from Chris's friend Jim 'in case of emergencies' and this definitely qualified, because she would absolutely follow us otherwise.)

Part of me hoped the pills wouldn't work, so we couldn't do this. But finally Chris's eyes drooped shut. Kevin carried her gently to her room – then blurred back down to the rest of us.

'All righty guys,' he said. 'Monster time!'

34. Evie

The vampire mustiness hit the second we stepped outside.

'Felix,' I hissed. 'Get back in –'

Too late. Something blurred out of the dark and grabbed him from behind.

'So this is where the runt's been hiding, eh?'

The guy holding Felix was all bulk, biceps bulging through the bloodstained combat jacket he'd clearly stolen from someone two sizes smaller than him.

I raised my stake, and Bulk laughed. 'I wouldn't, mutt. Unless you think your friends there can handle all my buddies.'

I glanced around. *Crap!* Four more vampires, lurking by the gate. Kevin could handle them, but what about Kate? It would only take one, pulling puppy-dog eyes while Kevin was occupied ... Plus, I'd have to be really sure I could get to Felix before Bulk ripped his throat out. I wasn't.

Kevin dropped his stake, and Kate stepped back and gripped my hand.

Well, that was a short rebellion.

'Fine.' I threw my stake down too. 'Now, let him go.'

Bulk's fangs snapped down. 'Nah, I need a snack!'

Felix whimpered – before stamping hard on Bulk's toes, smashing his fist back into the evil vamp's nads like Kate had shown him, and shoving him into the guesthouse.

Bulk gripped his head and shrieked.

I almost cheered, but then my head smashed against the path, and a vampire leapt on top of me, crushing the air out of my lungs

In the distance, I heard Felix yell, 'Hey, count these!' followed by a pitter-patter of seeds, so he was clearly keeping Bulk occupied. And a blood-curdling scream to my right said Kevin and Kate were busy too.

Meanwhile, my vampire's glowing eyes were on my neck, and I couldn't move under his giant mass. *FudgeFudgeFudge!*

He jerked my head to one side, teeth grazing my jugular – before vanishing backwards off me! I jumped up as Kate loaded her dart gun – and shot him.

The holy water hit instantly. His eyes bulged as he shrieked, foaming at the mouth.

'So that works,' I said.

'Yep!' Kate nodded towards another vampire, the owner of that blood-curdling scream, still howling as he flailed in the snow.

Over by the gate, Kevin had just head-butted one vampire, then slammed another onto the stake-shaped spikes of their picket fence. And Felix was in the guesthouse with Bulk, who'd collapsed, sobbing, as he tried desperately to count seeds through the brain-burning torture of being somewhere he wasn't invited.

'I'm gonna put him out of his misery,' I said.

'Hey! No killing,' said Kate.

'Unless we have to!' yelled Kevin, stomping on someone's chest. 'And we do. Check by the gate.'

Kate blurred off, so I raced into the guesthouse and flung Bulk against the reception desk. He snarled, then whimpered and tried to thrash his way back to the seeds, even as I gripped his head in my claws and twisted. I swear he looked relieved, right before he exploded. Felix gulped as I brushed myself off.

'I think you're scarier than them,' he said.

'Thanks.' I grinned. 'Come on, it's quiet out there, let's go.'

It *was* quiet as we re-joined Kevin and Kate.

The air was thick with red dust, and the snow was scattered with the clothes of now-exploded horde members. Kevin tucked his stake away, but Katie's fist was still clenched around hers. I think she was shaking.

'There's gas cans by the gate,' she muttered. 'They were gonna burn the place down. Chris is inside. If we'd left them, and the holy water had worn off ...'

'I know,' I said. 'Look, if this is too much –'

'I'm fine!' she snapped, before taking a deep breath and straightening up. 'I just wasn't ready yet, that's all. You're not going without me!'

She slipped the stake back into her waistband, forced a badass scowl, then vanished. A moment later, I heard her car rev in the parking lot.

'Come on, slowpokes!' she yelled. 'Let's go storm this castle!'

* * *

The gate to Ashton's base wasn't even closed, never mind locked.

Felix's heart pounded as we approached. Mine broke a little. He was so tiny and powerless. And, sure, we had bagloads of seeds waiting for him to toss out the car window once he made it back. It was just that he had to make it back first.

We couldn't talk – they'd hear us – so I decided, screw it, and pulled Felix into a giant hug instead. He seemed surprised, then relaxed. Kevin leaned over and punched him gently(ish) on the arm, before joining in the group hug.

Felix pulled back and stretched his hand out awkwardly to Kate – who yanked him into a proper embrace, and kissed him on the cheek. He pulled away, laughing silently, like we were all nuts, then turned to the gate, gulped and walked through.

My stomach knotted up. Waves of nervous energy pulsed through my body. My head was white-hot pin-prickly.

OK, calm down, I thought. *Breathe in. And. Out. In. And –*

There was an agonised scream from the garden. And then two.

My body pulsed. Fido was begging to play, but we'd be in there soon – fighting vampires, finding Mom, killing Batman. So I focused that energy into my muscles, and felt them burn with power.

Kate's phone lit up. She answered, wordlessly.

'Front's clear.' Felix sounded terrified. 'Kate, Kevin – come on in.'

'Invitation accepted, thank –'

'Oh, frak! Bye.'

'What? Felix?' The line went dead. 'FELIX?'

As if someone had given the order, the three of us turned and burst through the front gate at once. I could smell Felix on the wind. It took all my focus not to race off to help him. Ashton was stronger than Kevin; Kevin needed us with him.

That's what Felix wanted, I reminded myself

The front door was wide open, and the hallway was empty. Judging by the numbers being yelled from the garden, we had Felix and his seeds to thank for that. And we had Ashton's army to thank for the blood stench inside. It turned my stomach – and made Kevin's and Kate's grumble hungrily.

'Dude!' I whispered.

But then some extra-strength blond blur appeared out of nowhere and smashed me into the wall. So that changed *that* subject.

'You had a wolf on your tail!' he told Kevin – then paused, noticing Kate. 'Well, you're new.'

His leer made my skin crawl.

'Thought Ashton said "bros only",' added his dark-haired Goliath of a friend.

'Yeah.' Katie tilted her head, all flirty. 'But I can be *very* convincing.'

Groooss.

She moved closer. Goliath laughed. 'How old are you, sweetheart?'

'As old as I'm gonna get.' Kate put her hand on Goliath's bicep, and winked at Blondie. 'How 'bout my friend takes

Ashton his present, and you guys show me the ropes here? You look like you'd know your way around.'

Goliath chuckled again, far too busy checking Kate out to notice her slipping one hand behind her back as she got nearer.

But Blondie did. 'Brett, she's got –'

I drove my fist through his chest and yanked out his heart. He didn't explode. Oh!

Goliath's eyes blazed. He grabbed Katie's wrists, and pulled her close.

'Bi–' he started, before erupting into innards.

Kevin grinned, wiping his stake on his shirt before wheeling around to knock Blondie off me and toss me the stake.

I jammed it through the heart in my hand, and Blondie went BOOM!

'Dude, we have tranqs, remember?' said Kate, shaking off the monster dust.

'I had temporary amnesia?' Kevin grinned impishly. Which charmed me, but not Kate. 'What? I *had* to. No-one talks to my progeny like that.'

'Ew.' Kate shuddered. 'Well, no more unnecessary killing, OK?'

'Yeah, yeah, yeah,' said Kevin. 'Jeez, it's like hunting with my mom. Now, let's get to that basement bar before –'

'Anyone else smell wolf?' said a voice from upstairs.

'That happens. Run!'

We did. I couldn't quite keep up with their vampy-blur-ring, but I wasn't too far behind. Unfortunately, neither was the pitter-patter of big scary murderer feet.

And they were getting closer. I reached the staircase, then stopped. 'You guys go ahead. I'll hold them off.'

'What?' Kate spun back on the middle step. 'No.'

'Katie, *go*. I'll be fine.' I pulled my dart gun from my pocket. 'Find Mom, kill Ashton, just –'

'Kill me? Well, that's rude.' There was a click, as a gun-safety unlatched right behind me, and something hard pressed against my skull.

'Hey, Kev!' added the voice. Ashton's voice.

Oh. Crap!

'KATE, STOP!' Kevin dived to tackle Katie as she blurred forward.

They hit the top step together, and Kevin held her back. She was snarling.

'Those are silver bullets,' he said. 'Pointed at your sister's head. If he pulls that trigger, she'll die. *For ever.*'

Kate's eyes burned furiously.

Ashton chuckled, and must've passed his pistol to a hench-moron, because suddenly two of them grabbed me. One shoved the gun against my temple, as Ashton wrenched my gun away and stepped forward to examine it.

I examined him too – and could not see the appeal. He was a generic mass of cheekbones, hero-jaw and dumb, shiny hair. The sort of handsome you wanted to punch repeatedly in the face. Especially when he flashed a huge, ding-y smile.

'Oooh, tranquillisers. Very useful here, eh, boys?' He laughed, then lobbed my gun out the front door as the ten-or-so brawn monsters chuckled mindlessly.

'Wow, you've really got the dumb henchmen tropes down, eh?' muttered Kate.

'Kate –' warned Kevin.

But Ashton cut him off, blurring to yank my sister forward, then fling her down so hard her head cracked against the fancy floor-tiles.

'KATIE!' My muscles pulsed furiously.

That gun barrel dug against my skin but, honestly, the urge to snap was so strong my fangs were already down when Kate caught my eye and mouthed: 'Don't!'

Ashton spotted her – and turned around, back to me. 'Ooh! I see. Little Pup's got control over those pearly whites?'

He kept hold of Kate, dragging her with him, over to me.

'Don't touch her!' Kate snapped. 'I swear to –'

'Oh, shush, you!' Ashton shoved her over to two random hench-idiots. One found the stake in her waistband and jammed the point against her chest, as Ashton dinged his stupid smile in my face.

'Hey, fellas,' he said, 'check out the fangs and crazy wolf-eyes? My boy found a pureborn! And he's brought her straight to us. How thoughtful, Kev!'

He flashed a gloaty grin. Kevin's eyes glowed.

'Aw,' laughed Ashton. 'You got a little crush, buddy? Or are you in it for the yummy scent, hmmm?'

He leaned in to sniff me, froze, then lifted his head and sniffed again – before blurring over and burying his face in Kate's neck.

'HEY!' I snapped.

But he'd already spun back around to face Kevin.

'You're a *dad*?' He sounded impressed. 'Fellas, I'm a grandpa! And my pretty little grand-daughter smells just like that wolf expert I brought home. Which is gonna be very useful. Thank you, Kev.'

He gave an obnoxious salute, and I would have been angrier about him trying to have any claim on Kate – but my brain had snagged on the words 'wolf expert'.

'Where is she?' I growled. 'Where's my mom?'

'*Your* mom?' Ashton eyebrows shot up. '*Two* Wilder monsters, and my boy brought 'em both to kill me? How disappointing!'

He leaned forward and inhaled – his mouth millimetres from my neck – making hungry sounds creepier than anything I'd seen in the movies. I tried not to wince – he'd like that – but his breath on my skin made me want to tear it all off.

'You wanna talk disappointing?' snapped Kevin.

And suddenly all eyes were on him. He was up off the stairs, jaw flexing angrily, stake out. Ashton stepped forward, one hand up to keep the brawn brigade back, and said: 'Buddy, drop the stake.'

Kevin glanced at the muscle-bound mob, and shook his head. 'Nah, I'm not that dumb.'

'Kev.' Ashton's eyes glowed, Katewards. 'Don't make me be the bad guy here.'

'Oh, *me* make *you* the bad guy?' Kevin laughed.

There was a snorted half-snigger from the back.

Ashton blurred forward, flattening Kevin with a punch, then grabbed the stake and flung it across the hall – into the chest of an Archie Andrews-esque vampire. Poor Archie looked so surprised before exploding. He wasn't even the one who'd laughed.

'All right, fine.' Kevin was back up, wiping the blood from his nose. 'You're a freaking saint. Happy? Look, I came to talk, but you're not making it easy. Someone gimme my stake back!'

He said it so confidently one of the hench-idiots actually moved. Ashton blurred, ripped the moron's head off, and was over with Kevin again before the gore even turned to dust.

'Apparently, I have to say this,' he announced. 'No-one arm the intruders, OK?'

Another time, I might've chuckled there. But right now I was busy replaying the other thing Kevin had just said. About wanting to talk to Ashton.

And so was Ashton, apparently. He turned back to Kevin. 'So, you popped by for a little catch-up, eh? With a pureborn wolf and mini-Sinéad baby-vamp? OK, go ahead, bud. I'm all ears.'

He put his arm around Kevin – who ducked out of the way, and shoved Ashton back into his crowd of henchmen. *YES!*

'Don't touch me,' Kevin snarled.

The hench-idiots 'Ooo'd'.

Ashton stood up and brushed himself off, smiling. 'Buddy, I love you. but I'll rip you in half if I have to.' His grin gained a psychotic edge. 'I'll breathe you into my lungs, then dust your daughter and drain every last drop from your delicious wolfgirl. If that's how you want it?'

'Of course it's not!' said Kevin.

I wasn't exactly in the position to be getting tummy-butterflies but, if I had been, Kevin's hero-scowl would have done it. Until he added, 'I was coming to make a deal, but your jerks tried to torch my house. With my sister inside.'

Wait, what?

Ashton's head tilted. 'A deal?'

'Kevin?' I said.

'Shut up, Red!' snapped Kevin, before turning back to Ashton. '*Nobody* hurts my sister. Understand? Tell them. Right now.'

My stomach twisted. *No!*

Kevin wouldn't make a deal with Ashton. He was stalling, right? He wouldn't actually sell us out to … save his sister?

Crap. I glanced at Kate. She'd do it – I knew she would. And I'd burn the world down to save *her*.

'OK!' Ashton held his hands up and stepped back. 'If that's all you're cranky about, sure. No-one touches the guesthouse lady!'

There was a murmur, until Ashton wheeled around – eyes blazing. Then it was a full-on cheer. Ashton raised an eyebrow at Kevin. 'Better?'

Kevin nodded. Ashton grinned. *No!*

'That's my boy!' Ashton flung his arm around Kevin, who didn't even flinch. 'Now, how about we head to my throne room and talk about this deal, eh?'

Kevin, no! I thought. *Please! Shove Ashton's arm away, or shoot me a wink or – do something,* anything, *so I know you're still ours.*

But he didn't. He just pulled his glasses off, folded them up neatly, then crushed them and tossed them aside.

'Let's go, Dad.'

35. Kate

The blood stench was everywhere.

And it only got stronger as Ashton's brute squad dragged us downstairs, to the fanciest room I'd ever seen: a proper bar on one end, a cinema-style screen at the other and full-length mirrors set in ornate panelling along every wall.

Ashton was checking himself out in one as a microwave whirred beside him, filling the room with even more warm-human-blood scent.

I wish I felt ill, but it just made me hungry.

Kevin, who was lounging by the bar looking right at home, smiled and waved as my stomach growled. 'Well, someone's peckish, eh?'

'Hey, you want some too, pumpkin?' Ashton grinned at me. 'Plenty to go around, a nice warm glass of Summer –' He paused, then looked to the crowd around for a prompt.

'Wilson,' said someone.

'Summer Wilson!' Ashton clapped his hands, then pointed like whoever said that was getting a prize. 'How could I forget? Yeesh, she strolled in, looking for her boyfriend and Would. Not. Shut up! "Nobody ghosts me, Stan. I'm calling your wife, Stan.'" He leaned towards the microwave: 'Good luck with that, ya crazy broad!'

His guys laughed, like good little minions, and Kevin joined in *so* easily.

'Asshole,' I muttered.

There was a blur, then a crunch, and Evie yelped in pain.

I snapped my head around to see her spit blood and a couple of teeth at Ashton, who was sucking some stray splats from his still-curled fist.

Every impulse urged me forward, even as the freak holding the stake jammed it harder against my chest.

Evie shook her head at me. Her teeth were already growing back – she was OK. But the scent of her blood set my stomach rumbling, alongside every other vampire's.

Ashton chuckled. 'Aw, is mini-Sinéad hungry for sister-blood?' He swiped his finger through a smear by Evie's mouth and held it out to me. 'Go ahead, Grandbaba. Delicious pureborn yumminess … no?'

He shrugged, sucked his finger clean and stepped back. My eyes burned.

'Leave her alone!' I snarled.

'Nah, that's no fun,' said Ashton. 'But behave and maybe I'll hurt her a little less?'

He picked something out of the puddle of Evie's blood and held it up gleefully. 'Hey, a canine tooth! Geddit? *Canine!* I'm hilarious. Here.' He caught my hand, forced Evie's tooth into my palm, then curled my fist around it. 'In case you need something to remember her by.'

Psychotic son of a bitch! It took all my self-restraint not to say that out loud. But I'm sure Ashton could tell I was thinking it. He patted me on the cheek, then headed back to the bar and popped the microwave open as it dinged.

'Mmm,' Kevin moaned, inhaling. 'Come to Papa.'

'Kevin, stop!' yelled Evie. 'This isn't you.'

Kevin flicked out of his blood-scent reverie with a chuckle, and zipped over to us. Or to Evie. He tucked a strand of hair behind her ear and smirked.

'It's Kev,' he said. 'And I hate to be *that guy*, but – this *is* me. I even warned ya, but I guess you really are that stupid, eh?'

Evie managed not to growl, but couldn't stop her eyes glowing.

'Aw, don't be angry, Red.' Kevin pouted. 'It's just a little double-cross. Not like I'm actively killin' ya. And, hey, without you I might still be at home, trying to cling to that old life, eh?' He stepped closer, until his face was almost touching hers. 'You got me fighting again. And killing. And drinking human blood.' He sucked his lips in, like he could still taste me on them. But his focus was all Evie. 'We made a good team, Little Red. But I'm not here to be *good*, am I?'

Evie's heart was racing.

I hated that everyone could hear it, because she didn't look scared. Her eyes fixed on Kevin's, darkening at the edges as they rippled gold. I could *see* her imagining a million ways to tell him to fudge off. But then Ashton clinked two tumblers onto the bar and Kevin blew Evie a kiss before blurring back to join him.

'Here ya go, little guy.' Ashton passed Kevin a freshly filled glass, then tapped his own against it. 'To family reunions, eh?'

He took a swig. Kevin didn't.

Ashton frowned. 'Something wrong with your drink, buddy?'

'I just want a clear head for this conversation,' said Kevin. 'I'm not your buddy. You tried to kill my sister. Twice. But I *am* your son, can't escape that. So, if I come back, I'm not your sidekick. I'm your partner.'

'Partner?' Ashton's eyes burned. 'Kev, these are *my* men.'

'OK, bye.' Kevin put his glass down, and front-flipped towards the door – in full show-off mode. Ashton sighed, and blurred in front of him.

'Where are you gonna go?' he said. 'I've got your friends, remember?'

Kevin shrugged. 'Keep 'em. Lock 'em up with your new mad scientist, wherever she is. I don't care.' He feigned trying to push past, even though we all knew Ashton wouldn't let that happen. Still, the senior psycho was gentle as he shoved him back.

'Buddy,' said Ashton, before correcting himself. 'Kev, you can't go. We found it.'

He pulled his phone out, tapped the screen a few times and held it up.

'See that red dot?' he said. 'That's the wolf camp. I've got a contact near by. He can lead us there. But I don't wanna do this without you.'

He held out his hand. Kevin hesitated.

'It's like we always planned,' said Ashton. 'It's fate, Kev.'

'Right, our glorious purpose.' Kev sighed. 'OK, but *if* I stay, it's for the camp. And you listen to my plan. Your goons

268

listen to me. And if anyone touches Chrissy, even if she tracks us down –'

'BOOM!' agreed Ashton. 'I promise. But *my* guys do what I tell them.' He paused, before adding, 'Course, I'll be telling them to listen to you. That's what second-in-command means, Kev.'

He nudged his hand toward Kevin, who hesitated – and then shook on it.

Ashton actually squealed with delight. 'That's my boy!' He blurred, grabbed the drinks, and brought them back to Kevin. 'Now, a toast. To the family business.'

'The family business.' Kevin lifted his glass.

'NO!' yelled Evie. 'Kevin, please. That's from a *person*!'

Kevin smirked. 'Meh, not like she's using it now, eh? Still, maybe you're right. I should pay my respects.' He held his drink up. 'To Summer Wilson, who used to visit my guest-house with Stan over there – who I did not know was married to someone else. Hey, Stan!' He waved across at a salt-and-pepper-haired monster in the corner, who waved back, reluctantly. 'You're a real dick, you know that?'

Kevin downed the blood, flung his glass across the room and zipped over to rip Stan's head off. He whooped giddily as the gore misted up, encompassing him.

Then he looked around. 'Oops. But we all hated Stan, right? You should've seen what he did to my shower-head.'

He front-flipped back to Ashton, landed unsteadily and sniggered.

'Sorry about that,' he stage-whispered. 'I think my tolerance has dropped.'

Ashton chuckled. 'Well, let's build it back up then.' He pointed to a familiar, moose-ish-looking vamp near the bar. 'Kyle! More Summer for your new boss!'

'I'm Linc,' said Moose.

Linc? I knew that name – better than Ashton, apparently, who scowled dangerously at the correction, until Linc muttered 'Never mind,' and jumped behind the bar to start pouring.

Kevin spun around, tripping over his feet as he faced us. 'You girls want in on this? It'll blow your tiny female minds, I promise.'

Tiny. Female. Minds. I bit my tongue and glared at him.

'Aw, judgy Katiekins.' Kevin ruffled my hair. 'Y'know, you'd be an awesome hunter if you just got past all that human moral squickiness. 'Cos you're *not* human.'

'But she's still good,' snapped Evie. 'Kevin, *you're* still –'

'Good!' laughed Kevin. 'Is that what I was? Letting evil stalk the streets, because using my abilities to stop bad humans is so wrong?'

'Murder's wrong,' I said.

'Yeah?' Kevin sneered. 'Better to run off and leave a monster in your basement, is it? How d'ya think that's worked out for your neighbours?'

I felt a cold jolt.

No. Zoe would have said something. *Zoe and her odd texts …*

Ashton snorted. 'Now, see, fellas? That's what I mean: the hypocrisy of humanity. Mini-Sinéad's so kind and sweet that she just doomed her entire street. Oh, that rhymes! Someone write it down. I'm a genius.'

He waited for the obligatory minion-fawning, then turned to Kevin.

'Listen, Kev,' he said. 'Great work, bringing the girls. Very nice gifts. But, you know, we can't keep them both, right? I mean, who's gonna be able to focus when ...'

Evie shifted uncomfortably as Ashton gazed at her.

Kevin's jaw set. 'We'll get less distractible guys, then. I'm not being sentimental here, Dad. We need them. Kate can fight and teach. She'll whip these idiots into shape if they keep the blood in their brains long enough. And Red's our Trojan wolf.'

'Trojan what now?' said Ashton.

Kevin grinned. 'Told you, I have a plan. Red'll do anything as long as we've got her mom and sister, right? So we send her to join the wolf camp, she invites us in – and *bam!* Bye-bye fleabags.'

Ashton stared at Kevin for a moment, then burst out in a huge proud smile.

'Hear that, fellas? Trojan wolf!' He hugged Kevin. 'My boy's a genius!'

There was a dissenting grunt from the corner. Ashton's face darkened, as he dropped Kevin to glare at a biker-looking vampire with a shaved head.

'Something up, Trent?'

Trent looked tempted to run. Instead, he stepped forward. 'You're buying this? We coulda had those girls two nights ago, if he hadn't killed everyone but me.'

Ashton's fist started to curl, but then someone else piped up.

'Yeah, he tried to kill *you*, three weeks ago. Now he's our boss?'

'He literally just killed Stan!'

The mutters of possible-mutiny continued, until Ashton blurred forward, ripped Trent's heart out and bit straight into the middle. Trent exploded.

'Anyone else questioning my judgement?' snapped Ashton.

The unconvincing silence was overwhelming. Ashton sighed. 'We can't dust 'em all, Kev. Gotta do something.'

'Like what?' said Kevin.

Ashton thought for a second. 'Ooh, I know!'

He grabbed Evie and pulled her towards Kevin. I couldn't help snarling. Ashton ignored it. 'Hey, scrappy – do that pureborn claw thing I've seen?'

Evie gulped, and did it. Ashton smiled. 'Great, now rip your arm open.'

'NO! Evie –'

Kevin's head snapped towards me. 'Do it, Red. Or I'll do far worse to your sister.'

Fury flooded Evie's face, and she locked her glowing gaze on Kevin as she gouged her claw into her arm and dragged back. Blood dripped along my baby sister's skin, landing in thick red splotches on the floor.

I felt ill. And ravenous.

'Smell that, guys?' Ashton smirked. 'Pureborn blood's like nothing you've ever tasted. The flavour, the buzz, the power ...'

'Power?' repeated Kevin.

'Power,' said Ashton. 'All that pureborn magic surging through your veins? It's one hell of a rush, and I reckon Little Red's got just enough inside to give my second-in-command the boost he needs. So, go ahead, Kev. She's all yours.'

Kevin stepped forward, hungrily, then stopped. 'What about the plan?'

'I love it!' said Ashton. 'And, look, Red's bleeding everywhere. A little excess mixed into Mommy dearest's tea, and we'll have a whole new wolf. Now, come on, Kev. Show these guys whose side you're on. Kill Little Red.'

All eyes were on Evie's arm, and the blood oozing from her cut. Her face was fearless, but her racing heart gave away her terror as Kevin ran a finger along her skin, scooping up as much blood as he could.

'Kevin!' I screamed. 'Do this and I swear to God, I'll …'

'What, exactly?' laughed Kevin. 'Katiekins, if there was anything you could do, you'd have done it by now.'

He smirked, keeping his eyes on me as he licked Evie's blood off his finger. The monsters holding me had to tighten their grip so hard my bones cracked, and that stake jabbed a bloody pin-prick in my shirt.

'You twisted, sick son of –'

'Ashton? I know.' Kevin turned back to Evie. 'Well, Red, it's been fun, but –'

'Yeah, yeah.' Evie's eyes flashed. 'Blah, blah, blah villain speech. I get it. Evil Kev can *BITE ME!*'

Kevin didn't even bother to quip back. He grabbed my sister, plunging his fangs into her neck. She gasped, then whimpered. I screamed, and kept screaming as I tried to struggle loose and rip his head off.

The guys holding me looked at Ashton questioningly.

'Ah, let her,' he said. 'It adds to the drama.'

Blood trailed from Kevin's mouth, down Evie's neck and splattered onto the ground, as she jolted in his grasp.

Her heart was still pounding, but she was starting to look groggy. Kevin kept drinking.

Kevin. The guy who'd saved my life and made me pizza.

Who'd comforted me when I sobbed, and jumped between me and Evie when I didn't have the control to keep her safe. Kevin, my friend, who definitely had a crush on my little sister. That Kevin.

He was going to kill her.

36. Evie

Everything coursed through me at once: the pain, the power ... my blood.

My body jerked, but couldn't change because all that white-hot energy was flowing out of me and into Kevin. Kate screamed my name, and a lot of other things I can't repeat here. My head was starting to spin, as Kevin's voice echoed around my mind:

'... can't believe you're real'

'... just a little double-cross'

'... you're magical'

'... we're in sync'

'... not like I'm actively killing ya!'

My hand found his, through the flailing, and I gripped weakly.

He won't, I told myself. *He's not ...* He couldn't be.

'Good boy, Kev,' laughed Ashton. 'Can you feel it? The magic? The power?'

Kevin nodded.

'The strength?' said Ashton.

Kevin nodded again, slipping his hands to my waist as he drew his fangs back. He pressed his lips against my neck, gently, before licking the blood from his mouth and looking up. 'Wolf on!'

'Hmmm?' said Ashton.

That was all the warning I got.

Kevin spun around, launching me towards Kate, then blurred into Ashton – fangs out. I caught Kate's stakeholder by the head, dragging him to the ground with me.

Wolf's so *on!*

Kate yanked free from her surprised captors, and smashed their heads together. I didn't see what happened next, but they exploded as I grabbed my guy's stake and slammed it into his chest.

Then I made the mistake of trying to stand up. 'Whoooa.'

Kate caught me, holy-watered the vampire running at us and pulled me behind an armchair. 'You OK?'

I nodded, but the room was spinning.

And Katie looked pissed off. 'Did you know?'

'What?'

'When I thought he was killing you! Did you *know*?'

Did I? 'No! I mean, I – I hoped, it felt like he was trying to tell me but –'

'You risked your life on a *feeling*?'

Seriously? She wanted to fight about this now?

'I risked my life 'cos they had you!' I snapped. 'Kate, we're in the middle of a monster brawl. Can we pick this up later? If we're still alive?'

Kate scowled, then nodded. Thank God!

I steadied myself, before peeking out from behind the chair. Kevin and Ashton were tearing strips off each other; fangs down, blood everywhere. The goons didn't seem to know if they should join in or not, but then Kevin smashed Ashton's face into a mirror, and the goons jumped to – *SMACK!*

My head had hit the wall. I'd barely had a chance to register the pain before someone's fangs were in my neck. Kate didn't even hesitate.

By the time my vision unblurred, she was forward-flipping through a spurt of gore to kick another vampire in the chest. Then my guy clutched his neck and collapsed, screaming. He'd been tranqed by ... someone?

I sank to the floor and looked towards the bar, where Felix was crouched, loading up one dart gun, with another in his lap. He flashed me a quick smile and tossed over the loaded gun before refilling the other for himself.

Warm gore splatted my face as Kate finished off her guy, turning to dust as she dropped to stake mine too. Her eyes were deep, furious amber, but she still remembered a quick 'Thanks' for Felix before turning to me and snapping: 'Stay down!'

Yeah, right.

She vanished over the armchair. I tried to follow but wound up wobbling instead. Felix raced over to help me up, holy-ing a nearby vampire as he did.

He took the loaded gun back, gave me his and a spare dart, and spun to shoot that Linc idiot, who was reaching for Ashton's gun at the bar.

'You're a good shot,' I whispered.

'I play a lot of computer games,' he said. 'You all right?'

'Totally.' Well, weak and decidedly *un*super, but I could stand, walk-ish and aim (hopefully). What else did I need?

Despite what Kate wanted, there was no safe place for a delicious-smelling wolf to hide in a roomful of hungry vampires, so we didn't try. Instead, Felix nodded towards Kevin, now battling the angry Ashton-goons *as well* as trying to stake his ex-mentor.

We aimed and fired. A couple of monsters fell away, shrieking.

'Love this game!' I whispered.

We edged closer, reloaded and went again, and again. And kept going until Kevin was free to keep slamming torn-up Ashton's face into the broken glass on the ground.

'Should we help?' Kate asked, joining us.

'What about the ...?' I trailed off before 'others', because *what others*?

The room was empty, aside from the screaming holied-up vamps – and a lot of red dust.

'Holy frak, Kate,' said Felix. 'You went full-Thanos!'

'Yeah, totally snapped,' muttered Kate. Her eyes were still glowing.

Our moment of geek was cut short by Kevin, who flew past us into the back wall. Ashton leapt to his feet and strode straight past us, his eyes fixed on Kevin as he snarled. Then he gasped and clutched his neck.

He didn't scream, but his face contorted as he dropped to his knees. He looked at Felix – who'd just lowered his gun – and squeaked in recognition.

Kevin peeled himself away from the wall and stood up. His face had fared better than Ashton's, but right now it looked confused.

'Sorry, Kevin,' said Felix. 'I know it's personal, but ...'

Kevin shook his head as he walked back.

I picked up his stake and handed it to him while he fixed his glare on Ashton. 'No worries, Felix. It's all personal.'

Ashton's eyes bulged with holy-water-induced pain. He looked almost heartbroken. 'Kev. My Kev. You – you wouldn't ...'

'Actually.' Kevin slammed the stake through Ashton's throat. 'Yeah, I would.'

He twisted hard – slashing the wood right through his ex-mentor's neck until the body came away. Then Ashton exploded.

'And it's Kevin, you freaking psycho!'

37. Kate

There should've been a thunder clap. Or a fanfare.

Or at least some heroic victory music. But there wasn't.

Just lots of silence. It took a second to realise why.

It'd stopped.

The screams from the floor, the numbers being yelled outside – everything. The only sound was the steady thump of a whole lot of hearts.

Evie gasped. 'It worked! All those pulses … guys, you're human again.'

Kevin certainly was. I could hear his heart race as he turned green and puked blood all over Ashton's jacket – but that didn't bode well for *my* humanity, did it?

He shoved his fingers down his throat again, purging himself of Evie and Summer, then leaned back against the cracked mirror, looking broken and self-loathing.

'Sorry,' he muttered. 'Didn't mean to spoil the moment, just –'

His gaze landed on the pitcher at the bar, and he puked again. I should've felt bad for him, but all I could think was how much blood there'd been in his stomach.

And how delicious it still smelt. My eyes burned.

'Kate!' cried Felix. 'No, it – it worked! You can't be –'

My heart didn't beat, but it still sank as everyone's attention landed on me in various degrees of disappointment, confusion and anger.

Felix genuinely looked like he might cry.

Evie just looked perplexed. 'But everyone else is human!'

'Everyone *Ashton* turned.' Kevin's jaw flexed, miserable. 'All us mass-murdering psychos. And the one good one is – what? Stuck for ever, 'cos I was the one who turned her?'

He grabbed his blood-splattered stake from the ground and held it out. 'Maybe this'll work. Go ahead, Chris'll never know.'

'What? No!' I snatched the stake and tossed it away. 'I'm not killing you, idiot. Look, we saved the town. We're heroes! And now I have super-powers. Yay!'

I smiled, desperately willing everyone to smile back so I didn't have to keep making them feel better about my crappy non-life. 'Let's just find Mom and get out of here, OK?'

Felix had been very apologetic in admitting he had no idea where Mom might be. Ashton's guys had kept him in a giant walk-in fridge for most of the day he'd spent with them, so he hadn't seen or heard anything they didn't want him to.

Still, someone had to know something.

There was a groan from behind the bar. I leapt across and yanked the groggy moose-looking bartender to his feet. 'Lincoln Wells!'

I'd finally figured out how I knew him. Miriam's 'little grandson' was a mass-murdering monster. I glowed my eyes. 'Your granny would be so disappointed.'

Linc squeaked and tried to wriggle from my grip, so I tightened it and dragged him over to the others. He smiled desperately when he saw Felix.

'Hey, I–I know you,' he said, like he was pulling some kind of clout. 'Felix tutored me in English, we're friends! Tell her.'

'Dude, flushing my head down the toilet until I agreed to do your homework does *not* count as me tutoring you,' said Felix. 'Plus, you literally *just* tried to kill me, so ... not sure what you're expecting here.'

Evie didn't quite stifle a giggle. I caught Linc by the throat and forced him back against the cracked mirror.

'Tell me where Ashton's got my mom,' I said. 'And maybe I won't rip you apart, like you've been doing to the nice people of Brightside. Got it?'

Linc swallowed, hard. His Adam's apple bobbed against my grip.

'I don't know,' he gasped. 'No-one does! We – we saw her come in, we never saw her leave. He never mentioned her again, he never told us to clean up, he never shared any leftover –'

'All right, shut up!' My fangs flipped themselves down. Linc shrieked, like I was coming for him. I grabbed him by the arms again, force-marching him past the remaining ex-vampires, still whimpering on the ground with residual pain.

Evie, Kevin and Felix trailed behind as we left the bar.

'You're going to show me the last place you saw my mom,' I said. 'And when we're done I'll let Felix decide what happens to you. Fair?'

Linc gave a sort of hiccup-sob, and strained around to look at Felix, who shrugged like he hadn't made up his mind yet. I tried not to let the tears of the serial-killing moose-hulk get to me. He'd known what he was doing.

Worse, he'd known the people he was doing it to.

I wouldn't kill him, but a few minutes thinking I might seemed like some sort of payback for what he'd done to people like Cass, and Sage, and Summer Wilson

'Fair?' I growled again.

Linc cringed and nodded miserably, so I grinned – as slow and cruel as I could manage, 'Good, then let's find my mom.'

* * *

'Find my mom,' I'd said. Like it would be easy.

Like we wouldn't have to scour the entire massive house, trashing every room we entered as we sniffed for Mom's scent. Like we wouldn't have to pick past confused ex-vampires with Evie wobbling woozily as Kevin clung to her, suddenly myopic – and feverish from lingering wolf-blood side-effects. Like Felix wouldn't sink further into despair with every empty room, because he hadn't 'saved' me and he couldn't miraculously uncover my mom either.

On the plus side, Linc's frightened snivels and the little trail of pee he left as I dragged him from room to room served as fair warning to the rest of the horde that we weren't as harmless as we looked. On the minus side, I'd just dragged him as far as we could go – all the way to the attic – and Mom wasn't there either.

I inhaled, deeply, all around the room. But the only things I could smell were air fresheners and mothballs. There were so many mothballs.

Something gripped at my chest. I couldn't breathe. I didn't *have* to breathe but this was different. This felt like I was suffocating.

'It's OK,' I mumbled. 'She – there's probably a – a barn, right? Or – or shed, or a big garage with fancy tractors or …'

My head spun, the room swam and my body managed to flash hot and cold at the same time. The world went spotty around the edges.

'Katie?' said Evie.

'I – I'm fine,' I muttered. 'I just…'

What if she wasn't here? What if Ashton'd stashed her somewhere else entirely, and we'd never know because we'd killed him. What if she was starving to death, all alone?

What if the last thing I'd said to her was – was *the last thing* I said to her?

'Bro, is she having a panic attack?' Linc's voice swirled around my brain. 'I've seen those. I've caused those! Thought she was some badass – *aah*!'

I didn't even realise I'd shoved Linc into the closet at the back of the attic, and was right on top of him – fangs down – until Kevin caught my arm.

'KATE!'

His voice snapped me back to reality. My fire dampened as I looked down at the petrified psychopath I'd almost murdered. The world was spotty, and unsteady, and everything sucked. But killing Linc probably wasn't the answer to any of that.

'I mean, he'd deserve it,' said Kevin. 'I just think *you'd* regret it.'

I nodded weakly and fought back the tears as he helped me up while Linc scrambled to his feet and raced for the door.

'Whoa, not so fast!' Evie tripped him, then did her best to tower menacingly as he scuttled backwards, like a ridiculous jock-crab. 'Felix, what's the verdict?'

Felix shrugged. 'Whatever.'

I let go of Kevin and navigated the swaying world long enough to join Evie, wrapping one arm around her waist before glowering down at Linc.

'You can go,' I managed. 'But, spread the word – anyone so much as touches Felix, Kevin or their families, and they'll have us to deal with!'

Evie clawed one hand in front of Linc. 'Just give us an excuse.'

Linc nodded dumbly, then leapt up and raced out the door.

Evie turn to me. 'You OK?'

'Me?' The room was still swirling; my chest was tight. I didn't want to answer, so it was good I could see Evie, trying to subtly rub at that angry spot between her eyes.

'What about you?' I said. 'Is your head OK?'

'Um, yeah,' she said 'It just –'

She stopped, as Kevin massaged *his* forehead, furiously. I could feel the stomach-drop in her expression, and she was about to say something when Felix piped up –

'Um, guys, there's a light back there. Look!'

Suddenly, nothing else mattered.

Felix leapt into the closet – feet crunching on the mothballs – and indicated a little crack in the plywood backing, right where Linc had hit. A faint yellow glow seeped through the edges. Felix whipped his stake from his waistband and slammed it into the crack, splitting that tiny gap into a proper hole. Light streamed through.

'There's something back there!' He grabbed the jagged plywood and pulled, until the sting of his blood hit the air. He didn't even flinch. 'Kevin, give me a hand!'

'I've got a better idea,' I said. 'Stand clear.'

The world steadied. My chest unknotted.

I steeled myself, then zipped forward and collided with the closet. It toppled aside, revealing a huge hole in the plasterboard behind – like someone had smashed the wall open, then pulled the closet across to hide it. Just like mothballs and air fresheners had hidden a certain, very human scent from the blood-loving psychos Ashton clearly hadn't trusted with his 'wolf expert'.

Suddenly, I didn't dare breathe.

Evie did, though. She inhaled, deep and long, then raced over to the hole – eyes gleaming! 'She's here! Katie, breathe. We've found her.'

My lungs burned. I didn't exhale.

Evie tugged my hand. 'Kate, come on!'

I shook my head.

'Katie?'

I was rooted to the spot. Fear and shame flooded my body

Mom was here. She was *right there*. Those impulses I was still struggling with should have sent me rocketing straight to her, like they'd shoved me out that window after Evie. But could I face Mom, knowing what I was now? What I'd done tonight?

'I can't,' I whispered.

Evie frowned, looking torn between staying with me and racing to Mom. I think she was waiting for me to tell her what to do. Instead, Kevin stepped forward.

'Hey, I get it,' he said. 'But she loves *you*, not what you are. Trust me.'

I did, but I still couldn't move.

Felix put his hand on my arm and added: 'Kate, Kevin and I never get to see our moms again. Yours is just through there – and she's going to be so proud.'

He smiled, like he was proud too, and I don't know why that's what convinced me, but it did. I zipped through the hole – Evie's hand still gripped in mine, Mom's scent buzzing in my lungs as we raced through that crawl space until –

'Mom!'

My mom! There she was, gagged and groggy, chained to a pipe and covered in grime. Evie ripped her gag down. I gripped the chains and yanked until they snapped. Mom tumbled free, into my arms. Her eyes flickered open – drowsily at first, then wide – and wild – as she realised she wasn't dreaming.

'Hey,' I said.

'Miss us?' added Evie.

'Katie? Evie! What … how … are you –?' Mom sat up, taking us in properly: the blood all over Evie; the red dust coating my clothes and hair; the stakes still jammed in our belt loops.

The first look to cross her face was fear, and then annoyance – like she was prepping to give out to us for whatever recklessness we'd just performed.

But that only lasted a split-second before vanishing under a flood of relief, and joy, and tears I hoped were happy.

'What the hell have you been up to?' She laughed. 'You mad yokes!'

She must've had so many questions – I know I did – but they were lost in the urge to wrap our arms around each other and squeeze, like the three of us were trying to merge into one mega-Wilder.

If it meant we didn't have to be apart again, I'd take it.

38. Evie

We almost lost time, sitting there hugging and sobbing, reassuring Mom over and over that this was real – without going into details on what exactly reality was now.

Too soon, Felix appeared to remind us we needed to get going.

Ashton's men were starting to move around, recovering from all that leftover pain, and we really didn't want to deal with them on top of everything else.

So we shuffled back through the crawl space, through the attic and into the main house, where Mom did her best to walk tall and glare at the ex-vampires, who lurked in the doorways backing away as Kate and I scowled at them.

As we made our way through the grounds outside, Mom filled us in on how she'd bumped into Ashton in Ray's. How he'd been *more* than happy to talk about the attacks. And laugh at her jokes, and tell her how beautiful she was. *Blegh!*

They'd met up again the next night, and he'd lured her to the farmhouse with the promise of a night cap, and the camp map. But, when he tried to recruit her to his wolf-hunting team, Mom refused. She wanted to *find* my folks, not murder them.

Besides, arming an entire travelling goon squad of complete strangers with weapons that could be used against me didn't exactly seem like the smartest move.

So Ashton had dragged her to the attic – hiding her from everyone, with the closet and the stench of mothballs and air freshener – and locked her up until she changed her mind.

'He kept me human,' said Mom, 'because he knew, even as a vampire, I'd run if I could. He knew there wasn't much that could keep me from my girls. I don't think he'd realised he couldn't keep you from me either.'

She smiled, proudly, then shivered in the freezing air as we reached the car. The black dress and pretty cardigan she'd worn on her date with Ashton weren't exactly the best protection against the Canadian winter.

Without thinking, Kate pulled off her dad's jacket and wrapped it around Mom, who immediately tried to shrug it off.

'Mom, you'll freeze,' said Kate.

'I'm grand, Katie,' Mom lied, through chattering teeth. 'Sure you're only wearing a T-shirt, you'll catch your death in ...'

And just like that, the air was thick with awkward realisation. Because Kate – perfect, blood-splattered, slightly snow-coated Katie – wasn't even shivering. Her cheeks weren't rosy-cold, like mine. Her breath wasn't coming out in juddering huffs, like Felix and Kevin's. She was just ... fine.

I half-toyed with the idea of breaking the weirdness by quipping that she'd already caught her death, but I wasn't sure anyone would appreciate that right now.

'Listen, Mom,' said Kate.

'Katie, shush!' Mom buttoned up Brendan's old jacket, then reached out to take our hands in hers. 'I've missed a lot. Clearly. And we have things to talk about, but – I love you, OK? Exactly as you are. You'll always be mine, no matter what happens, or what's happened, you're my daughters first. Understand?'

She yanked us in for one more hug, and I felt a warm rush as Kate broke out into a huge, genuine grin. The first proper smile I'd seen on her in days. Every worry she'd had about telling Mom who she was now dissipated, like vamp-dust in the breeze.

Mom knew, and she loved her anyway.

I could have told her that!

'Now,' said Mom, 'can we get some food? That fecker forgot to feed me for the last day and a half. I was getting ready to chew my own arm off!'

She laughed – we all did.

And Kevin promised to whip up something delicious, and we headed home, and we all lived happily ever after. Roll credits, add bonus scene.

The end

Well, not quite.

We did get in the car, where we called Officer Jonson to report some 'suspicious activity' in the farmhouse. We didn't say 'swarm of ex-vampires', and he probably wasn't going to figure that out. But a mob of missing assholes trespassing on the property of a definitely dead owner? He'd have enough to go on.

We weren't even at the cemetery when my head buzzed, angry and bee-like, for the second time that night. I fought back the urge to jam my thumb between my eyes, and looked at Kevin instead. He was wincing uncomfortably in the passenger seat, rubbing at his forehead like he was trying to scratch it open.

Crap!

I took a deep breath, focused on that 'bee' in my head and – firmly but calmly – imagined myself squishing it down, like pressing the 'end call' button on my phone.

The buzzing stopped for a moment, and Kevin relaxed, confused. Then, out of nowhere, the bee sprang back to life and he yelped in pain and frustration.

It was so sudden, Felix slammed the brakes on – jostling us all forward.

'You OK?' he said. 'Is everyone OK?'

Kevin nodded, so unconvincingly I knew he wasn't himself because if there was one thing Kevin Goodman-Harris could do, it was lie. *Craaaap!*

This had happened in the attic too. I'd buzzed, and he'd flinched, and I'd wanted to say something but then we'd found Mom and everything had been wonderful, and I know

292

it sounds stupid but I *really* hoped if I ignored this, maybe it would … go away?

Or, maybe it would turn out to be Stalker Rom buzzing in my head, and I could sneak out and rip through him for ruining my life while Kevin took a couple of Tylenol and slept off his injuries from his demonic duo's battle royale.

But that wasn't it, was it?

He'd drunk my blood. It was in his veins as he'd turned human again. *If* he'd turned human again. Panic pricked my forehead.

How long did it take for an infected person to change?

Felix was right beside him, trying to call Telehealth in case Kevin had gotten a concussion that hadn't healed. How fast could Kevin lose control and maul him?

'I need some fresh air,' I announced. 'Kevin, walk home with me, eh?'

Kevin nodded. He was trying to stay calm, but his eyes looked panicky – and they were flickering orangey-gold. OK, this was real.

And if he didn't know, he at least suspected.

He unbuckled his seatbelt and threw his door open, stumbling out into the snow and grabbing hold of the nearest tree to stay upright.

Felix hung up on the nurse-line and turned to me. 'Oh. Not a concussion, then?'

I shook my head and unclipped my own belt.

Mom took my hand. 'Evie, hun. I don't think you should be running around town late at night with –' She glanced towards Kevin, meaningfully.

Right. Because Mom knew stuff. But she didn't know about me, not really.

'I'll be fine,' I said. 'We just defeated a whole army of vampires to find you, remember. *I'm* the scariest thing out there. And besides –'

I pulled up my jacket to show her my gun, horribly aware that we didn't have any tranqs – just silver-and-holy-water darts. The holy water was useless, obviously, but the silver without anything to knock him out or numb the pain? Last resort only.

Mom looked at Kate uncertainly, as the buzzing in my head intensified – like someone had knocked an entire beehive over in my skull.

Kevin's sharp intake of breath told me he'd felt it too.

I didn't have time to argue. 'I've gotta go, I'm sorry. Love you.' I squeezed Mom in a huge hug, then scrambled out and over to Kevin.

Behind me, I could hear Kate convincing Mom to stay in the car, let Felix drive her home to rest and have a sandwich. She took a *lot* of convincing.

Eventually, though, Kate won and the car took off, leaving the three of us alone.

Kevin dropped to his knees in the snow and roared. Kate's gun was out before I could blink. But it wasn't like that. He punched the ground, pummelling the white powder over and over. He looked furious. Pained. And totally broken.

'Kevin,' I said. 'It's OK.'

'It's not!' he sobbed. 'My joints are pulsing, My head's buzzing, everything feels hot and tingly – and I'm not like you, Red. I won't be able to control this.'

He pulled Ashton's gun from inside his jacket and held it out to Kate. She took it, slipped it into her waistband, then pulled him to his feet.

'Stop trying to get me to murder you, you mopey emo,' she said. 'We don't even know what you *are* yet. Mom said Robert turned as soon as he injected Madison's blood. You've been – whatever's happening – for half an hour now. You're fine.'

I mean, he clearly wasn't, but coming from Kate I almost believed it. So did Kevin, until the snow crunched, and he hit full panic-mode again.

'Kate, please,' he said. 'Something's happening, I can feel it. My head's like a beehive, and I'm not going to hurt anyone else. I can't.'

'You won't,' I said. 'That's not what that is. The bee feeling's just … us. Being near each other, thinking about each other. Our own wolfy detection system.'

That was supposed to be comforting, but Kevin's gutted expression said otherwise. 'So now it hurts to be near you?' The snow was still crunching towards us, but he was too forlorn to care. 'You guys are the one thing that's made me feel anything other than shit in the last twenty-three years. I liked having people I could just be broken with. I don't want to have to steer clear of either of you.'

The urge to just kiss him – like that would fix any of this – was so strong I had to bite my lip to keep from crushing it against his. Instead I focused on squashing that bee again, hanging up the phone on the buzz between us.

And then it stopped.

Just like that. Like someone had flicked a switch. The sudden quiet was so creepy, so controlled. It wasn't just me, squishing the buzz.

Someone had swiped the bee away completely.

'I don't think I did that,' I said.

'No, I did!' said a voice.

A cheery, familiar voice that set my stomach churning. The three of us turned towards the trees at once. And right there, weaving his way through the woods – his curly dark hair coated in snow, and a charming grin on his rugged, woodcuttery face – was Stalker Rom.

'Hi, Evie.' He waved with his free hand.

His other hand was busy, dragging Zoe King with him.

She was gagged – and freezing. They'd clearly been trekking through the snow a while – but she still managed to yell something that sounded like 'Run!' as they drew close.

'Don't run!' said Rom, with all the same boyish sincerity he'd had on my doorstep, before he'd clawed through my arm. 'Or I'll have to bite her. Which I haven't so far, by the way. She's still human, for now.'

He said it like he deserved a cookie for restraint. But then he grabbed Zoe's pony-tail and yanked her head aside. His fangs were out, suddenly, poised right against Zoe's neck. Zoe bit down on the gag, and didn't whimper. She couldn't keep the fear from her eyes, though.

'Stop!' yelled Kate.

I slammed my arm out, catching her before she could blur forward. There was no way – even at vampire speed – that she could be sure Zoe wouldn't get hurt. And we'd clearly caused her enough harm already.

Beside me, Kevin growled, so I squeezed his hand gently until he settled, then let go and stepped forward.

'Leave her alone!' I said. 'This is nothing to do with her – she's just our neighbour.'

'Is that all she is?' Rom's freaky demon eyes flashed towards Kate, and his mouth twisted into a smug grin. 'All those texts meant nothing, eh?'

Kate flushed furiously, and strained against my arm.

'Stop!' I said. 'It's me you want, right?'

Zoe gave a muffled yelp of protest, shaking her head in a 'No, don't!' kind of way. Rom tightened his hold on her pony-tail, until she couldn't move at all.

It must have hurt – she winced, but she didn't yelp.

I stepped forward, reassessing everything I thought I knew about sweet, slightly basic Zoe King. She'd clearly adapted to the role of 'brave monster-defier' as easily as she had to 'spirit squad captain' (and 'book club captain', right before I quit).

No wonder Kate loved her.

'You'll let Zoe go, right?' I said. 'Me for her.'

Rom nodded. Kevin growled again.

Rom snarled back, before re-focusing on me. 'Evie, I've come all this way for *you*. For the only other pureborn I've ever met.'

I tried not to let my eyes burn as Rom kept going.

'I picked up your signal by chance,' he said. 'I tracked you down because I was curious, but then I saw you.'

He smiled, all sincere, and my hands tingled. His fangs were in, his grip on Zoe was loosening. But he was still too close.

'I watched,' he continued, 'I observed, and admired and – aaaagh!'

Rom bucked back, losing his hold on Zoe as a silver-filled dart hit him in the leg and burned through his veins. I spun around.

Kevin's eyes burned golden orange, his fangs were half-down and I could see the urge to wolf-out rippling along his muscles. But he stayed him (or mostly him), as he reloaded his tranq gun and fired again.

Rom hit the ground. His body flailed, desperate to go full-wolf while silver sapped his power to do anything except scream.

There was a lot of screaming.

'Um, thanks,' I told Kevin, 'for saving me from the Big Bad Wolf.'

'You?' Kevin laughed. 'I was saving *him*, Red.'

He leaned forward, almost nose to nose with Rom. 'You had about two seconds before Evie ripped your head off, creep. Now, say "Thank you".'

Rom snapped pathetically, and Kevin laughed again. In between the twists of agony, my monster stalker actually had the nerve to look betrayed.

Kate was already over with Zoe, undoing her wrist-binds and untying the gag from around her mouth, before pulling her close. For heat, obviously.

I swiped the gag, and used it to shut Rom up, then tied his hands, as Kevin stripped down to his T-shirt and handed the extra layers to Zoe.

She shivered gratefully, pulling everything on before snuggling back into Kate. Kevin didn't exactly look human right now, but he was with us so I guess Zoe was just going with it.

'Th-thanks,' she stammered. 'I'm Zoe, by the way.'

'Oh, I know!' said Kevin, a bit too eagerly. He cleared his throat, took my arm and jerked his thumb towards a random tree. 'And I, um, need to go – over there now, with Evie. Now. Bye!'

Zoe tilted her head, confused, as Kevin pulled me aside and Kate groaned in 'embarrassed crush' (a language I spoke really well all of a sudden).

'Figured, we should let them have their moment,' he whispered. His new wolfy warmth radiated through his shirt, as he pulled me close. 'And hey, did you notice? No bees.'

'No bees,' I agreed. 'I guess it wasn't us, after all. Just Rom, looking for me.'

Kevin growled at the memory, and his arm muscles pulsed. My stomach butterflies went into overdrive.

'You're not wolfing out,' I said. 'That's good.'

Kevin nodded. 'Yeah, I'm focusing, like we've been practising. But I'm still burning. I need a distraction.'

'Like wh– oh!'

The 'oh!' was muffled, under the delicious warmth of Kevin's lips. His fangs skimmed my tongue, sending weird thrills through me, and his slightly clawed hands curled against my body. I kissed him until he felt human again, then pulled back to catch Kate and Zoe decidedly *not* looking at us, as they had their own conversation.

'So it was all him?' Kate sounded hurt. 'Every text?'

'Of course it was,' said Zoe. 'Kate, he was desperate to find out where you'd gone. To kidnap Evie and – and I dunno, form a new pack or something? Why would I help him do that to her? Or to you? You're my … friend. Right?'

Kate nodded, crestfallen. 'Right.'

'My insanely cool, impossibly beautiful friend?' said Zoe. 'Who'd maybe want to come watch a movie with me some night? Or ... you know ...' She hesitated, then leaned in until she thought I wouldn't be able to hear and added: '*Not* watch it?'

Kate didn't need to breathe, which is probably just as well, because that tiny intake followed by nothing told me she'd forgotten how to anyway.

Kevin gave a tiny *whoop!*, then blushed as I looked at him.

'What?' he whispered. 'I'm really invested in those two.'

'Alrighty!' said Kate suddenly. Loudly. All full of life and confidence again. 'The big question is, what do we do with this idiot?'

She nodded towards the still-squirming Rom.

Kevin shrugged. 'I mean, I know what I'd do. But that's probably the wrong answer right now, in front of company, right?'

Zoe laughed. '*Company's* been stuck with this jerk reading my texts and the fanfic in my Notes app. Do whatever you want, no Stockholm syndrome here.'

Wow, yeah. I did like her. Kate looked torn between shocked and impressed.

'We can't kill him! He's all incapacitated. And helpless.' She pinched his cheeks and ruffled his hair. 'Like a widdle baby, see?'

She was positively giddy on Zoe – and Mom, I guess. The whole night really. It was wonderful. She deserved an actual moment of glee in all the madness.

'What *do* we do with him then?' I said. 'We can't let him go: he'll kill someone.'

There was a moment of silence. Well, no, there was a moment of muffled screaming. They were all moments of muffled screaming right now. Thanks, Rom.

But aside from that, *we* were silent. Until:

'Actually,' said Zoe, 'I think I know something that might work.'

39. Kate

TWO MONTHS LATER

'Wait, she's dead? Like, *dead* dead?'

'Super-dead,' I said. 'But she saved her little sister.'

'Yeah, *"sister"*!' Rom actually did air quotes. He was taking this so personally.

'It's just a show.' I laughed. 'There's two more seasons, *and* a musical episode.'

'A musical?' Rom looked slightly placated as he stretched across his bed – in the big silver cage in our basement – to pick up his sketch pad.

I'd bought him that. I figured expressing himself artistically might take the sting out of *not* being able to express himself murderously any more. Although, honestly, I think Evie's old silver meds had taken the edge off that urge too.

Or maybe he was just happier now?

Maybe, compared to being a lonely orphan wandering Canada looking for a new pack (his old pack having been killed by a certain anti-werewolf vampire militia), being stuck in a basement with a rag-tag band of monster misfits wasn't so bad?

Sure, it was no hunting-and-eating-people, but maybe he was learning there was more to life?

'C'mon, slayer,' he tried. 'One more episode?'

'It's Kate,' I said. 'And no.'

I didn't really mind 'slayer'. It was hardly the worst thing he'd called me since we'd locked him up here – like he'd done to Zoe, until I'd accidentally texted our location with a photo. In fact, 'slayer' almost felt like a term of endearment. Or possibly grudging respect, for the vampire who'd dusted half of Ashton's army?

Either way, he'd had enough screen time.

'I've got enzyme assays to graph,' I said. 'But if you're bored, you can always re-read Zoe's Jane Austen collection.'

Rom growled, and went back to doodling as I got stuck into home-school. I was actually quite enjoying working alone; it meant I'd been able to pick up a few more advanced placement classes. Plus, I had Mom's lab all to myself while she was off lecturing, so I could use my free time to try to figure Kevin out.

Or figure out what he was, at least.

His blood slides were … weird. From what I could see, Evie's wolf-blood kept trying to rejuvenate Ashton's dust, to 'heal' Kevin back to the vampire he'd been when it entered his system. Then, the semi-revived vampire blood started curing the wolf-infection – which weakened Evie's blood, so the vamp-dust stopped 'healing'. Which meant the wolf-blood could get stronger again, which meant it tried to re-vamp Ashton's dust which – as Kevin had put it – meant: 'I'm basically just one big cycle of self-destructive monster failure.'

'What's new, eh?' I'd joked, and Evie had thrown something at me.

But we were past that now. We were happy. How could we not be?

The front door slammed, and three sets of footsteps raced through the hall.

'Katie, we're *hoooome*!'

My heart leapt.

Zoe was first down, as always – flinging her bag onto the futon with a quick 'Hey Rom' before pulling me out of my chair for a much nicer type of 'Hello'. Her lips tasted like strawberry bubble tea.

'How was school?' I asked, between kisses.

'Not enough vampires,' she said. 'Did you get your fancy genius work done?'

'Some of it. But it's very fancy and geniusy so ...'

Zoe giggled, then wrapped her hug tighter, and kissed me again. 'God, I love your big sexy brain.'

'I love yours too.' My body fizzed.

I still couldn't believe I got to do this with Zoe. *My* Zoe, finally.

Felix had given me a stern phone lecture, about six weeks back, when I'd been panicking because one day she'd outgrow me, and I'd be left behind *remembering*, like a sad Sarah McLachlan song.

'I wouldn't trade a second of Cass,' he'd said. 'So just – take the memories. Make them worth the pain. It's better than not making them at all, I promise.'

He was right, of course.

No-one's guaranteed tomorrow but that doesn't mean we give up on today. Especially when *today* can turn my 'big sexy brain' to mush with a grin and a kiss.

'Get a room!' called Evie, sliding down the bannisters to join us.

'I had a room,' I said. 'He's taken it, remember?'

'Well, if you'd prefer me to share with Evie ...' said Kevin, descending the stairs with a big tray and the smell of delicious pie.

He grinned as I glowed my eyes at him.

It was all playful, though. I actually loved sharing a room with Evie. I'd always wanted to when we were little, and she hadn't sleep-wolfed once since we'd stopped trying to chemically suppress her wolfy side.

Plus, the house had never been tidier than since Mom moved Kevin in, so we could monitor him and keep him in daily silver-and-sedative shots, which also meant Chris and Jim (the blood guy) could finally enjoy the alone time they'd apparently been craving for years.

'All right, who wants a slice? Fresh from Home Ec.' Kevin indicated the pie, proudly. 'It's blueberry. And vegan, obviously, Kate. And, not to brag, but I totally nailed the crust – Ms Myers basically said I should go pro.'

'Didn't you run a hotel kitchen for five years?' asked Zoe.

'Kinda.' Kevin plated the first slice and handed it to Evie. 'But I wasn't getting graded on that. Oh, and I got a stinking A-minus on my creative writing assignment.'

'How dare they?' gasped Evie, in fake outrage. 'Don't they know who you are?'

Kevin laughed, and kept serving the pie as we caught each other up on our days. Even Rom got a slice. He and Kevin weren't exactly best friends, after Rom's Evie-stalking and Kevin silvering Rom up, but at least they'd moved on from constant death threats. That was progress.

Evie had just suggested seconds when my laptop rang, and a video-call popped up, filling the screen with a picture of Felix and Cass. *Right on time, as always!*

We all crowded onto the futon, grinning into the camera with an ear-drum-popping 'FELIX!' as I answered. He couldn't see me, of course, but I smiled anyway.

Video Felix grinned back. 'Happy Friday. No, wait –' He held up a plate. 'Happy *Pie*-day! Kevin, that photo you sent was taunting me, I had to buy some.'

'From Miriam?' I asked.

'Of course from Miriam,' said Felix. 'She's going through a tough time. Linc's been implicated in all those murders. Her "friends" are freezing her out. Heather felt so bad for her she actually invited her over for coffee. But then Jubilee threw up on her and Gaius's diaper exploded while she was holding him, so –'

'Revenge babies!' grinned Evie. 'Yes. The twins have your back, dude!'

Felix laughed.

He really was trying with Miriam, but I couldn't blame him for enjoying a *little* baby-shaped karma. I was just happy to see him smile.

'Anyway, enough Miriam,' he said. 'Family Day's coming up. Who's got plans for the long weekend?'

He didn't say it like a question. It was more: Who's got two thumbs and an awesome plan lined up?

So I said: 'Is it … us?'

'It's us.' Felix grinned. 'Check it out.'

He clicked a button, and his face was replaced with a full-screen map, marked with a cluster of red dots over a town called Summerville.

'Mysterious murders,' he went on, 'weird animal attacks, missing *brains*. Something creepy's going on in Summerville. So – road trip?'

'Road trip!' Zoe grabbed my hand excitedly.

And Evie and Kevin both gave a 'Hell, yeah!'

Which just left me, with everyone staring at me, and the boys chanting: 'Road trip! Road trip! Road trip!'

'Come on,' said Evie. 'Whaddya say?'

I sighed. 'What do I always say when Felix suggests a creepy monster-hunting weekend instead of, I dunno, a sleepover movie marathon or something normal?'

The map vanished. Felix's face returned.

'Hell, yeah?' he said hopefully

'Hell, yeah!' I grinned. Or maybe I whooped.

As long as I was with my little monster family, there was nothing I'd rather do.

Acknowledgements

Evie and Kate Wilder have been with me, in one form or another, since I was sitting in a tiny Toronto apartment, missing my family and writing a new, found family (with monsters). They've been there through chaos, new babies, cross-continent moves and, now, a global pandemic. So, I should really start by thanking them for sticking with me all these years – even when I tried repeatedly to pack them away.

But the Wilder sisters would still be battling monsters in my head if not for the help and support of my very own rag-tag band of magnificent misfits:

My husband/science consultant Dave, who believed in this book even when I didn't, and always said it would be The One. (I mean, you're The One, Dave. But the book's a close second.)

Amber Caravéo, my dream agent. Thanks for taking a chance on my beloved monsters and helping them grow, before finding them the perfect home. I'm so lucky to have you in my corner.

The entire team at Little Island – a ginormous 'THANK YOU' for all your wonderful hard work. And Jonathan

McFerran for bringing my characters to life with your amazing cover art. This book owes so much to you all!

My Team Skylark agency siblings, who've been there for me through edits and subs and goats. Special shout out to Sarah Taylor Todd, Lee Newbery and Naomi Gibson for reading my early drafts and reassuring me they love my characters almost as much as I do – and to Lesley Parr for the emotional support Oz GIFs. Thanks for keeping me sane, guys.

My fellow 2022 debuts. I'm honoured be part of such a wonderful and talented group. Strap in, Patricia! It's world domination all the way down.

Sarah Webb and D. Stevens, two absolute gems, who've been there since the *very start*. Thanks for everything. Many pints are owed!

My Marvellous Maple Buddies, Elaine Kelly-Canning and Jamila Allidina. Thank you for being my very own found family (and Canadian fact-checkers). And James Looney and Derek Conlon, who listened to me rave about my monsters for years. Next Porterhouse Tuesday is on me, I promise!

Marcus Vance, who helped a stranger on Twitter calculate how long it would take to microwave human blood back to body-temperature, no questions asked. Thanks for not making that weird!

Tracy McEneaney, Jennie Loughran and everyone at Waterford Libraries (in fact, librarians everywhere). Thanks for feeding my reading habit, and introducing me to the Buffy Comics Collected Editions! I'd be a lot poorer without you.

My early readers – Paul Shortt, Ellen Brickley, Seán Cooke and Barry Gavin; my teen betas – Caoimhe, Kiera and

Emily; and, of course, my mom, Monica, and mother-in-law, Deirdre, who hate anything creepy, but read this anyway because I wrote it. Thanks for all the support, feedback and running-commentary texts. You're all amazing!

And Dad, you've read everything I've ever written, and refused to let me give up on any of it. I'm still here for the 37s, if we can get past that first sentence.

Big Bad Me is a love letter to family, and I'm lucky to have been blessed with the greatest! My wonderful siblings – Róisín, Seán and Sinéad; my in-laws – Greg, Fintan, Emma, Jody, Sharon, J.B., Jenni, Mungo; and my many, many wonderful and gorgeous niblings. You mean the world to me, so thanks for being part of mine.

Finally, my absolute favourite trilogy: Aoibhinn, Liam and Mara. Thanks for making every day magical, for being Evie and Kate's biggest fans – even if you're too young to read their story – and for all the hugs, quips and kisses when I needed them most. I'm your biggest fan too. I love you 3000. Always.

BABY TEETH
by Meg Grehan

The blood
Feeds the hunger
That threatens everything

It starts when Claudia offers her a yellow rose.

Immy has been in love before – many times, across many lifetimes. But never as deeply, as intensely as this.

Claudia has never been in love this before either. But then, this is her first time with a vampire.

The forbidden thirst for blood runs deep in Immy. And within her mind clamour the voices, of all the others she has been, their desires, and their wrongs.

A unique verse novel by the award-winning author of *The Deepest Breath* and *The Space Between*

Praise for *Baby Teeth*

"Emotionally rich and gloriously queer."
Kirkus, starred review

"Grehan's verse novel skilfully charts uncertainty, temptation and the course of a strange, desperate love."
The Guardian

"By linking vampirism to themes of queer desire and community as well as repeating personal cycles, Grehan freshens an old trope, building both a central romance and lifetimes-long connections that are by turns realistically sweet and thorny."
Publishers Weekly, starred review

ABOUT THE AUTHOR

Aislinn O'Loughlin grew up in Dublin, on a diet of fairy tales and horror stories – often at the same time (her biggest fear was the Big Bad Wolf escaping his story to eat her).

After writing several books in her teens, Aislinn worked as a storyteller and creative-writing teacher before moving to Toronto, where she sometimes took her kids to daycare in a sled (yes, really)! These days, she lives in Waterford with her scientist husband, three brilliant children and two evil genius cats. The Big Bad Wolf is welcome any time.

ABOUT LITTLE ISLAND

Little Island is an independent Irish publisher that looks for the best writing for young readers, in Ireland and internationally. Founded in 2010 by Ireland's inaugural Laureate na nÓg (Children's Laureate), Little Island has published over 100 books, many of which have won awards and been published in translation around the world.

RECENT AWARDS FOR LITTLE ISLAND BOOKS

Book of the Year
KPMG Children's Books Ireland Awards 2021
Savage Her Reply by Deirdre Sullivan

YA Book of the Year
Literacy Association of Ireland Awards 2021
Savage Her Reply by Deirdre Sullivan

YA Book of the Year
An Post Irish Book Awards 2020
Savage Her Reply by Deirdre Sullivan

White Raven Award 2021
The Gone Book by Helena Close

Judges' Special Prize
KPMG Children's Books Ireland Awards 2020
The Deepest Breath by Meg Grehan

Shortlisted: The Waterstones Children's Book Prize 2020
The Deepest Breath by Meg Grehan

IBBY Honours List 2020
Mucking About by John Chambers